A
STRANGE
AFFINITY
REBECCA
ROOK

SOUNDTRACK: A STRANGE AFFINITY

A Strange Affinity's Playlist is available on **Spotify**.

1. "The Ecstasy of Gold," by Ennio Merricone.

2. "I'm Only Getting Started," by Avi Kaplan.

3. "Bang, Bang (My Baby Shot Me Down)," by Nancy Sinatra.

4. "In Hell I'll Be In Good Company," by The Dead South.

5. "Way Down We Go," by KALEO.

6. "Change On The Rise," by Avi Kaplan.

7. "Cornbread and Butterbeans," by Carolina Chocolate Drops.

8. "Something's Rattling," by Benjamin Gibbard.

9. "Can't Find My Way Home," by Blind Faith.

10. "The Railroad," by Goodnight, Texas.

11. "Ain't No Grave," by Crooked Still.

12. "Danger and Dread," by Brown Bird.

13. "Wayfaring Stranger," by Jack White.

14. "Graves," by Whiskey Shivers.

Contents

CHAPTER ONE

Death and a blackbird were her only companions on the quiet plain.

A weather-worn, wrought metal fence encircled the town's lone cemetery, guarding the dead from the living who resided in nearby Agate Creek. Glory stood before the patchy dirt that covered her father's grave. Five months of a cold winter combined with a late start to spring hadn't done much to disguise the ground into which her father was welcomed last September.

Next to his grave lay the healing sod that marked her sister's plot. Both had simple grey stone slabs etched with the right names and dates, more permanent than many of the wooden markers throughout the cemetery. Lily's had a floral motif on her headstone, bluebells and forget-me-nots. Glory's father had insisted on it. In contrast, her father's headstone was plain. Her mother was absent, having died just after Lily had been born. She had been buried in another town.

Lily would like the bluebells, Glory thought.

Her blackbird companion fluttered to a different headstone, distracting Glory. She knew Mrs. Buntwell expected her to return to the general store soon, but Glory didn't move. Instead, she glanced around. Young maple trees hugged the metal fence along the north and east side of the cemetery. No wind cooled the sunshine that shimmered down upon her.

She watched as a procession of mourners and a small wagon with a closed pine casket made its way along the carved dirt road. Glory didn't recognize any of the tired faces, made further haggard by grief. Judging by the dated church clothes and the dilapidated shoes on some members of the procession, Glory suspected that another wagon train bound for the Oregon Trail must have stopped in Agate Creek, which rested near the halfway point on the journey, to bury their dead before moving on.

Glory turned to leave. She had done enough grieving to know that she preferred privacy for her tears. She didn't want to intrude on another's grief.

Funerals should not occur on sunny days.

Her blackbird companion had long since left, and the procession was at the final bend of the road that led to the cemetery. She could hear the creaking of the small, uncovered wagon that carried the casket. Glory stepped through the gates and as she did, something caught the corner of her eye: Two men stood near the graves of her father and sister. She stopped and stared. Tailored clothes, new boots, well-groomed blonde hair, and similar enough in build and appearance to be family. Glory watched them for a bit longer, and then turned away.

Visitors, she thought. *No business of mine.*

The walk from the cemetery into town was longer than most people liked to travel by foot. Many chose to ride or to drive a carriage out here. But Glory welcomed the exertion in exchange for the quiet. Late spring had softened the flat prairie, and the well-trod roads were lined with wildflowers and weeds. In full daylight, the flat lands stretched out from the town and the cemetery as far as one could see. No hills and few trees broke the visual monotony. During the summer, the haze of hot days across the prairies made her feel as though life were an illusion that would wink out at any moment. The snowbound winter days were just as bad, the land carpeted with white and grey and dark. Glory liked spring best. Fresh buds and new greens created bright and irregular textures that she trusted better than any other season. It seemed bumpy, rocky, *real*.

A small town situated off an Oregon Trail route, gossip was that Agate Creek would not remain small for much longer: The arrival of the railroad companies just over a year ago, coupled with the recent discovery of a tin mine located to the southwest, made the town attractive to merchants, miners, and even the families who'd had to abandon the arduous journey to Oregon. Some of the main streets in town were cobbled now, and it seemed to Glory like new buildings grew overnight.

Soon enough, Glory arrived at the outskirts of town. She walked down the wooden planks that fronted the new businesses. These shopfronts had fresh paint not yet faded by the combination of wind, sun, and dust. A gaily painted sign in the window of an otherwise empty shop, garnished with bright blues and yellows, prompted her to stop. Glory stopped to read:

"Healing, Herbs, and Health: Receive Guidance from a Magician with a True Affinity for the Healing Arts. Proprietor: Monsieur Cuthorpe. Grand Opening Soon."

A new magician in town? Intrigued, Glory peered into the window but only saw empty shelves that lined both sides of the narrow shop. A counter stood at the back of the shop and dozens of crates and trunks were stacked on the floor. Nothing stood out as striking or unusual. It seemed so...uneventful. Rather like her Mrs. Buntwell's general store, or perhaps a pharmacy. This *was the magician's shop*? Glory leaned back, disappointed.

"Good afternoon, Miss Gloriana."

A deep voice interrupted her thoughts. Glory groaned inwardly. Just her luck to have the pastor of the Agate Creek Church catch her peering into a magician's shop. She turned to face him.

"Good afternoon, Pastor Brooks." Glory gave a half-hearted smile – and braced herself for the forthcoming lecture.

"I hope you have better endeavors to occupy your time, Gloriana." Despite his youth, or because of it, the dark haired and unmarried pastor had narrow-minded views about women's roles in the world, the proper behavior for the citizens of Agate Creek, and the recent legality of magic in the United States and all affiliated Territories. Glory disagreed with Pastor Brooks on the first two issues, and thought he lacked a sense of adventure with regards to the latter.

"I'm simply curious," Glory replied. "Isn't it exciting, to have a new magician in town?" Glory knew that she stirred the hornet's nest and was promptly rewarded when Pastor Brooks furrowed his brow.

"Exciting?" he echoed, doubt and an edge of anger clear in his voice. Pastor Brooks shook his head. "Regardless of our nation's regrettable decision to make magic legal, magic remains forbidden by God." He smiled but the warmth didn't reach his eyes. "I hope you agree."

Glory smiled with her teeth. "But I thought magicians were born with their abilities?" She furrowed her brow in pretense, as if puzzled. "Those who are born with magic can't help having it, right?"

Now it was Pastor Brook's turn to sneer. "That remains a matter of debate. It still is against God's word, and His law transcends that of man."

What an ass. Fortunately, she was interrupted before she could respond aloud.

"Pastor Brooks and Miss Gloriana! What a delight to see you both this afternoon." The syrupy sweet trill came from a young matron who was popular in the Ladies Circle within the church; Glory only knew her from afar and had seen enough that she was reluctant to know more. As the young woman swayed up to them, and the town clock tower struck on a new hour, Glory seized her chance.

"Oh! Pardon me. I should return to Mrs. Buntwell," Glory said in a breathless tone. With a few further pleasant noises and an entreaty to see her next Sunday from Pastor Brooks, Glory escaped down the wooden walkway.

Glory shook her head to herself. She couldn't stand the devout young man. He had arrived a year earlier upon the prior pastor's death from a rattlesnake bite. Brooks had endeared himself to the more conservative families in town, and of course, none of these illustrious lineages had a magician within their ranks. Glory thought that these same families would likely disown a member, or hush up the manifestation of an Affinity, despite the United States government having made magic legal twenty years ago.

Too concerned about propriety and appearances.

A twinge of disappointed pinged through Glory. Though magic had been legal in her lifetime, and the right to practice magic protected, Glory had never met anyone with an Affinity. She had only heard that those with magic often applied their skills with one eye on the social temperature of the surrounding neighborhood. Religious tolerance for magical practices varied greatly, and many pastors, priests, and church elders frowned upon it. Often called the devil's work – *Even in 1886*, Glory thought, rolling her eyes – magic still had the stench of the unfamiliar and the dangerous for many. Most magicians felt safer in the cities, as some were driven out of the smaller towns and more rural areas.

Glory continued down the wooden esplanade and thought more about the new magician. *Maybe something interesting will finally happen in this town.*

CHAPTER TWO

The dawn came early, and cold.

Glory twisted beneath the linens and the thin blanket, trying to get warm. She shared the bed with another girl, Amelie, who snored but softly like a milk-drunk kitten. Glory supposed she should be grateful the warmth of another person during the cold nights.

Buntwell had refused to provide the girls she boarded a private room, citing the need to accommodate customers who actually paid. So Glory shared a tight space with a bed made of desiccated wood and rope springs, a stale hay rush mattress that smelled of damp, and was cratered with divots from the many bodies that came before hers.

I need to get up. I can't be late.

Glory winced to herself. She missed her own bed, in her own home, with thick blankets — not these thin, heavily used calico quilts made from remnants leftover from purchases at the general store. Glory especially missed waking up to the sounds of her father as he puttered in the kitchen, her sister already up and chattering at him. Her father had never cooked well so he kept to the simple meals: biscuits, bacon strips, roasted potatoes when he had them. Lily had tried to help but her father would often shoo her away or ask the younger girl to set the table instead. Lily had been a menace at most tasks that required any kind of sense, Glory remembered with a half smile.

When they caught the illness, they went so quickly. The debt incurred by the doctor's and the undertaker's visits had forced Glory to sell the very modest home they lived in. The two room cabin was drafty, and with no land, didn't fetch a high price. And with no place to go, no job prospects in sight, Glory had begged Mrs. Buntwell for room and board in exchange for working in the general store adjacent to the hotel. Mrs. Buntwell prided herself on her charity to the unfortunate, however parsimonious it truly was, and accepted the arrangement. Months into the agreement, Glory now knew something many people did not: Mrs. Buntwell was an unpleasant person who shouted at everyone who worked for her. But Glory need food and a place to stay. So Glory stayed.

Sorrow wrapped a tight fist around her throat, and Glory stared up at the ceiling, her eyes counting the knots and burrs in the wood.

Sometimes she resented them for leaving her behind. She hated that feeling — it made her feel so *guilty* — but sometimes the loneliness and the misery were too much to bear. It *hurt*.

With a sigh, she heaved herself out of the bed and when her feet touched the icy floor, the sigh turned into a hiss. She dashed toward chest of drawers, pulling out clothes in quick motions. Frigid air wafted through the room and Glory shivered as she dressed. *I hope breakfast is good. I loathe the porridge Mrs. Buntwell's cook makes.*

Before she left the room, Glory checked on the small, neatly repaired trunk tucked beneath the bed she shared with Amelie. She peered under the quilt edge and heaved a sigh when she saw the dark shape with the brass handles. Inside were the only remaining items and curios from her family: Several journals from her late mother, a badly embroidered handkerchief from Lily, her father's smith tools, and locks of Lily's and her father's hair. It had become a ritual for Glory to peer under the bed and ensure the trunk was safe every morning. She could not — would not — lose what was left of her family.

Glory straightened, trying to shake off her grief. She had another long day ahead of her.

The Gormans were the first family to arrive in the general store.

The ladies entered the neat shop much like they had entered Agate Creek last spring, on a train from Cincinnati: Loud, and festooned in bright colors and poor manners. The parents had encrusted their four daughters with virtuous names (Faith, Charity, Hope, and Prudence), and little else apart from a love for finery and for themselves. Agate Creek had soon learned that the Gorman Ladies would sweep into an establishment and insist upon being catered to through an extensive repertoire of huffs, sighs, and pointed looks.

Glory swallowed a sigh. She couldn't abide any of them. She continued to organize the combs, brushes, and personal toiletries located on the other side of the shop, away from the noise. But before long Glory heard the rustle of clothing behind her: One of the Gormans had found her. Glory sighed, and without looking up, retrieved the buttons, ribbons, and baubles tray. She then placed it on the counter.

"Here is the latest shipment."

A cough. Then a man spoke. "Ah, those are lovely. But I'm afraid they won't suit me."

Glory looked up as she realized her mistake. Two men stood before her, one in his mid-twenties and one only a few years older than her own sixteen years. Both had dark eyes and dark tailored suits made with expensive cloth. Tanned skin, severe features, and a curious shade of strawberry blonde hair echoed across both men.

Brothers, Glory assumed. She gave a small smile. "What do you need?"

The older man smiled again as he spoke. He gestured to the Gorman Ladies. "My brother and I are visiting our distant cousins here in Agate Creek."

Glory glanced between the loud family and two quiet men in front of her. She kept her face in a neutral expression. *My condolences.*

"We neglected to prepare for our trip and we need some supplies." The older man would have continued but Glory interrupted.

"Men's toiletries, shoes, and some clothing are available to your right." Glory pointed. "If you need anything else, I'll be here."

The older man beamed at her. "Thank you." He bustled away from the counter. The younger man remained.

"How long have you lived here?"

Glory paused her organization of the accessories tray, surprised at the inquiry. She did not expect such a private question from a stranger. Glory saw that his dark eyes remained on her face.

"A while."

He smiled. "I can't imagine living an entire life in one place," he teased.

Glory shrugged.

A pause. "I meant no offense."

Glory looked up. Without the wide smile, his face was severe again, and earnest. "You gave none," she assured him.

The corner of his mouth hitched.

"Seth, have you collected all the items you need?" The older man had returned, a short scrap of paper in one hand.

Seth shifted from one foot to another. He seemed impatient. "Buy two of every item on your list, and we'll survive until we depart." Mrs. Gorman let loose a high and terrible titter from across the shop. Both men shared a wince. Glory did not envy them their relations.

Her curiosity piqued, Glory watched the men step away and then observed the brothers through a few surreptitious glances. Glory saw that they tried to avoid any unnecessary interactions with the Gorman Ladies. They dawdled, taking their time to speak to one another in low voices. She continued to pretend to ignore the brothers and made efforts to truly ignore the Gorman Ladies.

Until Glory heard her name.

"Oh! Gloriana Rue?" The oldest Gorman sister, Faith, only a few years older than Glory, called out.

Glory stilled, then peered up.

"What in heaven's name are you doing here?" Faith said.

Glory thought the answer was obvious — and suspected the inquiry was malicious. "I work for Mrs. Buntwell now."

"Of course you do, silly." Faith rolled her eyes, a display of poor manners that would give her mother conniptions had the older woman seen them. "I'm just *delighted* to see you about and out these days."

"Thank you." Her answer was drier than a desert.

Out of the corner of her eye, Glory watched Faith saunter over to the older brother. She gave him an insincere smile and spoke in a low voice — but not low enough to escape Glory's hearing.

"Gareth, you are so kind to converse with Glory. Especially after all she has suffered. You see, both her father and her little sister have recently passed to their reward. Goodness, her father only died six months ago." A tsking noise. "Honestly, I am surprised she's here at the shop. I suppose she must work to earn her living now." Faith simpered up to Gareth, and spared a quick smile to the younger brother, too. She waited for the response to this information, her eyes bright with the expectation of approval for her choice bit of gossip.

A silence fell upon the shop, one as big and deep as the fabled canyons to the southwest of Agate Creek. Even Mrs. Buntwell and Mrs. Gorman had fallen silent, faint horror and discomfort on their faces.

Shock slicked through Glory, followed by a sudden, hot rage.

How dare Faith discuss her father and sister with *strangers*? How dare that thoughtless girl treat her family tragedy as gossip fodder? Glory fought back the tears that threatened and clenched her fists beneath the counter. Glory watched her knuckles whiten. Her chest felt hot, achy — painful. Fire traced across her chest and down her arms. She struggled to breathe.

CRASH.

A cacophonous rattle of metal echoed through the shop.

Glory jumped. What on earth had happened?

She stepped from behind the counter to peer at the back of the store and stopped short.

And stared.

Mrs. Buntwell had stored her practical, bulky, and less attractive agricultural tools, such as metal shovels, hand-trowels, small axes, hoes, and the like in the back of the general store. Usually these tools hung from discreet, sturdy hooks along the back wall and from the ceiling. But when Glory stared at the back of the store, she saw that all of the tools had somehow fallen off the hooks and had scattered across the floor in an untidy sprawl. Glory glanced up. The hooks were still screwed into the walls and the ceiling.

So how had the tools fallen onto the floor?

"Damn!"

Glory looked away from the mess. And stared.

The younger brother had entangled himself in the drooping ends of the linen curtain cloth sold by the bolt. His polished boots were twisted the fabric folds, and the buttons on his suit jacket had caught in the machine-made lace that Mrs. Buntwell had ordered from Chicago. He looked a fool, and by the sheepish expression on his handsome face, he knew it.

His brother snorted and shook his head. Glory almost smiled.

And unseen by the others, Seth winked at her as though they shared a secret.

Gareth promised Mrs. Buntwell that he would pay for any damage caused by his younger brother but the proprietor, relieved at having had a gentle and humorous distraction, assured Gareth it was no trouble.

"Come along, ladies, we have tarried for far too long here," Mrs. Gorman pronounced. She bestowed an indulgent smile upon Mrs. Buntwell. "So much to do when one has family in town, yes?" Not seeking a response, the Gorman Matriarch swept to the door, and paused to call out over her shoulder: "Simply deliver the parcels to our home later."

The Gorman Ladies filed out the door.

Glory saw that both Gareth and Seth offered Mrs. Buntwell the usual niceties. To her surprise, they then turned to Glory.

"Good day to you, Miss Gloriana. Have a pleasant afternoon." Gareth spoke with a natural warmth and cheer.

"Thank you."

The brothers left and through the window, Glory watched them converse with one another while they traveled the wooden esplanade until they disappeared from sight.

Mrs. Buntwell looked at the mess of metal tools scattered across the floor of the store and gave Glory a pointed look. "Clean this up, girl."

Glory stepped forward. "I will."

Mrs. Buntwell opened her mouth to continue but stopped when a weary man with dusty clothes and dilapidated boots entered the store. Glory did not know the man but recognized the unofficial uniform of an Oregon Trail passenger, and as Mrs. Buntwell bustled across the store to assist the man, Glory looked at the considerable mess that lay in front of her. And wondered again:

How on earth had this happened?

CHAPTER THREE

Glory trudged up the stairs. The day had been long and the work hard but she dreaded returning to the room she shared with Amelie. There was no privacy and no comfort in that rented, charmless space. Sometimes she even skipped dinner just to have a half hour to herself in that room.

Just outside of the door, Glory sighed to herself. Then she reached out to turn the knob—

The door swung open, and Mrs. Buntwell stood within. "It's about time you arrived."

Glory took a step back in surprise. *What is going on?*

"Get in." Mrs. Buntwell stepped to the side. "I'm making some changes."

Glory eased into the room, the stilled. Instead of the single bed she shared with Amelie, the room had since been rearranged. Three bunk beds now crowded into the small space, covered by thin mattresses and worn quilts. Glory peered behind one bunk bed and saw Amelie cowering behind the bed frame as if she were trying to disappear altogether.

"I don't understand." Glory turned to Mrs. Buntwell. "What is going on?"

"I'm taking in more boarders," Mrs. Buntwell announced. "You two will have new roommates tomorrow morning. I'm sure you'll welcome them."

Glory eyed the small room. "I'm not sure six of us will fit in this space." She tried to keep the doubt out of her voice.

"You'll make it work." Mrs. Buntwell's steely tone brooked no arguments.

Alarm trickled through Glory and she tilted her head for a moment. *Something is missing.* "Wait — what happened to our belongings? Where is my trunk?" Her voice rose higher and louder with each word. She had to find the trunk, now. She needed to ensure she had the last remnants of her family with her.

"Personal belongings are no longer permitted in this room." Mrs. Buntwell waved a hand. "They take up too much space."

Shock immobilized Glory for a minute. "Then what did you do with my trunk?"

"I threw it out back."

"What?!" Glory staggered in place; her hand reached up to steady herself against the wall of the crammed, hateful room. Fear rippled through her. *I can't lose that trunk. I can't.* "How could you do that? That's all I have of my f-family." Her anguish broke the last word. She saw Amelie fold into herself, further hiding in the corner of the room.

Mrs. Buntwell pulled herself up to her full height. "This is not your home. That trunk took up too much space so I removed it. I will not discuss this further." She frowned at Glory. "You're overreacting, child."

Glory fell back against the wall. She felt tears cascade down her face and splash onto her collarbones below. Her breath bellowed through her like it had when she ran races at school, years ago. Her body was heavy, achy, hot, and her fingers ticklish. Her head felt as though it were wrapped in a pillow. She felt a single thought make its circuitous way through the maelstrom within her body. Finally, it arrived.

No.

No. No. NO. NOOOO.

Glory inhaled several gasping breaths. *This is not happening. This cannot happen.* Hot anger rustled within and something deep inside erupted.

Crrrraaack.

Something exploded next to Glory.

The loud, violent noise rattled her. Stunned, she threw her hands up and staggered backwards. She heard faint whistles as small projectiles pummeled her body. Mrs. Buntwell screamed, then cowered to the side of the room. Glory peered up through the tears that had smarted her eyes, trying to see what had happened.

A pipe near the ceiling had burst.

A long split separated the tube into two and the metal had splayed apart like unraveled fabric. A chill chased down her spine when Glory studied the damage. *What on earth?* She glanced around and gasped.

The rest of the room was in shambles.

The wooden boards on the walls hung askew; the nails had been ripped out and scattered across the floor of the room. The bunk beds swayed and wobbled, the nails and the braces having been flung off during the explosion. Glory winced as one teetered over and slammed into the wall before tumbling to the floor. She jumped with the door to the room thumped to the floor, the hinges missing altogether.

Something trickled down her face. Glory reached up, then pulled her fingers back to examine them.

Blood. She was bleeding.

"*You.*" The single word was pure poison.

Glory glanced up, then swallowed hard. Mrs. Buntwell loomed before her, glaring down.

"You did this," the older woman said. She raised a fist and unfurled a single finger to point at Glory. "You did this, you rotten, horrid brat. You're... you're one of those freaks!"

Stupefied, Glory could only stare at the woman. "I don't understand. What are you saying?"

"You are a freak. A magician. Don't deny it!" Mrs. Buntwell drew back her hand as though to slap Glory—

A metallic screech ripped through the air.

Distracted by the sound, Mrs. Buntwell looked away — and Glory made her escape.

She pushed away from the wall, then wrestled the useless door out of the way, letting the heavy wood fall into the room. She ignored the squawk of anger from within and dashed down the stairs, taking two at a time in her haste. Glory bumped into a man on the stairwell, bounced off him and into the rail.

"Goddamnit! Watch where you're going."

"Stop her!" Mrs. Buntwell's voice filled Glory with fear. *Move, move, move.*

On the first floor, she ran down the hallway that led her past the kitchen and to the back of the boarding house and general store. She dodged other residents and cooks, then plunged outside in the cold evening leaving behind echoes of surprise and irritation. Something familiar caught the corner of her eye and she skidded to a stop, slamming into a nearby post.

Her trunk rested on the ground just past the kitchen entrance.

Relief rushed through her. Glory raced over, then hefted the small trunk into her arms, grunting with the effort. *Thank goodness it's still here.*

"Where is that freak?" Mrs. Buntwell's angry voice curtailed her relief. Glory glanced around, searching for a path to take. Footsteps stomped closer as though someone were running down the hallway through which she had just escaped and Glory fled down an alleyway, choosing the closest one.

Glory ran down the dark, narrow lane, tripping over garbage and loose debris, the trunk bumping painfully against her chest each time she lost her footing. Her arms screamed in pain but she refused to let go. Her breath sawed in and out of her as she dodged down one alley, then another, and yet another. She didn't follow any path or pattern — she just wanted to get *away*. Away from Mrs. Buntwell, away from that horrid boarding house. Away from it all.

A train whistle pierced the night.

Glory stopped at the sound, gasping for air.

The whistle warbled again.

The train. Glory tried to think past the loud heartbeat in her ears. *I could take the train. I don't have any money, though, and where would I go?* A loud rumble, growing louder with each moment, filled the night. *It's getting closer. I can't miss it. I don't know where it's going but I'm not staying here.*

Glory adjusted her grip on the chest, then started jogging to the train station. She quickly ran out of alleys and switched to the main roads, hoping the people out tonight were too drunk to notice her. She just moved forward, panting in painful gasps. *I'm almost there. I'm almost there.*

Glory almost cried when she at last saw the train station. She slowed down to avoid attracting notice and scanned the depot. She ignored the ticket office since she couldn't afford a train ticket anyways, and looked past the common waiting space, almost empty this late in the evening. Her gaze stopped suddenly, arrested by the sign.

Luggage.

The last carriage on the train was the luggage car.

If I can sneak into the luggage car, maybe I can stowaway.

Glory started forward, her arms protesting the continued weight of her small trunk. There weren't too many passengers around but plenty of train operators and staff. She kept to the dark shadows of the depot building, waiting to move forward whenever someone looked in the opposite direction. Around the building and across the tracks, taking care to lift her feet over the metal rails. Glory continued to the other side of the luggage car, bent low.

Finally she stood before the luggage car. She set her chest on the ground, then climbed onto the platform at the end of the car to stand in front of a narrow door. She tried to turn the handle but it wouldn't give. *Locked.*

Disappointed, Glory jumped down from the platform and gathered up her small trunk. She walked to the side of the luggage car, the one that faced away from the town, and searched for an opening of some kind.

There.

There was a small sliding door roughly the size of a window near the front of the luggage carriage. Glory crept closer and when she pulled on the door, it opened with a wicked groan. She stilled, listening for an alarm or a shout. Hearing none, Glory hefted the trunk on the carriage floor and pushed it forward. Glory then pulled herself up and slipped into the carriage, bracing her feet on the sides of the railcar.

Inside, Glory slumped against the wall. Relief and pain intertwined within her; her breath sobbed out despite her attempts to stifle the sound. *I made it. I'm here.*

Someone cleared their throat in the darkness.

Glory froze.

A single match was struck, and the flame moved in a slow journey to a lamp. The stranger lit the wick within. As the light grew and illuminated the carriage, Glory gasped at the sight before her.

Two men bearing a strong resemblance to one another stood in the luggage carriage, and stared down at her, surprise and wariness etched across their faces. Glory stared at their faces, recognition ringing through her like a bell.

"Well, this is a surprise," Seth Hill remarked. "Miss Rue, what are you doing here?"

CHAPTER FOUR

Madame Quinn's Tea and Coffee Carriage bustled with the muted hum of servers and customers as the Brothers ushered Glory from the luggage carriage. The decor was done in greens and golds, with finishes of pale pink. The train carriage had big windows framed with forest green velvet drapes. Thick carpets nestled under a series of small tables, each of them set apart from one another to give the customers an illusion of privacy.

Delicate teacups rested upon matching saucers and rattled with the motion of the train. Glory saw Madame Quinn had paid for high quality sugar in decorative shapes, and each of the tables were decorated with small platters of sweets, expensive fruits, and small sandwiches. Her stomach rumbled, and Glory winced. She hadn't had dinner and after the... event, she had only focused on getting away.

"Here we are, miss." The Hill Brothers stopped before a small table, snug against a wall wrapped in brocade paper and tucked away from one of the windows. Seth pulled out a chair, and after a moment of surprise, Glory murmured her thanks and sat, acutely aware of her torn and stained skirts.

Shame rose up within and she avoided the young man's gaze. "Thank you," she murmured.

"We are delighted that we found you, Miss Glory," Gareth, the older brother, beamed a smile at Glory.

Seth leaned forward in his chair, and to her surprise, began to serve the tea. Serving refreshments was usually a woman's responsibility. The surprise must have shown on Glory's face, for he grinned in response. "We don't stand on convention, and since we found you and coerced you away from the luggage carriage and into this, I'm happy to serve," he said. "Are you partial to tea? Or coffee?"

"Tea."

"Milk?" Seth asked. She nodded.

"Sugar?"

"Yes." Glory accepted the offered teacup and took a sip. Madame Quinn's carried a fine black tea, aromatic and bracing. The blend was much better than what Mrs. Buntwell sold in the general store. Seth then prepared a cup of coffee for himself and his brother. Glory sipped the tea again, then set the cup on its saucer on the tabletop. "Thank you for the tea. For..." Glory didn't know how to finish her sentence. What did they want from her? Why had they insisted on helping her from the luggage railcar? On feeding her?

She had forgotten what kindness felt like.

A short silence fell over the table.

Seth gave a nod. "We're glad to help. Magicians look out for each other. Many of us have afoul of mundanes a time or two."

Glory opened her mouth, then paused.

Seth continued. "We had planned to introduce ourselves to you because of our connection to your parents. Or rather, our desire to learn more about your mother's work. But now we've met you! Metal, am I right? You have an Affinity for metals?"

Yesterday. Father. Mother. Affinity. Glory stilled, her cup paused midair, as the words swirled around her. She felt like a dam about to burst, and all of her questions and concerns and emotions were ready to flood out. Mrs. Buntwell's accusations swirled in her mind.

Glory leaned forward, and tea sloshed over the lid and onto the tablecloth. "So I *am* a magician?" More words tumbled out, faster and unorganized. "It has only happened twice. I think. But I don't know how I did this... thing, whatever it is. And what does this have to do with my mother and my father? I thought only magicians had Affinities."

Glory came to an abrupt stop once her mind had caught up with her mouth. She saw growing shock dawn upon the brothers' faces. Dismay and worry crowded in, too. They exchanged a long look.

"Does that mean she doesn't *know?*" Seth demanded in a low tone.

"She must not," Gareth replied.

Seth turned back to me. "What do these words mean to you?" he asked. "Thornhedge? The Academy? Affinities?" He shot each successive word forward like bullets from a revolver.

Glory shook her head. "I understand that Affinities are what magicians call their ability. But I've never heard of Thornhedge or an academy. And how is this related to my mother?"

Seth turned to his brother, his eyes wide with disbelief.

"This does complicate matters," Gareth murmured.

Glory saw the clear bafflement upon their faces. They seemed at a loss for what to do or to say. "You said you know — or knew — my mother?" Glory suggested. "Did you know my father, too?"

Gareth gazed at Glory, his dark eyes intent. At last, he spoke. "Pardon our confusion, Miss Glory. This discovery, you see, changes things."

"I don't understand." Glory felt nervous. Her palms began to sweat.

Gareth cleared his throat, reminding Glory of a child preparing his monologue at a schoolhouse recital. He began.

"Your mother, Juliet Rue, is — was, my condolences — a scholar who created an inventory of magical abilities, which are commonly called Affinities. While doing so, she integrated the principles of natural philosophy and our community's knowledge about magical abilities into a resulting publication, a text called Rue's Inventory. In doing so, she furthered our community's understanding of magical inheritance. The simple mechanism of documenting these abilities had quadrupled our collective knowledge within the space of a single generation."

Glory felt stunned and short of breath, like the time she had fallen off a horse. "My mother did this? Are you certain you have the right person?" She shook her head.

"Oh, yes." Gareth pulled out a small black notebook and pencil stub from an inner pocket of his suit and waved it. "You see, we followed the census records. We also got a tip from a colleague at Thornhedge."

"And you say she was magician?"

Gareth and Seth glanced at each other, the quick look colored by confusion. "Er, yes, of course," Gareth replied. "She was. Mind, she wasn't known for her work as a magician. But she was a wonderful scholar."

Had her mother and father really had another life? A secret life? Glory took a sip of cold tea just to give her hands something to do. If all of this was true, why hadn't her father shared these details with her and Lily?

Gareth brushed away crumbs before speaking again. "With every generation, as far back as our myths indicate, there are a few members of the human species who have an ability that is something *more,* an Affinity if you will, for a particular skillset or a natural element. These Affinities set themselves apart from traditional notions or manifestations of hard work and talent at a specific endeavor because these same abilities transcend the natural order of the world. They are supernatural."

"Supernatural?" Glory echoed.

"How else would you have destroyed a wing of that boarding house?" Seth queried. He leaned forward, his thoughtful gaze on Glory, and she flushed at his close attention. "Yes, we heard the news but we suspect that Buntwell embroidered the truth to serve her own ends. Was that the first time you had used your Affinity? Or perhaps it was the incident at the general store? With the farming tools?"

Glory looked between the brothers. "I think so?"

"Ah. Do you... Forgive me, do you know what your Affinity *is*?"

Baffled, Glory looked from Seth to Gareth, and finding no help there, back again. "I don't know." Her hand tightened on her teacup, knuckles white as frustration trickled through her. *How could Father put me into this position? One in which* strangers *are telling me I have a magical gift?* Worry chased those thoughts and Glory shivered. *Was he hiding something?*

Glory set her teacup on the table. She leaned back in her seat. Took a deep breath. And another.

"Let's continue." Gareth sounded determined. "Affinities, the supernatural gifts that allow each member of our society to perform a task with extraordinary power and focus, are found among all races and on every known continent."

"Known continent?" Glory interrupted.

Seth grinned. "He loves the myths about Atlantis. When we were children, he was determined to locate the lost continent. He remains hopeful to this day."

"Ah." Glory smiled into the biscuit she nibbled on. The brothers' easy rapport and gentle teasing reminded Glory of her and Lily. Sorrow sluiced through her at the thought of her little sister. *Had Lily had an Affinity?* Glory would never know.

Gareth's cheeks reddened but he continued. "Affinities appear to be hereditary, as is the case in the Hill and Rue families." Gareth gave a nod to Glory. "But not all children inherit an Affinity. And these abilities may not present themselves even in families who possess generations of Affinities. I believe these failures to manifest an Affinity to be a chance mutation, not a moral deficiency or a curse, as some more ignorant people maintain."

"Regardless of where Affinities present themselves, there is also the matter of frequency. The observable facts are that Affinities remain rare among all populations. Given our low numbers, gathering consistent and accurate information — instead of myths and wild half-truths — has been difficult. Until recently."

Gareth paused, and Glory realized that she had only half-listened to the last bit of his lecture. She found herself turning over several questions within her mind at once. Glory looked up. "Why did you come to Agate Creek? My father left your Academy at some point, or else he wouldn't have ended up in that town."

Seth leaned forward once more, his eyes fixed upon her face. "We sought your father at the behest of a friend and colleague. We've never met him, only read of your mother's work. We only wished to consult with him, I promise you. Maybe even read through her journals, with her permission. Er, your permission, I mean." Glory watched his lips move and his fingers tap against the leg of his trousers. It seemed important to him, Glory thought, that she believed him.

She gave a slow nod.

A glorious smile broke out across his face, one that had her looking away. A flutter thrummed through her. "Do you know why my father left? Or when?" Glory only remembered Agate Creek and the surrounding flatlands; she had no memory of another town, of any other life. Of her mother.

Gareth had started to shake his head before she had finished speaking. "I don't know what prompted your father to leave us," he said, his eyes sad. "Perhaps someone could answer that, when you join us at Thornhedge."

Glory sat upright. Surprise filtered through her like sunlight. "Join you?"

Gareth seemed nonplussed by her reaction. "Well, yes."

Seth rolled his eyes. "Well handled," he said in a dry tone. "Excellent work." He looked at Glory. "He refers to Thornhedge Academy, where those with Affinities may get an education and develop their gifts. It is the premier institution of the West," he added with a distinct touch of pride in his voice.

Gareth harrumphed. "San Francisco has greater diversity in magical abilities."

Seth sighed. "Then it is *one* of the premier institutions of the West."

Glory was still confused. "Why would I attend Thornhedge?"

Now it was the Brothers' turn to be puzzled. "Why, to develop your own Affinity, of course," Gareth answered. "You clearly have an ability. You should have an opportunity to grow your gifts and to use them."

"You have a powerful one, based on what we heard about today," Seth added.

"Maybe there's been a misunderstanding?" Glory offered. She knew she grasped at straws. "Maybe I'm not... what you say I am."

Seth merely smiled. "No."

"Pretend that you did have an Affinity," Gareth invited. "Would you entertain the possibility of attending Thornhedge?"

Glory's face burned from embarrassment, but she forced herself to say the words. "I do not believe that I have sufficient funds for further education." *Or any at all.*

Gareth nodded his understanding.

Her heart sank. *Foolish,* Glory thought. *Foolish to get excited about this impossible endeavor.*

Then Gareth spoke. "I understand your concerns. Fortunately, Academy administrators insisted that tuition remain low or free for those who could not afford such sums." Some of her skepticism must have bled across her face, for he continued in a firm voice. "Which covers *all* expenses. We believe in the merits of a free education for all."

Glory sat back in her seat. "Oh." A pause. Then, in a cautious tone: "I would be able to attend on a scholarship of sorts?"

Gareth nodded. "I can wire them from the next town to let them know you're arriving soon."

Seth cleared his throat and he raised his eyebrows. "So, will you enroll in Thornhedge?"

Glory shifted in her seat, uneasy and overwhelmed. If she went, Glory could learn more about her mother's legacy. She could perhaps learn why her father had been so secretive about their family history. "I need to think a moment."

Gareth waited all of one minute before he continued, eager to persuade her. "Another inducement for you: With the Falstead Act, practicing magic is now legal and has been for a little over two decades." Gareth paused, as if searching for the right words. "I advise you to be cautious with whom you share your ability, though. Not all people welcome magicians."

Glory nodded. She remembered Pastor Brooks' aversion, his disdain for the new magician in town.

"No one wants a witch hunt," Seth muttered.

"Quite so." Gareth sipped his tea.

"Where is Thornhedge Academy?" Glory asked.

"In Denver, Colorado."

Gareth sipped his tea again, then looked at her. "So Miss Glory: Are you joining us at the Academy?"

Yes.

Her sudden response startled even her, and for a moment, Glory wondered if she had spoken aloud. She hadn't realized how quiet, how painfully empty, her life had become in the absence of her father and Lily. The thought of living a life like the one she had led in Agate Creek withered something vital within her. Glory looked down at her hands, wrung together in her lap and beneath the edge of table. She wanted the opportunity, desperately.

"What would I truly do with a *magical* education?" she asked.

"You have just now learned about Affinities, correct?" Gareth countered her question with one of his own. "I would wager that you have never been Tested properly. Upon completion of the Academy's Affinity Trial, I believe it's safe to assume that new opportunities will present themselves to you." Gareth's eyes twinkled with his enthusiasm, and for a moment, he almost looked as young as his brother.

"Have we alleviated your concerns, Miss Glory?" Seth's voice cut across her thoughts.

"Please also consider, Miss Glory, that if you join us at Thornhedge, you may find your mother's presence throughout the Academy." Gareth studied a plate of biscuits before choosing a lemon flavored one. He nestled further back into his chair. "I believe that rather than leaving your father here in Agate Creek, you would find him and your mother again in a new place."

Tears threatened. Glory looked away from Gareth and focused upon the thick carpet at her feet while she regained her composure, the worn tips of her walking boots that peeked out from beneath the ruined skirts she wore. In the discussion of Thornhedge, of Affinities, it had never occurred Glory that she could learn about her family history outside of Agate Creek.

Seth leaned forward in his seat.

"Miss Glory, I would like provide one last reason for attending Thornhedge," he began. His eyes, which were fixed upon hers, sparkled with a conspiratorial enthusiasm. "Thornhedge Academy houses scientists and natural philosophers, artists, and authors of great import from around the world. And once you have fully developed your Affinity, who knows what you will do? Where else you will travel?" He paused and he leaned even closer with an impish grin. "In short, Miss Glory, my brother and I are inviting you to a lifetime of adventure."

Chapter Five

At full speed, the train made remarkable progress across the plains. To Glory, who had never before ridden a train, the speed seemed truly magical — more real to her than the supernatural gift assigned to her by the Brothers. As the day dawned, she witnessed the landscape change in gradual bursts of new colors and textures. The plains grew drier, with less gold and green that morphed into a persistent rust brown. Scrub brush and short, dark green pines popped up in closer proximity to one another. The smell and the very feel of the air changed, dry and abrasive to her face in a way the hardest winds on the plains never were.

Soon Glory had another realization: Travel by train was... boring.

Apart from the landscape, there wasn't much to look at. The train wobbled to a stop in the few towns that dotted the plains. The travelers from these small towns seemed to comprise mostly small families and single men. The trunks and the luggage were sorted into the baggage railcar, the passengers settled into their respective cars, and the train would then rumble into motion soon after.

The train lurched forward, then back, in rapid succession.

The whiplash roused Glory from her nap. She gazed around the railcar with bleary eyes. "What happened?"

The train groaned, then slammed to a stop in a sudden, vicious motion. Glory was thrown from her seat and into Seth. She scrambled to get off the young man but, hindered by skirts and an unwillingness to put her hands on his thighs, Glory simply flopped onto the floor.

"What the hell?" Seth reached down and assisted Glory to her feet.

Gareth peered out the window, craning his neck to look up and down the sides of the train. "I'm not sure. We're not stopped at a depot."

The clamor of the passengers swelled, the noise flavored with confusion and panic. The train wasn't scheduled for another stop until Sweet Springs, a small mining town four hours east of Denver where most passengers would stay the night in a hotel. But that stop was scheduled for early evening, and when Glory glanced outside, she saw bright daylight on the rust brown land.

Then a shout echoed down the rail car.

"Robbers! The train is being robbed!"

As the shout died down, Glory watched the passengers break from the collective, frozen shock and began to scatter. Several men and women gathered guns from satchels and from holsters; older family members gathered children close to them and sank to the floor between the benches. As one, her companions grabbed Glory by her arms and ushered her to a seat closest to the aisle and away from the windows.

Seth brushed aside his long, tailored coat to reveal a pistol strapped to his left leg; Gareth pulled a short-nosed six-shooter from a shoulder holster hidden beneath his own jacket. The ease with which they handled the weapons spoke of longstanding familiarity and expertise.

Shocked, Glory could only stare at them. She had never imagined that these sophisticated men would be able to respond to a dangerous situation with such ready ease. Glory watched Seth peer out the window, and then still.

"Gareth." Seth's voice was low, urgent. "They are going after the luggage car." The brothers exchanged a look, and an entire conversation occurred between them. "One of us should stay with her," Seth stated.

"Yes," Gareth replied.

Seth turned to Glory. "Do you know how to use a pistol?"

Glory shook her head.

Gareth's shoulders sank and he heaved a sigh. "One of us definitely has to stay with her." He peered out the window. "Who's going out there?"

"I'll go." Seth stepped past Glory, then disappeared down the aisle and into the next car.

Glory looked throughout the railcar. Worried faces and hushed voices greeted her gaze, and she saw that several men and one short woman in cowboy chaps lined the windows on either side of the railcar, with pistols and even a few rifles at the ready. Two men stood at either end of the railcar, guarding the entrances. Everyone waited for something to happen, tense and nervous.

A shot rang out.

Glory jumped and clutched the hammer even tighter.

Gareth's head flung up. "Seth," he muttered. "What is he doing?"

"How do you know that was Seth?" Glory asked.

Gareth gave a grim smile. "It's always Seth." He peered out the window, then grunted in exasperation. He turned to Glory. "Stay here. I'm going to investigate."

"What?!" Alarm blazoned through Glory. *I don't want to be left alone here.* Two more shots broke the silence. Then the train rocked from side to side, and Glory staggered into the wall, her free hand scrabbling for purchase.

"Just stay here and stay away from the windows," Gareth ordered. "He's going to get himself killed," he muttered as he stepped past Glory and into the aisle.

Glory shrank into the walls and held the smith's hammer against her body like a shield. And she waited.

Several minutes passed.

And then several more.

Waiting for disaster to strike was the worst feeling, Glory found. A tense silence had fallen over the railcar, only broken by intermittent whimpers from the two young children a few seats down. Their grandmother rocked them against her body, her ornate violet traveling dress an oddly cheerful contrast to the fear and anticipation that resided in the railcar. She made shushing noises that the children ignored, worry pleating her brow in concern.

The train rocked again, and for a brief, terrifying moment, seemed to tilt to the side before slamming back onto the tracks. Glory dropped the hammer and grabbed an armrest with her free hand.

A man yelled out, "They're boarding the train!"

Several more gun shots served as an exclamatory of sorts.

A nearby man with a rifle shifted from one foot to another, unease clear on his face. "This is taking too damn long," Glory heard him mutter to his neighbor at the window, another man with a .44 pistol in one hand. "Why don't the conductors just decouple the baggage cars already? They keep this up, someone's going to die."

The other shook his head, with eyes trained on the window and his features pinched with worry. "I don't know. Something about this stinks to high heaven."

BOOM.

Whoosh.

An explosion rocked the train.

The blast flung Glory onto the floor; the subsequent shudder of the railcar as it slammed into the adjacent car tossed Glory into the wall. A second blast ripped through railcar, and Glory could hear and see several things at once:

She heard the next railcar groan against the one she occupied, a grotesque and awful metallic embrace.

She heard the screams of the frightened children.

She smelled smoke.

She heard her heartbeat in her ears, an arrhythmic percussion that accompanied the fear that flooded her body.

How would they survive this?

The men in the aisles and neighboring compartments shouted:

"Fuck, fuck! This is it."

"Stay down and hold on!"

Hold on? What is happening?

She felt the car tilt off the track, and pitch further and further to the side.

Then the railcar tipped over. Off the tracks, and onto the hard, brown land below. Glory curled into herself and braced for impact.

Glory woke to the sounds of gunshots.

She didn't know where she was. She tried to sit up and gasped from the pain that thrummed through her body. Her face was wet and her hands shook. Glory probed her face in gentle motions, wincing at the soreness, and pulled her hand to look at it. Her fingers trembled as she examined the tips; her throat tightened with fear.

Her fingertips dripped with blood and tears.

Then she remembered: The train had tipped over. Pushed over, like a child's toy in a nightmarish nursery.

No wonder everything hurt.

Glory grabbed a nearby bench edge, perpendicular to where it should have been, and pulled herself up with slow and careful motions. Her body ached with every movement, but no bones seemed broken. Upright, Glory surveyed the wreckage: The railcar had fallen onto its left side, pitching the occupants into a haphazard and broken pile of humanity and luggage. Glory could see several unconscious passengers sprawled across the car walls on either side of her; she couldn't determine if they were dead or alive. She heard whimpers

from someone —she couldn't tell if they were children or adults —
and could smell spilled oil. And blood.

My trunk. Glory searched around her and found both items several
feet away, cast like dice in a game. *I can't lose it. Not now, not after all
of this.* They were remnants of her life with Lily and her father.

A blood-and-dirt stained hand thrust itself into her face, and Glory
flinched.

"Miss, can you stand? We're getting the live ones out first." A man,
a stranger in denim and a wool vest, pulled Glory into a crouch before
ushering her down the makeshift aisle. She stumbled and tripped her
away down the aisle, gathering her belongings. She took careful, ginger
steps over the spilled luggage and the unconscious bodies cast about
within the railcar. Glory could hear her heartbeat in her ears. She tried
not to look at those who hadn't survived. Her heart hurt when she saw
the still, open eyes.

At the end of the railcar, two men hoisted Glory onto the exterior
platform where she knew the conductors would stand if the train were
still on the tracks. From there, she half-tumbled, half-slid down the
platform and onto solid ground. Glory had no time to rest, though:
Another passenger, this one a small girl in blood splattered, brown
calico skirts slid down shortly after. Glory reached out a hand to
stabilize the child, then stepped back to look up and down the train
tracks. She saw that the detonations had knocked two cars off the
tracks; the others were damaged but still upright.

It's a miracle that it's not worse, Glory thought.

More gun shots erupted. Her head jerked up, and horror trickled
down her spine.

The train robbers were still here.

A dozen or so men in cowboy chaps on horseback, with red or
blue bandanas over their faces and with pistols in their hands, surged

closer to the train. In the distance and to the left of the toppled train, Glory saw a stagecoach hitched to a team of four horses that waited on a rutted road nearby, partially hidden by the brush. The coach was guarded by more men atop the coach. She saw the glint of metal muskets flash through the sunlight. *Ready to carry away stolen goods from the derailed trains*, Glory thought. She remembered the still bodies within the railcar and felt a wash of fury sweep away a fraction of her fear. These robbers had killed for mere profit.

Glory glanced at the luggage train, certain that it had already been breached, and stopped.

And stared.

Seth and Gareth Hill nestled atop the luggage car a few railcars down, shoulder to shoulder and knees spread apart in a wide stance, as they faced down the robbers. Their fine clothes were torn and stained, and Glory could see that Seth had a red goose egg on his forehead from where she stood. Glory watched Gareth man a repeating rifle and use it well. The older brother aimed in slow, careful, and steady motions before he squeezed the trigger.

Crrrack! A flash of gunfire before a robber squalled and tumbled off his horse. Gareth cocked the rifle and aimed again.

Glory glanced at Seth and paused. *What in heaven was he doing?* Seth frowned in concentration and stared into the distance, his raised fists in the air and his guns at his knees. Sweat and blood shimmered across his face and as he bit his lower lip in concentration, it bled red down his chin. A rattle shook the earth beneath Glory. A groan that sounded like a landslide tore free from the ground. *An earthquake?* She followed the sound, the gasped.

A shard of rust red rock had erupted out of the ground to pitch the robbers' stagecoach onto its side. The robbers cascaded off the coach like raindrops as it tipped over. The horses screamed and reared in fear, white eyes and frothed flanks. They lunged forward, dragging the tipped stagecoach behind them.

Glory whipped her head to stare at Seth. He had done that. A sense of awe trickled through her. A magician could do *this*?

A gunshot rang out — and Seth cursed. Red bloomed across his right arm; he had been shot. Gareth stepped in front of his brother, and tried to urge him back to cover, to safety. The robbers sensed their advantage and urged the horses closer, shooting in rapid bursts of gunfire.

Glory started forward, then stopped. *What could she do?* The Brothers needed to get *off* that railcar. She had to do *something*. She didn't know exactly what. But better to move than do nothing.

Glory started forward in a low crouch, and moved behind the railcars, keeping to the edge of the train tracks and out of view of the robbers. She couldn't do anything about her yellow dress, now stained with soot and blood, which made her such an obvious target. Glory stepped over a gnarled metal shard on the ground. Finally, she had reached the luggage railcar and ducked into the conductor's platform. Glory peered out around the edge of the railcar.

She squinted. Shock arced through her as she took in the scene before her. Was that... was that her trunk? With her mother's research?

It was.

The trunk rested on the ground about twenty yards away, a new dent on the side and the handles ripped off. No other luggage was present — just her trunk. Disbelief unfurled through Glory. Why would the robbers be after her luggage? That made no sense. *Maybe this is all that they must have had time to grab before the shooting started,* Glory thought.

A groan of pain interrupted her thoughts. Then, "Glory! Why in hell are you here?"

Glory glanced up. Seth stared down at her from the railcar rooftop. Horror and fatigue marred his features. Past him, she saw that Gareth had had to switch to the pistols he kept in his shoulder holsters. *He must have ran out of bullets for the repeating rifle*, she thought. Glory's heart sank. From her time in the general store in Agate Creek, she knew the range on pistols weren't sufficient to protect them from the remaining thieves. As though to punctuate her thoughts, Glory saw the robbers move forward.

"Get the trunk!" One of the men, this one in a black hat and a blue bandana, pointed to the trunk with his pistol. Another man, a red bandana over his face, rode forward with the reins in one hand and a rope in the other. He twirled the lariat in lazy motions, his intent clear.

They are after my chest, Glory thought. *But why? What was important to robbers?* Seth had only mentioned her mother's research journals. A shudder rippled through her.

No, she thought. *Something* cracked inside her chest. *No. I can't lose the last connection I have to my family.*

Raw power, hot and energetic, pulsed in her chest and then spread through her torso. It felt like lightning within her veins, and Glory smelled smoke and burnt hair. She had only felt this energy, this magic, a few times before and yet it was already familiar. The tips of her fingers were ticklish, and she flexed her hands.

And then, she knew what to do.

Glory lifted her right hand and twisted her fingers — and an iron metal bracket on the luggage railcar rent itself away the wood with a sharp crack. Splinters and shards flew through the air, showering Glory. She felt something slice her face; she ignored it. Another wave of her fingers, and the strip of iron arrowed through the air at the robbers. The thieves screamed and cursed, wheeling their horses to the side. The iron strip slammed into the abandoned stagecoach. The poor horses still attached to the overturned coach lunged forward, trying to escape the reins that trapped them in place.

Glory stared at the stagecoach, stunned. *I did that*, she thought. *It felt so... natural.*

She didn't have long to enjoy the feeling. The man in black and blue pressed forward once again, and Glory wondered at his determination. What value could her personal belongings possibly contain that he would risk himself so? She clasped her still raised hand into a fist. Two more railroad spikes ripped from the tracks with a metallic screech and sped through the air at the man.

The man's eyes widened over the nose of the blue bandana, so much so that Glory could see the whites of his eyes from where she stood.

And then he fled, jerking his horse's head to the right.

Whipping his poor mount, he aimed for the small hill a short distance away. The spikes continued until he faded from view. Then, Glory dropped her fist to her side. She couldn't *see* her makeshift weapons fall to the ground but she *felt* them reverberate through her skull as they clattered through the air. Glory swayed in place, then staggered a few steps to the side. The ticklish sensation had left her fingertips. Instead, they now felt scorched. *Tired*. She was so tired. And empty. Her head ached, as though she had had a recent bout of illness.

A step sounded behind her. *Someone else was there*. Glory stumbled around, wary, and her hand crept up.

"Whoa, whoa! Put the hand down," Seth barked. Glory saw him give her a thorough glance, and his frown lightened into sympathy; the panic in his voice subsided into a gentle reassurance. "It's alright. It's only me." A pause. "You're safe now."

Seth looked like she felt: Exhausted, dirty, and covered in blood. The sleeve of his shirt had matted with blood where he had been shot; he had fashioned a sling for his arm.

Seth frowned. "How do you feel?"

"Tired." Glory paused, searching for the right words. "Confused." She shook her head. "What were they after? None of this makes any sense."

His frown deepened as he studied Glory. After a moment, he spoke. "Gareth and I can explain." He surveyed the scene of wreckage, machine and human alike, before them. Seth turned back to Glory.

"Later. We'll have to talk later."

CHAPTER SIX

Glory settled into the hip bath with a heavy sigh. The warm water both soothed her skin and stung her cuts, and the metal basin pressed against her new bruises. Every bone in her body ached. She rested for a moment, savoring the quiet stall in the bathhouse. The shouts of laughter and the noise from the kitchen within the nearby hotel and saloon faded somewhat, and she drew a deep breath for what seemed like the first time that day.

Glory thought it a miracle, really, that all the passengers, dead and alive, made it into the destined town, Sweet Springs, late that very same evening. A shepherd had been grazing his flock in a nearby pasture and had heard the noise from the detonations and gunfights. He came to investigate, and seeing the wreckage of the train, he had left for the town to seek the sheriff and relief for the passengers.

One of the passengers was a nurse and had begun treating the injured immediately, persistent in the provision of her care even through the gunfire. Despite her own fatigue, Glory had helped the nurse as best as she could. Glory had felt grateful to survive, and had wanted to help, to do something useful.

So Glory had been shocked and then embarrassed when two of the passengers had refused her assistance. The young couple had backed away from Glory when she approached with a borrowed quilt, and the young woman, a short redhead with fair skin and freckles, had caressed the small gold cross she wore around her neck. Her husband, a short man with a bushy eyebrow that joined in the middle, curled a protective arm around the woman before snapping at Glory. "Get away from us."

Glory had stared in disbelief and hurt, her cheeks red with embarrassment and the proffered quilt lax in her hands. Why would this man treat her in such a manner? What was wrong with him? Then Glory had realized: The young couple had seen Glory use her Affinity. She heard an echo of Pastor Brooks in her head: *"God's law transcends that of man."* Apparently, these two shared his views on the subject of magicians.

Seth had been nearby and gathered Glory away from the couple. He had glared at the husband before telling Glory, "They are ignorant," he had said through gritted teeth. "Forget them."

She had followed Seth away, desperate to get away from the couple but unable to escape the discomfort the couple's disgust had left behind, like a smeared handprint on a freshly painted wall.

Later, Glory had been in mid-rip of a petticoat, to serve as makeshift bandages and slings when the unexpected reinforcements had arrived from Sweet Springs: More men, five wagons and two litters, the sheriff, the undertaker, and a doctor. The live and less damaged passengers had already removed the survivors to a single huddle on one side of the train. Three dead passengers were placed on the other side of the train, out of view of the children.

Another miracle, Glory reflected, to have so few deaths. Nevertheless, the county's only doctor, a young man in a bowler hat and with a black handbag, had looked sad and overwhelmed at the sight that stretched before him. It had been a long afternoon. The train passengers hadn't arrived into town until late that same evening.

"Miss?" A young woman called through the curtain that afforded some privacy to the bathhouse residents. "Are you done?"

Glory sighed. She was loathe to leave the hip bath but knew others were waiting, and stood up. At least dinner would be soon, and with it, some answers.

The hotel's crowded dining room was a simple affair with calico tablecloths, wooden chairs, and oil lamps. From what little Glory had seen of Sweet Springs from the wagon ride into town, the small settlement had translated its former mining glory into the profitable business of being a train stop on the way to Denver. Despite being smaller in size, Sweet Springs had more hotels and saloons than Agate Creek. Glory had even spied a brothel attached to the one of the larger saloons, with women in silks and black lined eyes lounging on a balcony above the entrance.

The Hill Brothers stood when Glory joined them at their table, a courtesy that startled her a bit. In the general store in Agate Creek, she experienced little courtesy from Mrs. Buntwell's customers and she was even less accustomed to the courtesy that gentlemen showed ladies. Glory settled herself into a chair, and the Brothers followed suit. Seth managed to hide his wince as he bumped his injured arm on the chair arm. *He's not wearing his sling,* Glory thought.

"How are you feeling?" he inquired, smoothing the pain from his face.

"Exhausted." Glory said.

A young man arrived with platters of food, distracting her. Her stomach rumbled. Glory hadn't realized how hungry she was. The dinner meal matched the dining room: a simple and serviceable array of cornbread, stew, and beans. Glory ate in silence and with focus. She still felt hungry once she had cleaned her plate; she tried to be discreet as she pursued the last crumbs of the cornbread. She looked up to find the Brothers watching her with identical looks of knowing amusement.

Glory blushed and placed the fork next to her plate.

Gareth gave a quiet chuckle, but Seth laughed out loud. Glory's blush deepened and she could feel the heat rise from her cheeks.

Seth caught it. "Don't be embarrassed," he urged. "Using your Affinity, especially in such an enormous display, always drains you.

You need to eat and then rest in order to regain your strength, especially when you're new to this. That's simply the way of it."

Glory looked at the Brothers' plates. Both brothers still had food to eat. She gave Seth a skeptical glance. "Really?"

Now it was Gareth's turn to laugh out loud. "Seth is right, I promise you. We are adept at using our Affinities; we've done this for a long time. With proper training and much practice, you can learn how to use your Affinity safely, in ways that won't compromise your health."

Glory gave a slow nod. She hadn't known that the use of her gift would induce such hunger. She felt her brow furrow. *I don't know anything,* she realized. Exasperation soured her enjoyment of the food, her peace in the dining room. She wanted to ask so many questions but where would she even start?

"What are your Affinities?" Glory finally asked.

"Mine is simpler to understand, so I'll start," Gareth said. "I'm a mender. I can mend small breaks or cuts, or other kinds of damage, in most materials." He nodded at Seth. "I mended his arm earlier this evening. That's why he's not in a sling."

Glory frowned. "So... you're a healer?"

Gareth shook his head. "If my ability limited itself to other humans, I suppose I would be. However, I can restore most materials or things to their original state. For example, I can re-attach a blade that has broken from its handle. Or I can fix a sapling bent by the wind or rain. But there are definite limitations to my Affinity: I can't re-root a fallen, fully grown tree. Or rebuild a home destroyed by a fire." Gareth shook his head. "My ability is merely useful, I'm afraid. Nothing out of the ordinary."

Glory disagreed. How useful that Affinity would have been in in the general store! Or in her father's home. She gave Seth with an expectant look.

He gave a rueful grin. "Mine is more complicated. Simply put, I'm manipulate soils and the geology of the earth."

Glory stared. "I don't quite understand."

Seth grinned; Gareth chuckled. This topic seemed to be an inside joke for them. He turned back to Glory. "Essentially, I can magically intuit the composition of the minerals that make up the land beneath our feet, and I can manipulate it. Because of that ability, I can also find water."

Gareth continued when Seth paused. "It's a rare ability, and the diagnosticians at the Academy had a devil of a time figuring out what it was. They were flummoxed. Many of them thought he had some kind of botanical Affinity."

"It wasn't until I had perfected my trick of stone and soil eruptions did they finally realize that I'm a soil man, not necessarily a plants man," Seth said, with a lazy grin.

"Your ability is rare?" Glory asked. She looked at Gareth. "And yours is.. not?"

"An Affinity can manifest in any kind of ability," Gareth replied. "We have students and faculty with every possible magical ability, and with varying strengths in those abilities. That being said, there are common types of Affinities that many magicians have. Culinary, botanical, and healing abilities or some variant thereof are the most common. Which makes a certain kind of sense.

"Many of the faculty at Thornhedge subscribe to Mr. Darwin's ideas on evolution and natural selection, and believe that magical abilities in humans were shaped by the same forces that shaped non-magical human genetics — luck, environment, and existing potential for magical abilities within humankind. As humans evolved over millennia, it's obvious that magical abilities responded to specific environmental pressures, such as the ability to safely grow, select, and prepare foods, or to heal oneself and family members from illness and injuries."

Gareth frowned as though something had just occurred to him. "Apologies. I often lecture at the Academy, where I'm confident that my audience is familiar with some of the foundational knowledge upon which my lectures are based." He paused, seeming to struggle with this next query. "May I ask about your educational history?"

Glory didn't understand. "My educational history?"

Seth rolled his eyes. "He wants to know if you can read, write, and do arithmetic."

Gareth glared at him. "Yes. But I believe diplomacy matters."

Glory smiled at the Brothers, relieved and a little amused. "My father had the largest library in Agate Creek, and beyond. He wasn't satisfied with the local schoolhouse because he thought our schoolmarm didn't challenged her students enough, so he insisted that Lily and I read from his library to supplement our education." Glory's smile deepened as she remembered the quiet afternoons in her father's study, nestled in a chair next to Lily whose feet couldn't quite reach the ground and reading the texts assigned to her by her father. "My father valued education and developed entire lesson plans based on questions Lily or I would ask. So, in response to your question, I am familiar with Mr. Darwin's work."

"Lily?" Seth inquired, his brows raised.

Glory's smile faded. "My sister. She passed a year ago." Glory cleared her throat. "The wasting sickness."

"Our condolences on your loss, Glory," Seth murmured. It was the first time he had used her given name. Glory nodded, her eyes fixed on her empty dinner plate.

She wondered what gift Lily would have had.

"Well, Gary, now you know." Seth seemed determined to lift the spirits around the table. "She can read."

"Very droll, Seth." The older man shook his head. "Let's return to my original point: Magical abilities were likely shaped by the same principles of natural selection that shaped human evolution. This hypothesis also provides some understanding for the origin of magical abilities: It simply assumes that humans always had the potential for magical abilities, and these abilities simply manifested in time and in response to specific environments."

"So magic is inherited then?" Glory asked.

"Yes, and no." Gareth grimaced. "Magic *can* be inherited from magical parents. However, a magical lineage provides no guarantee that each family member with have an Affinity. Likewise, a non-magical lineage can produce a child who does have an Affinity." Gareth paused, and muttered almost to himself, "The very randomness of how Affinities manifest does point to a genetic basis for the origin of magical abilities."

"And my mother studied this?" Doubt echoed through Glory's voice. "Truly?"

"Yes," Seth assured her. He studied her a moment, his brows pleated in puzzlement. "What else are you worried about?"

Glory hesitated, then spoke. "Why were the robbers after my luggage? Is that connected to my mother?"

The Brothers stilled and exchanged another glance. "That we can't reveal, unfortunately."

Glory frowned as irritation rippled through her. "Why not? It's my trunk, my family belongings."

"We're working on a project assigned to us by the Academy leadership. We cannot divulge our goals or tasks to anyone who hasn't been authorized," Seth said.

"What, you're magical Pinkertons?" She looked from one brother to the other. "Spies?"

Seth blinked, then laughed out loud. "Damn, there's no getting anything past you."

Glory didn't acknowledge the confirmation. Instead, her frown etched deeper into her brow. "What kind of investigation would possibly require my mother? Or her work?"

The Brothers simply stared at Glory, their resemblance strengthened by the identical expressions of impassivity. *This is a serious matter for them*, Glory thought.

Gareth broke the brief silence that fell over the table. "We should adjourn. We have a long day tomorrow."

As Glory readied for sleep in the shared hotel room where two other young ladies slept nearby on a large four poster bed, she reflected on the night's conversation. What the Brothers didn't say was even more telling than what they had shared: The answer to the mystery they wouldn't speak of lay in her rescued trunk.

Perhaps the answers to her own mystery could be found there, too.

INTERLUDE

H e stepped back.

Nothing. All this effort, for *nothing*.

Disgust twisted his face. Alternating waves of frustration and fury flickered through him. He gazed down at the corpse in front of him, the limbs in neat repose, the head tilted up with a slack jaw and the long brown hair pushed back from the pale white blue scalp. A precise incision marred the forehead, the straight line a boundary from which the skin had been forced apart and the flaps peeled back to make room for his inquiry.

He gave a sudden curse and flung the surgeon's forceps across the cramped studio. The metal clanged against the damp wooden walls with a muffled thud.

This girl had seemed so promising, truly rife with potential for his work. She had a unique ability, a prerequisite for his attention and labor: She had an Affinity for bees and beekeeping. With her magic, she partnered with the bees in her hives and in the adjacent neighborhoods in this small boomtown to develop flavorful honeys and even colored beeswax. She was a local celebrity of sorts.

He had wanted that gift for himself.

He *needed* a gift, to belong.

He pushed away from the operating table and made himself go to his erstwhile desk (a few flat wooden planks atop two worn sawhorses), to sit down and transcribe the details of operation — the manner of death, the incision, the proposed location of an Affinity within the body — and in the specific ways he had failed. It took him longer than he liked and he vibrated with restrained anger by the time he finished his notes; he loathed each of these failures and despised having to document his errors. He felt a sense of growing doubt and desperation with each corpse he left behind. What if he couldn't succeed? What if it were impossible? He shook off those thoughts, and continued collecting observations about the young woman's autopsy.

He would succeed. He *would*.

The alternative didn't bear thinking about.

Finally, the notes seemed as complete as possible, even to his exacting standards. He closed the cover of the large journal with a short-lived sense of relief; he wouldn't have to revisit this entry for a while. He ran a finger down the red and gold spine of the journal: The young beekeeper's autopsy fell near the middle of the thick, leather bound volume. So many entries, so many experiments, and with little to show for it. His shoulders sagged, weighed down by bleak despair.

He put the journal aside and stood. In quick motions, he wiped down the surgeon's tools (scalpels, saws, forceps, and more) in whiskey before packing the items into his neat satchel. He hated bloodstains on his luggage. He removed the apron, his fingers fumbling with the tight knots behind his back and near the nape of his neck. Yanking the garment off, he cast it over the body. Then he gathered the volume with his notes, his research, and tucked it into the satchel.

He left the cramped room, and its contents, without a second look.

He needed to find a new lead.

CHAPTER SEVEN

Their arrival in Denver was uneventful: Glory and the Brothers had simply boarded a different train which then conveyed them to the city. The Brothers then hired a cab to take them to the Academy. Denver was unlike anything Glory had ever seen.

She watched the streets pass by like pages in a book. Each neighbor-hood seemed to tell its own story, some dominated by family homes where others seemed overrun with shops and businesses. The sheer size of the city felt never ending, with cobbled roads and freshly paint-ed shopfronts. The scents and noises were insistent, almost invasive; the former mostly offensive while the latter was a cacophony.

After a while, it was clear to Glory that they were headed to the outskirts of the city: The homes here were built with wood rather than brick, with more land between these edifices. Livestock and children ran freely upon the land. The road, though well maintained, became well worn dirt tracks rather than cobblestone.

Soon they arrived at Thornhedge.

The Academy was less one great manor but rather several of them, organized in a series of square courtyards, and lined in two- or three-story grey stone buildings. Large windows adorned every floor and roses, pansies, and bluebells edged each courtyard. Cobblestone paths zig-zagged the courtyards, and Glory saw several individuals walking them. Were they students? Faculty at the Academy? She couldn't tell.

Out of the cab, Gareth and Seth followed the steps that led up to a large central grey building which, to Glory, looked identical to the other grey buildings on the campus.

"This is the Registrar's Office." At her blank look, Seth clarified. "Where you are formally admitted into Thornhedge."

"Oh." Nerves crawled up her spine and wrapped around her throat in a light squeeze. She took a deep breath. "What do I need to do?"

Gareth chuckled. "Regrettably, a lot of paperwork." He walked up the steps to the ornate double wooden doors and opened one. "Welcome to Thornhedge, Glory."

The foyer near the entrance was simple, with dark wood panels and a black and white tile floor which marched up to a large wooden desk. A matron sat behind the desk, picking away at a typewriter, a device Glory had only seen in the post office in Agate Creek. A discreet nameplate identified her as Registrar Staghorn. She sported spectacles and a graying blonde bun, and peered up at the small party as they approached.

"Yes?"

"We're here to enroll Gloriana Rue into Thornhedge Academy." Seth placed a hand at Glory's back and ushered her forward.

"Rue?" She repeated, then tilted her head to the side. "Any relation to Abraham and Jules?"

Gareth cleared his throat. "Glory is their daughter."

A small smile edged up one corner of her mouth, and she looked over Glory, casting a glance up and down the stained, torn, and tired traveling dress. Glory stood straighter but a slight tinge of embarrassment stained her cheeks. They hadn't made time to find new clothes after the train robbery in Sweet Springs; she couldn't help the state of her dress.

"It will be good to have a Rue back on our grounds." The Registrar stood to retrieve a large folio from a nearby bookshelf, then sat back down and flipped open the book to a half-completed page. She picked up a pen. "Full name?"

"I'm sorry?"

"Your full name, please."

"Oh. Uh, Gloriana Rue."

"Age?"

"Seventeen."

And so the questions continued. The Registrar had a quick hand and added her notes to the folio with rapid strokes of her pen. She inquired about Glory's highest level of completed education, academic strengths and weaknesses, all prior residences, even hobbies. Glory didn't have any hobbies; at least, not since her father and Lily had passed. She had been too busy trying to survive. So she shrugged and said gardening. It wasn't exactly a lie: Being around flowers and gardens made her feel closer to her father.

The only hiccup during the interview came soon. "Affinity?"

Glory looked at Seth, then Gareth. How could she describe her ability when she didn't understand it?

Gareth came to her rescue. "She needs the Trial. We think that she has an Affinity for metals, but she needs further testing to determine the strength and scope of her ability."

The Registrar's eyebrows flew up. "Metals?" she echoed. She cast a curious glance over Glory once more. "Hmph. Curious. Well, I'll put her down for Ravesbroke. He'll figure it out."

The Registrar scribbled a few last notes into the folio, then looked up. "Welcome to Thornhedge, Miss Rue. Eden will be here shortly to escort you to your new residence." She stood and rounded the large wooden desk. Glory was surprised at how tall the Registrar was. "You will receive your course schedule, books, and other supplies after your Trial with Ravesbroke, which is scheduled for tomorrow. You should rest today." The Registrar gave Glory a kind smile.

"Thank you."

"Ah, Eden, thank you for coming." The Registrar moved to usher forth a short brunette with tan skin and blue eyes. "This is Eden Garcon. She is also a student at Thornhedge, and has graciously agreed to guide you through your first few weeks here." The other young woman gave her a bright, bubbly smile that reminded Glory of the expression she herself gave to customers in the general store in Agate Creek: Determined geniality.

"Thank you." Glory offered a small smile.

"I'm afraid this is where we leave you, Miss Glory." Gareth smiled.

"Wait. What? Where are you going?" Glory couldn't keep the worry out of her voice. The Brothers were the only people she knew at Thornhedge or even in Colorado. If they left, she would be alone in a foreign place. With magicians. Glory shivered. She suddenly missed Agate Creek for a moment, where she knew everyone whether she wanted to or not.

"Not far. We'll leave you to get settled into the ladies' dorm, and we will see you tomorrow for your evaluation with Ravesbroke." Seth stepped forward and lowered his voice. "We wouldn't miss that for the world." His eyes twinkled down at her.

Glory nodded. She still held onto some worry, and it must have shown on her face because Seth continued. "If you can handle a train robbery, you can handle Thornhedge," he said with a grin. "We have far fewer gunfights here. You may even grow bored."

Glory followed the polite young woman out of the Registrar's Office and through a maze of courtyards. Eden kept up a cheerful monologue as she pointed out areas of interest or function. As they moved forward at a quick clip, Glory realized with a ripple of shock that the train robbery had only happened yesterday. She still had the bruises on her side from being flung from the car interior. They had ripened from red to purple.

Now she was at an academy of magic. *How quickly things change*, Glory thought.

Eden continued her introductions. "Here is the dining hall. We dine for breakfast, lunch, and dinner but the hall is almost always open. If you ever get hungry, just bother the cooks. They will rustle something up for you."

"This is the library. It's gorgeous inside, and there are many study carrels for the Academy's students and faculty. You can use all of the books except for those reserved for the faculty or restricted from student use." Eden continued but lowered her voice. "The restricted texts often have problematic or even illegal craftwork. For research purposes only, of course." Glory studied the three story building with a pair of stone crows guarding the staircase that led up to the double doors in the entryway. *What did forbidden magic look like?* she wondered.

"Student dorms are divided by sex and age." Eden pointed to the north, then the south before finally pointing to the west. "Boys reside on the north side of campus, girls on the south, and the faculty apartments and cottages are to the west." At this point during the tour, Glory realized that Eden had done this tour many, many times. She remembered the genial smile in the Registrar's Office, the one that felt a bit forced. Glory wondered why Eden volunteered to do these welcoming activities. Did she do this because she wanted to? Or was there another reason to serve as a hostess of sorts for newly arrived magicians? "Workshops, studios, gardens, and other spaces needed Affinity work are largely to the east side of campus but are found everywhere, really."

"The grounds and gardens feed the campus and are maintained by magicians with botanical Affinities."

Glory interrupted the flow of information at that point. "How many people are at Thornhedge?"

Eden considered for a moment. "We have a little over seven hundred students, I think, and around two hundred faculty and resident scholars. Thornhedge is smaller than the other academies due to its location. Denver is still growing, you see. I have heard that Chicago has over two thousand people. Of course, the schools only have a certain percentage of the entire magical population."

Glory frowned. "What do you mean?"

Surprise crossed Eden's face. "Well, many magicians never get a Trial at all. Or their families won't let them attend an Academy, or they may not be able to afford the costs, despite the scholarships offered by the Academies." Eden's voice lowered and flush stained her cheeks at this statement, and Glory wondered why. "Because magic was only very recently legalized, the Academies still don't reflect the entire population of magicians in the United States. There is still a great deal of stigma and bigotry." Eden scowled. "Some of our students at Thornhedge were turned out from their own homes because their families discovered they could do magic."

Glory's brow furrowed. "But...isn't one born with an Affinity? You don't have a choice over that, right?"

"Right." Eden's lips pressed together. "Blaming someone for having an Affinity is like punishing the sky for being blue. It just *is*."

"That's awful." Glory's heart twisted inside her chest. Her family was gone but they had loved each other fiercely.

"Speaking of Affinities, what is yours?" Eden nodded at a passing student, a tall boy with locs and a smith's apron.

"I think I have an Affinity for metals." Glory recited in careful tones, trying to remember what she had learned from Seth and Gareth.

"Apparently that means I can manipulate and shape different metals."
Glory looked at Eden to see if she got it right.

Eden's mouth hung open and her eyes were rounded in shock.

Glory felt uneasy. "Is something wrong?" She shifted from one foot
the other.

Eden's mouth snapped shut. "No, not at all." She grinned and the
unease within Glory melted away like snow beneath bright sunlight.
"On the contrary, that's an incredible ability. I've heard of metal magicians, but I've never met one. Did you know what your ability was
before you came here?"

Glory shook her head. "I didn't know *anything* before I came here."

Eden sighed. "Everyone else gets the fun abilities," she complained.

Glory gave a small smile. "Why do you say that? What's yours?"

"Botanical. I can grow plants and manipulate botanical specimens."

"But that's useful," Glory protested.

"Exactly — useful. Not exciting or innovative." Eden sighed again.
Then she straightened.

"Here are the classrooms designated for the general education curriculum. Unlike most schools in the States or the Territories, all students — men and women — receive the same education." A note of
pride rang through that statement. "Here are the workshops dedicated
to Affinity-based curricula. The infirmary is in the next building,"
Eden added.

Glory examined both buildings, then turned to Eden. "Are Affinities so dangerous that you require medical assistance?"

"Sometimes. Often, for the beginners." Eden gave Glory a small
smile.

The answer did not reassure Glory.

Eden finally paused in front of a rectangular, two story building in the ubiquitous grey stone. Flowers lined boxes at every window, and Glory saw that curtains blew from the open windows on the breeze of the sunny day. "Here you are. I'll show you to your room."

Eden led Glory up the short flight of steps, and through a single, discreet door into the residence hall. From a quick glance, the building seemed to be composed of long hallways, covered with dark wooden wainscoting and wallpapers with a lush botanical pattern of flowers and curling leaves, and rooms on either side of the walkway. A simple office with a desk and chairs abutted the foyer but no one was present. "This is the hall matron's office," Eden said. "She's usually here in case you have any needs or questions. Bathing facilities and restrooms are located on both floors, at opposite ends of each floor."

Eden continued to the wooden staircase. "Your roommate is Franny Seale." Glory trailed after Eden, dread slowing her steps. *Maybe this won't be too bad*, she thought. A roommate could be a new friend. *Maybe.*

Once upon the second floor, Eden knocked on one door. After no response, she fished out a keyring from the reticule she carried and upon a cursory examination, inserted one of the keys into the lock. Glory wondered. Eden pushed open the door, then stood to the side.

"This is your room."

Glory stepped into the room and glanced around. While no one was present in the room, half — more than a half, she realized — was clearly lived in, with clothes laying at the end of one bed and upon both chairs. Bright light streamed in through two long windows, nestled within thick curtains that were pulled apart. The wainscoting from the hall followed into room but in a simple white; the wallpapers had a roses and fern theme. A small bookcase rested against the wall, adjacent to a desk and one of the chairs, which housed some items of clothing. A heavy floral perfume wafted through the air and Glory coughed a few times. Through watering eyes, Glory saw her new bed. Narrow and long, the linens looked fresh. A thick quilt hung over the bed's edge.

"I'll leave you to settle in," Eden said with a smile. Glory glanced at her and saw the dark circles above the cheerful smile for the first time. *She looks tired,* Glory thought. *So why did she help me?* "If you have any questions, you can ask the hall matron downstairs."

Glory nodded. "Thank you. For the tour. I would never have found this place by myself." Glory peered down the hall, then at Eden. "Do you live in this hall?" *Please say yes. I need a familiar face.*

Eden shook her head. "No, I live in another women's hall across the way." She pointed out the window.

"Oh." Glory nodded again, trying to hide her disappointment.

"Well, I'll see you tomorrow morning," Eden began. At Glory's inquiring look, Eden clarified. "For your Trial? You can't start classes until Ravesbroke assigns them, and he can't do that until you undergo your evaluation." Eden turned at the doorway and looked at Glory over her shoulder with a final smile that felt too big for the young woman's tired eyes.

"You should rest up. Tomorrow will be a long day."

CHAPTER EIGHT

A combination of nerves and boredom had Glory up with the dawn.

After Eden had left the prior evening, Glory had met her roommate later that evening. Franny Seale was a tall, willowy brunette with pale skin, and their introduction was made mercifully short by her immediate and complete disinterest in Glory. Franny had an Affinity for culinary arts, Glory learned, and a large existing social circle, judging by the small crowd of exuberant young women who escorted Franny to dinner. Hungry, and having heard of their destination, Glory had followed the group from a distance to the nearby dining hall.

The sheer size of the hall, and the number of students and faculty had caught Glory by surprise, and she had paused at the hall entrance, overwhelmed. She heard shouts of laughter, thumps of bodies as they slid into bench seats, and the silverware against plates. Roasted meats and something sweet tickled her nose. Buffets lined the front of the room while tables took up the remainder of the room. The dining rooms were larger than the one within the new hotel in Agate Creek, by a wide margin. Varnished wood covered the walls and floors, and dark emerald velvet curtains made up the decor. Simple tablecloths adorned the table tops and the cutlery was functional, not decorative.

Then she looked over the people: Members of every race and gender crowded the aisles and the buffet at the back of the hall. Men and women sat together and chatted in animated voices. Most of the students — Glory estimated well over half, really — had African, Indian, or Mexican heritage. A group of older men and women sat at polished tables free from the dents and scratches that marred the rest of the long tables in neat rows throughout the room. The teachers, Glory guessed. She scanned the room. Every table was almost full. *So many people*, she had wondered with awe. *And there are* more *Academies throughout the States and the Territories?*

After a moment of indecision, Glory had simply wrapped a small plate of food in napkin and returned to her room to eat alone. She had re-read a favorite novel she had found in the dorm collection until she fell asleep, tossing and turning until dawn.

Glory woke with gritty eyes and morning breath that tasted like death. Her bruises ached in tandem with her heartbeat as she struggled out of bed and into her clothes, trying not to wake her roommate.

A quiet knock had come as Glory had just finished buttoning her only spare gown. Glory crossed the room in quick strides. She cast a quick glance at Franny as she opened the door, and a loud snore answered. *Well, she isn't a light sleeper*, Glory thought. She turned to face the visitor.

Eden stood in the hallway. "Good morning." She beamed.

"Good morning to you," Glory replied in a quiet voice. The loudest snore Glory had ever heard disrupted the brief silence, and the young women grinned at each other.

"Are you ready?" Eden asked.

"Uh, yes, I think so."

"Then I'll take you to Ravesbroke."

Eden led them out of the residence hall, and across the courtyard to yet another set of buildings and courtyards. Glory glanced around and around, trying to take in everything. Eden noticed.

"Don't worry. You'll be able to find your way soon." Eden shook her head. "It's overwhelming at first but then you get used to it."

Glory nodded. She hoped that was true. "Is it difficult?" Glory found herself voicing the question without quite realizing it. "The Trial, I mean?"

Eden paused. "Not terribly. Mostly it's frustrating."

"Oh."

Eden seemed hear her puzzlement. "See, there's no wrong answer in an Affinity evaluation."

Glory gave her a skeptical glance.

Eden chuckled. Glory noticed that Eden seemed more relaxed, more approachable this morning. "Truly. You are given a set of tools, and then asked to perform a task with each tool. The evaluators, Ravesbroke in your case, assess how you engage with each tool and task, and use the observations to determine your Affinity."

"And no one has failed a task?"

Eden shook her head. "It doesn't work that way. You have a single Affinity, an ability for a specific kind of magic. So you can't possibly succeed at *all* the tasks."

Glory nodded but still didn't understand. Another thought occurred to her. "You said it could be frustrating. How long do these events take?"

Eden sighed. "If you're lucky, an hour or so." She gave a wince. "If you're not, if you have a rare Affinity, you could be in Ravesbroke's lecture hall for the entire day."

Glory stared. "What? An entire day?" As they climbed the stairs between the floors, Glory swallowed hard. What if she failed today? She winced to herself. Would they send her home? Where would she go? She had no one waiting for her in Agate Creek.

"The rarer an Affinity, the longer it takes to diagnose." Eden paused in front of a set of double doors that led into a red brick building. "Here we are."

Eden wasted no time in ushering Glory to Ravesbroke's office. A podium stood beside the closed door, and Eden wrote Glory's full name into the careworn leather-bound text with neat, small handwriting. Four other names resided on the same page, but Glory couldn't make them out. Eden straightened and turned to Glory.

"Ravesbroke will be in that lecture hall." Eden pointed to a door to Glory's right, and two doors down. "He's probably already started with the first student."

Glory paused. "Are... do you plan to watch the Trial?" Glory didn't know if Eden had expected or wanted to attend the test. Privately, she half-welcomed the idea. She would have liked to know at least one person in the room. And where were the Hill Brothers? They had promised to be there.

Eden shook her head but smiled. "I'm required in my classes this morning. But good luck." Glory watched the other girl walk away, then forced herself to walk over to the door Eden had pointed out. She turned the knob slowly, hoping not to attract attention, and peered within. Despite her caution, several people glanced at her with curiosity. Glory gave up on being discreet and stepped through the door. The large room was a lecture hall with desks and seats edging three of the four walls. Large windows lined the far wall, and the room was bifurcated with a long and narrow table at the front of the room. Several objects littered the desk surface, and Glory saw a blonde young man — almost a child, really — standing in front of the narrow desk. A tall man with grey hair, a robust beard of the same color, and a round stomach stood on the opposite side.

He looked up as Glory entered the room and frowned. "New student?"

"Yes."

"Be seated over there." He waved in the general direction of three other students (two boys and one girl, all of whom appeared younger than Glory). "I'll get to you when I can."

Glory blinked. *Not what I expected*, she thought. Glory took a cautious seat near the youngsters and smiled at them. They nodded or smiled back; all of them looked as nervous as Glory felt. She glanced at the door. The Hill Brothers still hadn't appeared. A pang of disappointment thrummed through her and she felt her shoulders sink. She turned away to watch Ravesbroke and the boy in front of her.

Ravesbroke walked around the narrow length and watched as the blonde child first handled a pot filled with flowers and soil. Ravesbroke shook his head. Then the boy assembled a small sandwich, using worn cutlery and plate ware. Ravesbroke shook his head again and made a note in a ledger. He began to pace behind the boy as the child drew a picture of an orange and lemon nestled within a basket. The man ignored the resultant image, and instead seemed to focus on the boy's actions. He bent to scribble another notation.

As she watched Ravesbroke, Glory had a nagging sense of recognition. And then it came to her: Ravesbroke resembled the tailor back in Agate Creek, who had made the wardrobes for the town's businessmen. There was little physical resemblance but rather their manners were alike: The tailor had muttered to himself as he measured a man, took notes, and paced between the fabrics and the tools of his trade, comparing texture, fit, and style. He could not, would not, be hurried in his process.

Glory sighed. *This may take a while.*

Finally, something seemed different: Glory watched the child pick up a toy building set, the worn wooden sticks and blocks painted in faded, once-bright colors. The set had clearly been well used. Puzzled, Glory wondered if the boy had simply given up on the evaluation and had began to play instead. But a look of quiet, intense focus filtered onto his face, and after a brief huff of breath, the boy moved. His fingers flew over the set in nimble motions, first sorting the pieces into small and neat piles. In a matter of moments, the boy had assembled the foundation of a structure in quick and deft movements, and over the next few minutes, finished the edifice. Somehow, the odd-shaped and well worn wooden blocks had been transformed from a child's toy into a small castle: Four turrets atop walls that surrounded a courtyard and with a drawbridge.

Glory stared. *Incredible.*

Ravesbroke had backed away several paces, to examine the boy through narrowed eyes during the assembly. He gave a nod. "Architecture," he muttered. Glory watched as Ravesbroke marched up to the ledger, and again bent over the text. This time he withdrew a notepad from another drawer and wrote on that paper. Tearing off the paper from the pad, he handed it to the boy.

"Take this upstairs," Ravesbroke instructed the boy. "Give them the Trial results." He waved the paper. "They need this in order to finalize your class schedule." Ravesbroke gave a small smile, obscured somewhat by a large mustache. "Congratulations, young man. You have an Affinity for building. Very useful, indeed."

The boy grinned, and left the room, paper clutched in his fist.

Ravesbroke glanced at his ledger, then looked up. "You." He pointed at the other young woman. "You're next. Come here."

And the process started anew. Glory watched as Ravesbroke examined the young woman first, then the remaining two boys, from every angle as they completed one task after another. He paced. He huffed. He sighed. He chewed the edges of his mustache. He made notes in the ledger. He frowned, then made more notes. And then *something* would shift as one of the teenagers completed a task, and even Glory could see what Ravesbroke sought: Eyes narrowed in a sudden and intent focus, accompanied by quick, sure movements that seemed as though the student were creating a dance with their hands, and then — a stunning transformation.

Glory watched in awe as the young woman held one of the worn wooden blocks used in the castle to its original state: The paint peeled off as if steam cleaned, and the nicks and grooves had filled in. Glory started as the piece of wood grew in length and started to branch off new twigs before Ravesbroke intervened.

"Forestry," he muttered. He paused, then tilted his head in the opposite direction. "Possibly other greenery." He ushered the young woman out, Affinity papers in hand.

It seemed to Glory as though Ravesbroke took his time diagnosing the remaining two boys ("Healing," he declared first. Then, "Culinary"). The last boy almost skipped from the room in his excitement. Nerves clenched and unclenched her hands into fists, and Glory hid them under her knees, clenching the fabric of her skirts.

Glory heard Ravesbroke call out. "You're next."

She looked up, then stood. Walking over to the long table, Glory noticed Ravesbroke studying the ledger in front of him. He leaned again over a document in his portfolio, peering at the neat scribbles within. "The Hill Brothers reported that you have an unusual ability." His eyebrows flew up. "One associated with metal? Or possibly wood," he added to himself. He looked to Glory for confirmation.

She nodded.

"And you're a Rue?"

"Yes."

"Any relation to Jules?"

"Yes. My mother."

Ravesbroke looked up, a small smile almost buried beneath the mustache and further seen in the creasing corners of his eyes. "It's good to have you here." He looked around. "No siblings? Weren't there were two of you?"

How did he know that? Glory wondered. "My sister Lily passed away two years ago."

Ravesbroke cleared his throat. He shifted a short stack of pages on the table and seemed uncomfortable. "My condolences."

"Thank you."

Ravesbroke cleared his throat again. "Shall we get started?"

"Yes." Glory stepped closer. "Only... I'm not sure what you want me to do."

A frown scattered across his face. "You've never had a Trial?"

"No."

"And you've never used your Affinity?"

Glory began to feel foolish, like she had erred in some way. "Uh, no."

"But you're a Rue?" Ravesbroke pressed. "Of the Rue and Volt lineages?"

"Yes?" Glory remembered that Volt was her mother's maiden name. "Do lineages matter here?"

"Only to other scholars." The man chuckled as he waved away that concern. "But you do have an Affinity?"

Glory shifted from one foot to the other, worried. *What if I'm a fraud? Will I be thrown out?* She forced herself to stand up straight. *Remember. Remember what you did.*

"Well?"

"I m-made things fly."

Ravesbroke stopped. "What now?"

Her voice grew stronger as she repeated herself. "I've made things fly. Metal objects. Or lifted things."

His eyebrows shot up again. "Hmph." Ravesbroke made a note in his ledger. "Now I'm quite curious. Let's start with the usual tasks, rule some obvious abilities out."

And thus began the next three hours. She performed task after task for Ravesbroke. She made inedible meals, and then arranged flowers before gardening in a small window box. Ravesbroke made notes, muttered to himself, and then removed the debris. Glory was next tasked with building an edifice of some kind with the wooden toys. Her pitiful log cabin bore no resemblance to the earlier glorious castle, with its simplistic frame and mismatched roofing. As if to underscore her singular lack of talent, the cabin walls fell when Glory removed her hands.

She blushed. Ravesbroke only made another note.

Writing and arithmetic were simple exercises, written on blank paper with a crude pencil stub. The results yielded no special attention from Ravesbroke. Glory then recited a sonnet, feeling foolish for the entire duration, to no great acclaim or interest. Drawing and watercolors, both simple botanical illustrations, were passable but not exceptional.

Glory managed to stick herself with a bone needle *and* snap the thread before Ravesbroke took them away from her. A small bird and a baby rabbit were brought for Glory to handle. While she enjoyed the warmth and softness of the bunny, she didn't feel anything beyond that. Glory ran her fingers through water and fire, and at Ravesbroke's bidding, breathed in deep gulps of air.

Nothing.

Ravesbroke then departed the room and brought back a young man with a small bandage on his finger. Glory was unable to heal him or offer anything beyond a rueful smile and a shrug. The young man smiled back and departed.

Ravesbroke had stopped taking notes altogether at this point. "Nothing?" He asked. "You are not sensing an attraction, or sense of *rightness*, for anything?"

Glory shook her head, and she could feel the embarrassment heat her cheeks. "I'm sorry."

Ravesbroke smiled, a grim curvature upon his face. "We will finish this Trial." It sounded like a threat rather than a reassurance. "Let's try the metals then. We'll see if the Brothers were right." Ravesbroke left to retrieve a wooden crate from underneath the opposite end of the table, and removed a parcel rolled into a tight curl and wrapped in worn leather. He laid the furled roll on the surface, and with a snap of his wrist, opened the package.

Ravesbroke motioned Glory forward. "Try these."

He handed her a hunk of metal, or rather, several pieces of metal in an interlocked puzzle of conjoined links. Glory turned the metal links over in her hands, feeling the material warm and start to tingle against her palms. The color of the metal, a copper burnished from frequent use, seemed to sharpen and then glow. Her fingers tickled with the sensation.

"Solve it."

Glory look up, distracted. "What?"

Ravesbroke nodded to the puzzle. "You feel something, yes? Then *use* that feeling."

"How?" Glory turned the links over again. "With tools?" Doubt echoed in her voice. Somehow, she didn't think Ravesbroke sought that solution from Glory.

The man grunted. "You are at an academy for magic." He sighed. "Use *magic*."

"I don't know *how* to do that," Glory countered. Still, she turned the links over and over in her hands. She frowned. The metal continued to warm. It now felt almost pliable and loose in her hands. Almost bendable.

"Listen to your instincts." Ravesbroke leaned forward, eyes on her hands. "What do you *want* to do with this copper? What should this object really *be*?"

Glory sighed. Privately, she thought those questions were somewhat nonsensical. But on the heels of that thought, an image filled her mind: A copper shield. Her hands caressed and massaged the metal. These links should melt, and smooth into a round disc. A handle for the back, and with reinforced edges for stability after repeated blows. She felt a squawk of resistance at the back of her mind: It felt as though the copper informed her not through words but through a sense, a feeling, that there wasn't simply enough material to make a full-sized shield. In response, Glory shrank the shield's perimeter in her mind's eye. If not functional, she thought, then the shield could be ornamental. Vines and flowers erupted from the disc's newly flat surface and wove themselves around the edges of the circle. Upon reaching either end, the motif wove into itself. The edges pulsed, shifted, and at last, settled into the right shape.

Glory felt an abrupt fatigue steal over her body, and an ache settle between her shoulder blades. She gasped out a breath, light-headed for a moment. Sparks shot across her vision, and she shook her head to clear them.

"Well done." Ravesbroke's voice, rich in satisfaction, interrupted Glory's thoughts. She looked up.

"Huh?"

"*Look.*" Ravesbroke gestured at her hands.

Glory looked — and felt her jaw drop. She held a replica of the vision in her mind. The copper shone in the sunlight, the ornate edges rich with lilies of the valley and briar vines casting faint shadows that gave depth to her work. Questions roiled inside, competing with emotions: disbelief, pride, joy.

Fear. *How did I do that?* Glory swallowed hard. *What am I capable of?*

"Congratulations, Miss Rue!" Ravesbroke beamed at her, his earlier reserve forgotten. "You have a magnificent gift." He scribbled more notes into his portfolio and muttered under his breath. Glory caught snatches and fragments: "...an Affinity for metals... unusual but quite strong. But she is Jules' daughter..."

Glory placed the copper disc on the table with care. She didn't quite trust her own hands to be steady. It felt as though the world had tilted, and that she was watching from a place just outside of her body. She had manipulated the metal, and she had felt the after-effects Seth had warned her about: Fatigue, aches, and now hunger. Though Glory was astonished by what she had done, she couldn't deny that she now felt a sense of rightness steal over her body. Like the magic finally awoke from a deep slumber. She wondered how she hadn't realized that something was missing within her all this time.

"Miss Rue?"

Glory tore herself from her thoughts and focused on Ravesbroke. "Yes?"

"How are you feeling?"

"Too much. Everything." Glory shook her head at her own immediate response. "Confused, mostly."

Ravesbroke smiled. "That's understandable." He leaned forward, eyes intent. "Do you understand what I mean when I say you have an Affinity for metal?"

Glory searched for the right words. "I assume it means I can do magic with metallic objects?"

Ravesbroke smiled again. "An Affinity is so much more than 'magic with metallic objects'," he quoted. "An Affinity is an understanding, a knowing, of the fundamental nature of the material or phenomena before you. Once you comprehend and appreciate what's before your eyes, you will be able to shape it into something different. To transform everyday objects into art or function or both." Ravesbroke paused. "An Affinity is a call to know at least one thing deeply in this life. Your gift is associated with metals; thus, you will need to know, work with, and befriend metal."

Ravesbroke smiled, an oddly tender expression for his severe face. "We magicians are fortunate. Our gift is a lifelong companion and an invitation to stay curious about the world around us. You have a rich life ahead of you."

Excerpt

Research Notes, J. Rue

July 14th, 1878

South Dakota Territory

I had a devil of a time finding young C., an irony not lost on me once I convinced him to trust me and I finally learned of his gift.

He had found work as a hostler and errand runner for a local livery in one of the most desolate towns I've stumbled across in the South Dakota Territories.

Young C. is roughly fifteen years of age. When I pressed them for accurate data, they had simply shrugged. Fifteen was as close as they could figure. My heart twisted in my chest when I heard this; a child should be cosseted, spoiled on a birthday — not completely ignorant of the date on which they came into this world. And C. hasn't had an easy time of it, no. The child was kicked out of their home by their parents after an accusation of thievery (for how else would the child know the exact location of the missing comb with semi-precious stones?). Looking over the child and seeing how they defy easy categorization into a gender, I suspect that the parents had been looking for a reason to do away with a (to them, at least) strange child.

Selfish, lousy bastards.

I approached C. multiple times with my request — six, in total. I had offered half of my lunch to C. on my fifth request and while he had taken it, he did not grace me with an interview until my sixth visit. Finally, C. believed that I only wanted to have a conversation with him. After that, C. became positively voluble, perhaps from loneliness. Or perhaps the novelty of having someone listen to him with full attention was too rich a treat to pass up. Regardless, I was allowed to purchase a real meal for C. and to hear about his Affinity.

For as long as he can remember, C. has always been able to find lost items and sometimes even lost people. The first time the gift manifested, C. had found a missing reticule: The schoolmarm had thought she had misplaced her bag somewhere in the small shack that served as the local primary school; however, C. knew in an instant that an older boy had taken it, stuffed into his schoolbag. With all the delicacy of a young child, which is to say none at all, C. announced to the room the location of the absconded purse. The teacher was pleased but didn't inquire how C. obtained this knowledge nor had anyone else. Everyone had assumed C. had seen the classmate take the reticule.

But C. knew different. He was different, in more ways than one.

The older boy later gave C. a thrashing for his good deed.

From then on, C. began to test and explore the Affinity. Items and objects were easy to find; the location of an item could be assisted by gazing at the prospective recoveree or being in their home or having another piece of the absent item. People, C. acknowledged, were much harder. Trying to locate a lost human felt like searching through dark mud while wearing a blindfold: Often fruitless and very uncomfortable.

C. confided that his mother in particular was disturbed by the often uncanny facility with which they could find an object. C. had soon learned not to demonstrate the Affinity at home; otherwise, the air seemed to leave the room and a frost descended upon the household. Everyone would then ignore him.

(I shake my head even as I write this. What a sorry, vile family. They have no idea how precious and remarkable their child is).

Finally, the missing comb incident ended with C. on the streets with two changes of clothing, a bedroll, and little food. C. had four hard months catching naps whenever possible and taking any odd job that came his way. Finally, the livery hired him on a trial basis — and that was six months ago, C. told me with clear pride in his eyes. The job comes with a clean bed, meals, and a modest paycheck.

This child is too good for this small-minded town.

So, in summary, the Affinity is the ability to locate lost items primarily, and to locate lost humans secondly and with less accuracy. The gift manifested early on, as C. believes he was eleven when he had located the schoolmarm's missing reticule. C. uses the gift almost daily and for items great and small, animate and inanimate; once, C. led a farmer to an escaped hog that had wandered two acres away.

I concluded the interview in time for C. to return to work and avoid being late. While my field research has concluded, I am not quite done with this miserable town. I've wired the Avamere Academy in Chicago to inform them of a prospective new student that may join their ranks. It's my hope that I can convince C. to take a chance on a new adventure, to enroll at the Academy in Chicago to get an education and to learn about his gift.

I hope I'm successful in my efforts.

—J. Rue

CHAPTER NINE

G lory woke the next morning — and wished she could turn over and roll back into sleep. Yesterday had been a blur of paperwork and bureaucracy. She must have visited seven buildings scattered throughout the campus, with multiple offices in each. Apparently even a magic academy required paperwork.

After he had completed her diagnosis, Ravesbroke had dismissed Glory and sent her on a journey to the Office of Affinity Registration. There, she had been required to hand over the portfolio Ravesbroke had entrusted to her: His summary of her Affinity, and his recommendations for the combination of curriculum and practical workshops needed. The Office of Affinity Registration was a quiet, small, and dusty cube of a room, staffed by a young man (a fellow student at the Academy, perhaps?) who seemed grumpy at the sight of Glory.

The next office Glory had been required to find was in a different building. Simply titled Curriculum on the ornate double doors that opened to reveal a spacious sitting room. This visit took a great deal longer. Glory was told that her time at the Academy would comprise of a general curriculum, a magical one, and a series of workshops, which would serve as a practical tutorial of sorts in how to develop and use her own Affinity.

Glory had answered a barrage of questions about her prior schooling in Agate Creek. As the scholastic interrogation unfolded in the spacious room, sitting upon a comfortable chair an sipping tea, Glory felt as though she at last understood why her father had insisted on such an unorthodox education: Despite keeping the knowledge of her Affinity from her and denying her the opportunity to practice, Abraham must have *expected* that Glory and Lily would have attended Thornhedge. He had anticipated their entry into the magical community. Otherwise, why had he insisted on a supplementary curriculum of classics, literature, natural history, and much more? One so ill-suited for frontier life in remote Agate Creek?

The examiner seemed satisfied by Glory's responses to her quizzing, and then placed her into a suite of courses designed to pick up where Glory left off at her father's passing. Upon receiving her course schedule, Glory was then hustled off to another corner of the Curriculum

Office and had to put aside the mystery of her father's seemingly contradictory educational choices.

The corner of the Office was dedicated to identifying the practical experiences that would refine and enhance the use of one's Affinity. She needed, Glory was informed, practical and hands-on experiences to supplement her general and magical studies. These very experiences would give her control and finesse over her gift. When Glory handed over her course schedule, the woman at this desk glanced at it and made notes in yet another portfolio. Then the woman did a double-take and traced a note with her finger. Her eyebrows flew up, and she cast a quick glance at Glory.

"Metal?" She asked, surprise in her voice.

Glory nodded. "Yes, ma'am."

"Hmm." The woman's gaze returned to the notes. After a moment, she added her own comments to the notes.

Glory glanced around the Office and saw that it was busier than the Office of Affinity Registration, Curriculum, or even Ravesbroke's office, filled with more employees and with what she assumed were students. The sunlight had filtered through the windows and indicated that it was late afternoon. Glory had been astonished. How had the day passed so fast?

"Miss Rue?" A voice had interrupted her observations, and Glory had turned to look.

The woman had held the portfolio out to her. "Here is your complete schedule. You will find your course schedule, list of required texts, and your workshop schedule. Classes occur Monday through Thursday. You will need to go into Denver to purchase your textbooks; be sure to go to Carville's. She'll have what you will need. You will likely need to purchase additional tools for your metal smithy. Perhaps your ambassador can do that with you, show you around a bit."

"Ambassador?"

"Yes, of course. All new students receive them." The woman checked her paperwork. "Eden is her name, I believe?"

"Oh." Glory nodded. "Yes." *Well, now I know why she was so helpful.* A

"Classes are already in session for the academic year but you will start classes the day tomorrow afternoon." The woman had smiled.

Glory had left the office, dodging two irate students who argued over something she lacked the context to follow. The hallway outside was crowded, more so than earlier in the day. A meal sounded appealing — she was still hungry from using her Affinity earlier — but she couldn't remember how to get back to the dining rooms. Glory double-checked the packet of papers in hopes of finding a map of thornhedge but nothing. *Maybe there is a map in my room,* Glory thought. She thought she knew how to get back to her room.

Outside the spring air felt brisk against her face. She watched the students all around her as they filed between the different buildings, using the worn brick paths bordered by coiffed shrubbery and flowers. The students were a mixed bunch to Glory's unfamiliar eye: The population seemed an almost even split between men and women. The youngest student Glory saw looked to be about eleven or twelve while the oldest student (or at least, Glory had assumed they were a student based on the notebook and texts they carried) seemed to be just shy of their twenties. She didn't recognize a single soul. A pang of loneliness echoed through her chest.

With some envy, Glory realized that the proximity to Denver ensured that the students' sartorial sensibilities were greater and more refined than those found in her hometown. Glory looked at the silks, muslins, and high-quality linens and cottons with gorgeous patterns, embroidered designs, and other pleasant details, and felt a bit dowdy in her practical day gown. Perhaps someone could recommend an affordable seamstress or dressmaker, Glory thought. The dress lines were slimmer than she'd see prior to Denver, and many of the female students seemed to favor a blouse and skirt combination, rather than a day dress or something even more formal. Glory supposed that was sensible for a magic school.

She had been reassured that her tuition and most school-related expenses were prepaid, with an additional stipend for supplies. Anything not covered by the stipend would be covered by a scholarship administered by the governing board of the Academies throughout the United States and its affiliated territories. Glory had been surprised to learn how widespread the magical schooling system was established, given how recent the legalization of magic had been. She suspected that many of these schools had existed for a long time prior to the Falstead Act of 1859. They were simply allowed to be open about it now. But she didn't have anyone in whom she could confide to confirm her suspicions.

Walking down the hallway that led to her shared room, Glory heard voices within. As she reached to open the door, it was opened from within and Glory found herself staring at an unfamiliar young woman, roughly the same age as her. Beyond her Glory could see her roommate.

The tall and blonde young woman gave Glory a discreet appraisal. "Franny's new roommate, I believe?"

Glory swallowed hard. "Gloriana Rue. Hello."

"Charmed. Tiny Peterson." The woman with what Glory hoped was an ironic nickname swung the door further open to let the other two women out. "Franny, your new roommate is back."

"Oh." An explosion of ruffles came into view. "You have a message. I'm supposed to ensure that you receive it so I placed it upon your desk." Franny pointed with a distracted wave of her hand, then squeezed past Tiny and Glory, out of the room and into the hall. "Have a pleasant evening." The two women traipsed down the hall, discussing someone named Harry.

Glory stepped into the room, closing the door behind her. She crossed the room to search for the note. The message was not on her desk but instead on her new bed, resting upon a stack of linens and a quilt. Glory picked it up, noting the elegant script that spelled out her full name.

It was from Seth, and brief.

Miss Rue,

My deepest apologies. Gareth and I have been called away on business for the Academy, and we're not able to refuse this task. I wish you well during your Affinity diagnosis and registration, and I hope the first weeks at Thornhedge prove satisfactory. If we may, my brother and I would like to call upon you when we return.

Seth

Glory let the note fall back upon the stack of linens. Disappointment seeped in like fog and she felt her shoulders sink. She hadn't expected the Brothers to stay a permanent fixture in her life at Thornhedge — but neither had she thought they would leave the day after depositing her at the academy. Glory felt chilled and rubbed her arms. Now what? She knew no one at the school, other than Eden — who was an ambassador, not a real friend. She couldn't even remember where the dining rooms were. How would she navigate this new place? Especially the magic?

Glory sat at her desk and rested her head in her hands. She could feel a faint headache coming on, no doubt created by a lack of food and fatigue from using the Affinity. She also felt dusty and overwhelmed.

She thought she had a tin of biscuits in her satchel and decided that they would suffice for this evening.

She would deal with everything tomorrow.

Glory woke to bright sunlight seeping into her windows and the considerable noise of her new roommate getting dressed for the day. She peered over at the other side of the room from beneath her quilt and saw that Franny was already dressed in a light blue day dress, tucking books and papers into a satchel. Soon after, she left.

Her stomach rumbled, and Glory decided to get up. She dressed in her only day dress, the light yellow print faded with age and use. She was pleased that someone had provided each woman an ewer of fresh water, a sliver of soap, and several linens for washing. Glory had started transferring the rest of her meager belongings into a chest of drawers when a knock at the door interrupted her work.

Eden offered an exuberant smile. "Good morning."

"Good morning." Glory smiled at her, a bit puzzled. *Why is she here?*

Eden offered a small return smile. "How are you feeling today?"

"Good. I think." Glory thought that was mostly the truth.

Eden nodded as if she had heard what Glory hadn't said. "The first few days are always overwhelming for the new arrivals. Between the testing, moving into new lodgings, and getting your course schedule, it's simply hectic."

A sense of relief stole over Glory. "Yes, it is, a bit," she admitted.

"It's normal, I promise," Eden said. "You'll adapt within a week or so, and soon this will feel like you have always been here."

Glory wasn't so sure but she didn't want to disagree with the friendliest person she had met thus far at Thornhedge so she simply nodded in response.

"I'm not sure if the Office told you this but you will need to go into Denver proper to get your textbooks and some other supplies." Eden's gaze took in the scene behind Glory, her few items on the bed. "You can purchase any other items you may have forgotten at home, too. I would be happy to escort you, as your Ambassador."

Glory paused and then decided to ask. "What exactly is an Ambassador?"

Surprise sketched across Eden's face. "Oh. Didn't they tell you? When a new student arrives after the start of the academic year, they get an ambassador, whose responsibilities include acquainting the new arrival with the campus and answering any questions you might have." Eden sounded like she was reciting from a manual. "So I'm your ambassador. Have you had breakfast yet?"

Glory shook her head. "No. I can't quite remember where the dining hall is," she admitted in a sheepish voice.

Eden groaned. "I am so sorry. Let's get breakfast."

CHAPTER TEN

The dining hall was noisy and crowded with the breakfast rush. "Quickly," Eden urged. "They have just put out fresh biscuits," She glanced back at Glory with a grin. "Those are my favorite."

BOOM.

Glory jumped, her heart racing in her chest. "What *was* that?"

Eden simply shook her head.

"No magic in the dining rooms, Andrew!" A matron from the buffet called out. "Report to me after breakfast."

A young man at a nearby table, presumably Andrew, groaned. His shoulders sunk as his tablemates laughed at and shoved him.

"That happens at least once a week." Eden sighed.

"So he is not allowed to do magic?" Glory felt confused, like she was missing something. Thornhedge was an academy for magic, yes? Then why weren't students allowed to do magic? She snagged the toast, eggs, and tea from the buffet line, then followed Eden to a nearby table.

"No magic outside of classrooms, workshops, or dorms. So in common areas like the dining rooms, the library, and the public walkways, magic is restricted." In a delicate motion, Eden rescued a glob of jam about to fall from her biscuit with a napkin. "Not all students know how to control their Affinity yet. So the restriction of magic use in public areas is a safety measure for everyone."

Glory remembered the damage she had done back in Agate Creek, and winced to herself. An Affinity wasn't something to be careless about.

Eden placed the napkin near her plate. "I've been given a pass from my classes this morning in order to show you around, answer questions, that sort of thing." Eden paused. "Whenever you're ready, we can get started."

Glory finished her meal in short time. "Let's go."

After ascertaining that Glory both had her reticule, and sufficient funds for the trip, Eden ushered them to a cab stand at the east end of campus. There, Glory was surprised to see two horse-and-buggy equipages, waiting and ready. Eden explained that the Academy had arranged that service; there was almost always someone who needed a trip into Denver.

Ensconced in the buggy, Eden kept up a running stream of cheerful commentary. Glory remained quiet and took in the unfamiliar noises, the smells, and the sights. They soon arrived on a bustling street named Colfax. Every kind of shop imaginable lined the corridors of the street: Fabrics, off-the-rack clothing, and dressmakers, books, stationary, hats, even an entire shop dedicated to notions such as buttons and ribbons. The street felt like a bazaar from the Arabian Tales that Glory had read as a child: Colorful, loud, and filled with diverse peoples and new surprises. Men, women, and children wove between one another, and carried parcels and bags and crates.

Eden threaded them through the crowded sidewalks. "Let's stop at the bookstore first." She gave Glory a quick smile. "It's next to my favorite sweet shop."

The bookshop, simply called Carville's, smelled of paper, leather, and glue. Glory inhaled deeply. The smell of books reminded her of her mother, and his bafflingly well-stocked library in the middle of the prairie. The bookstore was larger inside than Glory anticipated, with neat rows of books and newspapers atop polished wooden floors; the aisles were lined with lush rugs. Crowded but somehow hushed, the shop had a gun safe just inside the door with a sign: "Guns and firearms must be safely stowed here. No exceptions!"

Eden led them to a back wall, adorned with shelves of books underneath a sign that simply read "Thornhedge." The other young woman found most of the books in short order. Glory was bemused by some of the titles but then gave herself a mental scolding: She was enrolled in a school for magic. Of course the textbooks would have titles such as, *Affinities: A Course in Magic* and *The Ethics of Magic*. A few more general texts, covering philosophy, natural history, chemistry, mathematics, and classic literatures, rounded out the list.

Then, a familiar name jumped out at her: Juliet I. Rue.

Glory stilled.

Seth and Gareth had told her that Juliet was a scholar, but that knowledge had never felt real until Glory saw the texts on the shelf. She reached out and ran a finger down the spine of the first, then a second text, and traced over the name. A decision made, she scooped all four texts off the shelf and into her pile. She wanted to read them, to know more about her mother's prior life, the one filled with magic and scholarship and adventures. Her past seemed glamorous and interesting. *Why would Father hide this from Lily and I?*

"Ms. Carville?" Glory heard Eden's voice near the register and looked up. "I can't seem to find these two texts."

The woman behind the counter looked up at Eden's question and smiled before walking over. Only a few years older than her own seventeen years of age, Ms. Carville wore split skirts and a man's button-down shirt with the sleeves rolled up. With practical boots on her feet, she barely stood taller than Glory. Stick straight brown hair was pulled back into a braid and green eyes peered through spectacles over a chin dimple.

Glory placed her mother's books on the counter where the cash register rested. They were *not* light texts. She watched the older woman scan the lists of required magical texts.

"Hmph." The woman frowned at Eden. "I thought you had a botanical Affinity." Glory could hear the unspoken question in her voice.

"Oh, no. These are for Miss Rue, a new arrival at Thornhedge." Eden gestured at Glory with a smile.

Ms. Carville fastened her gaze on Glory. The scrutiny startled her; most people didn't stare at another person with a look that could peel an apple without a blade.

"So you must be the metal magician," Ms. Carville said with a swift smile. Her voice was soft spoken, an unexpected contrast with her practical appearance. "The gossip mill has been rampant. Don't get many of those here. Or anywhere, really." Ms. Carville tilted her head, considering. "Very useful skill, especially in these times."

Glory cleared her throat. "I hope so. I have to figure out how to use it."

Ms. Carville's gaze settled on the stack of her mother's texts. "Rue," she murmured. Her eyes flew up to Glory's face. "Any relation to our author?"

"Distant family," Glory lied. She didn't want to share the truth with this stranger, not when she had so many unanswered questions.

Ms. Carville didn't look convinced. "Well, Rue is a solid scholar of magics. Dispelled a great deal of quackery."

"Like what?" Eden had leaned up against the counter. Her intent gaze on Ms. Carville, combined with the faint blush on her cheeks, made Glory suspect that the sweet shop was not precisely why Eden had wanted to come to the bookshop first. Glory swallowed back a smile.

Ms. Carville shrugged. "Well, the usual myths. You've heard them: People possessing multiple Affinities, switching powers between magicians, or even stealing them." Ms. Carville shook her head as she wiped away nonexistent dust off the countertop with a bandana. "Utter nonsense, of course. But hopeful fools are everywhere, I suppose. Rue did an excellent job describing the inheritance of magic and she did her fieldwork at a dangerous time, when magic was illegal and public expression of an Affinity could land a person in jail. Or much worse." Ms. Carville sighed. "Those years were rough on the Affinity community. Magicians have always had to hide what they were for centuries. But the violence just before and shortly after legalization was especially hard on us. It's still not safe, not as long as we have movements like God's Word terrorizing the country." Ms. Carville made a moue of distaste.

Glory and Eden spoke at once.

"God's Word? What's that?" Glory asked.

"Where is she now?" came Eden's query.

Ms. Carville grinned. "One at a time. About fifteen years ago, Rue just vanished. No one that I know of has heard from her, or her husband, Abraham, since." Glory ignored Carville's quick glance.

"Oh." Eden looked disappointed.

Ms. Carville turned to Glory. "God's Word is a religious group of churches and evangelicals who protest the legalization of magic in the States and the Territories. They claim to be peaceful but..." She trailed off, her face grim and her mouth a tight line. "Other magical communities have reported homes and businesses being burned down. We had one magician crushed to death in New Mexico."

"Crushed?" Glory echoed. She felt sick. She hadn't realized how dangerous it could be to be a magician.

"Weighted down with rocks upon his chest, like the Salem Witch Trials." Anger flickered through the other woman's eyes and the corners of her lips turned down. "Ignorant bastards," she muttered.

Eden placed a hand on Glory's elbow. "We're safe at Thornhedge, Glory."

Glory hadn't realized how much dismay had shown on her face. "I hope so." She turned back to Ms. Carville. "Were the killers brought to justice?"

Ms. Carville shook her head. "Justice is still a theoretical rather than a literal right for magicians. It will take more time for the populace to change their minds and for the courts to catch up." She sighed and looked tired for a moment. "Of course, the God's Word movement disclaimed any responsibility and even denounced the murders, claiming that wayward members of the flock had acted on their own. But the denial is all for show. They have active chapters across the country."

A short silence fell over the group. Then Ms. Carville cleared her throat. "This is a grim topic. Let's get you rung up." She emerged from behind the tall desk. "Those last two texts are in a different area of the shop. Like I said, I don't get many metal magicians here." She went to retrieve the books, leaving Eden and Glory at the cash register.

"Here we are." The bookshop owner bundled up the texts in brown wrapping paper before tying them together with colored twine, a sweet frivolity that seemed unexpected in the face of her practical demeanor. She looked up at Eden, then to Glory. "I assume you have more shopping to do? If so, I'll hold these here until you're ready to return to Thornhedge."

"Thank you." Eden beamed. A smile etched itself across the other woman's face, an answering warmth in her eyes. It seemed to Glory that Ms. Carville couldn't help but smile back. Then Ms. Carville shook it off. "I will see you later, ladies." She turned to the man who stood behind Eden and Glory. "How may I help you, sir?"

Eden fell back from the counter with a small, private smile and led Glory out of the bookshop. Glory's thoughts tumbled through her mind, one over another, like small pebbles in a fast-moving stream.

"Eden?" Glory asked.

She looked over. "Yes?"

"How dangerous is the God's Word... movement?" Glory didn't know what else to call it.

The buoyant smile from the bookshop dimmed. "It's bad," Eden admitted in a low voice. Glory leaned closer, straining to listen through the noise of the street. "We're safe at Thornhedge but many magicians have had to relocate suddenly when they attack. I know there are those who help magicians in distress, a whisper network of sorts." Eden hesitated, then continued. "In fact, Ms. Carville's father helped me get to Thornhedge through such a network."

Glory thought for a moment, trying to consider how best to phrase the question. "Were you in distress?" Her tone was gentle.

Eden smiled, an expression made more of determination than happiness. Her eyes were flint hard. "Not for long."

Glory didn't press. She knew a wound when she saw one. She changed topics instead. "How did you discover your Affinity?" She was hungry for knowledge about the magical world. She had so much to learn. She also missed the Hill Brothers. They had been generous, both with information and friendship.

Eden let out a chuckle. "It's not very mysterious, I'm afraid: A magician tried to set up shop in my hometown, which had the unfortunate name of Friendsville, and was run out of town shortly after. Despite magic being perfectly legal." Eden's tone had turned indignant. "Before he left though, he visited me and told me I had an Affinity." Eden gave Glory a rueful glance. "I had thought there was something wrong with me before I realized it was simply magic. He confirmed that I wasn't crazy, and then told me about Thornhedge. He even gave me fare to get here; the whisper network took care of the rest." A grim smile crossed her face. "I left on the earliest mail carriage the very next morning."

Glory noted that Eden did not mention her family even once, and she didn't comment on the omission. "How brave of you."

Eden snorted and Glory grinned, delighted by the unladylike sound. "It wasn't brave. Anything was better than a future in Friendsville. It's been renamed since. It's now known as Broken Whistle, which is not an improvement." Scorn dripped from the last words.

"After I arrived at Denver, Mr. Carville — Felicity's, I mean, Ms. Carville's father – escorted me to Thornhedge. I then found that they had the scholarship program." Eden's voice came to an abrupt stop. A flush stole over her cheekbones, and she looked to the ground.

It was clear to Glory that Eden thought poverty was a cause for embarrassment. Her heart twisted in her chest. *No one should feel shame for things over which they have no control*, Glory thought. But aloud, she simply said, "I'm grateful you're at Thornhedge."

Eden met her eyes, searched them. "I am, too," she said at last. Eden seemed to shake off the thoughts. "Let's get the rest of your supplies. Here is the stationary shop."

The next few hours passed in a whirl for Glory. The stationary shop had more types of paper than Glory had ever seen before, from frilly to monogrammed to plain. The notions store was next: buttons were organized by drawers upon drawers while ribbons dangled from the ceiling in spools that rested on rails. On Eden's advice, Glory purchased a small satchel to carry books and lecture materials across campus.

Next was a clothing store. When Glory confessed that her attire was perhaps appropriate for a prairie town but not quite so for Denver and the Academy, Eden had nodded and whisked them into a shop called Denver Woman's Clothing Emporium. The shop had, living up to its name, the largest array of women's garments Glory had ever seen. Upon perusing the racks and shelves, Glory selected a few blouse and skirt ensembles, relishing the lightweight feel of the cotton and the machine stitching of the seams. Eden warned her that Glory would need to purchase thicker clothing and heavy boots at some point in the future. The Denver winters were very cold, and the high desert weather was often unpredictable even in summer. After some back and forth, Glory added two pair each of split skirts and breeches onto the pile.

"Are we done?" Glory eyed the enormous pile of wrapped packages. She hoped she had brought enough money.

"Done for now." Eden grinned.

The noise and texture of the crowd outside had shifted: More people had filled the streets and sidewalks while they had shopped. With the sun nearly straight above, people seemed to be taking luncheon. Scents of beer and bratwurst turned Glory's head to the right, where she saw a vendor with a booth on wheels. A long line snaked around the vendor, and down the sidewalk.

An angry shout echoed through the street.

A crowd had gathered in the street. Or rather, two crowds: One group of men and women had formed a procession and marched down the avenue. The marchers held banners, wore sandwich boards over their shoulders, and carried an assortment of smaller signs.

Every one of the signs, Glory saw, denounced magic.

"Magicians shall not know God."

"Thou shalt not suffer a witch to live."

"Magic is an Abomination."

"Magicians are sinners. Death to the magicians."

"God's Word is the Only Law."

The men and women marched in silence, their solemn faces focused forward. No one in the procession smiled, and Glory shivered. The second crowd was looser and stood at the edges to the march. Buggies and wagons, laden with and driven by irritated drivers' intent on completing their day's work, yelled at the procession, urging them to walk faster or get out of the way.

The march continued the unhurried pace until a man in the front raised his hands to the sky. It must have been a prearranged signal,

Glory thought, because the rest of the procession came to a halt. The man with raised hands wore conservative attire that jarred against his unkempt beard and youth.

He spoke.

"The United States and its territories have committed sins against God," he intoned. His voice echoed across the now silent street, deep and flavored with fervor. "The Falstead Act of 1859 legalized the devil's work. It promotes and encourages the proliferation of evil magicians, devilry, and witches." Disgust dripped from his words. "Our holy book forbids this. It is clear: God forbade magic, as it takes us away from his grace and into hell," he thundered, arms crashing down to point at the ground.

He continued but Glory looked away. She trembled; she had seen enough. It reminded her of an uglier version of Pastor Brooks in Agate Creek. The crowd that lined either side of the street swelled, and she saw more than a few nods of agreement throughout the thronged people. It was clear that the young man's message resonated with several of the watchers. Glory felt a frisson of fear dance down her spine. Would these strangers countenance harm to her, or even her death, simply for being a magician? That knowledge seeped into her like ink staining cloth: *There are people in this world who thought those with Affinities should die*, she realized.

She could taste nausea as it filmed her mouth. She swallowed hard several times, and clutched the packages of her new purchases tightly to her torso.

The young man — he had to be a reverend, Glory thought — continued but Glory only heard snatches of the monologue over the rumble of the crowd: "Witches are the devil's sluts, to do his bidding, and to entice away our young people into a life of moral laxity and evil."

Members of the procession began shouting in counterpoint to the reverend's words:

"Amen!"

"Hallelujah, Reverend."

Murmurs rippled through the audience, a mix of agreement and disdain, forcing the reverend to speak even louder.

Eden gripped Glory's arm, and Glory jumped. "We should leave," Eden said, worry evident in her voice.

Glory nodded.

They began to push their way through the people closest to them and down the boardwalk but progress was slow. It felt like trekking through molasses to Glory. No one wanted to move aside, captured by the drama unfolding in front of them.

"Horseshit."

An angry oath rang out. Glory paused, looked up.

A stylish man, with expensive, tailored clothing and a hat with a modern brim, had stepped from the crowd and up to the reverend. "You are speaking utter horseshit," he repeated, his baritone voice shaking with fury. "There are no deals with the Devil, and no sacrifices in exchange for unholy abilities. Magical is a natural gift, born to a few." The man had to shout his last few words because the crowd's clamor had grown during his rebuttal, loud and angry and threaded with disbelief. Glory was shoved into Eden as another man struggled to the front of the crowd. In his haste, he stepped on her foot, and Glory yelped at the sudden discomfort.

The reverend ignored the stylish interloper. "Heavenly Father, I beseech you to protect my flock from this magician and all such similar minions of the Fallen One."

The well-dressed man rolled his eyes at the reverend and let loose with a disdainful laugh — and pandemonium broke out.

Several members of the procession rushed forward, swinging signs. The converged on the man, who no longer laughed. Instead, he had the good sense to retreat. In his haste to get to the laughing naysayer, one march member bumped into a man within the crowd of observers. Angry shouts followed, and then fists flew. That seemed to be the turning point to Glory: Violence had occurred, and it seemed to give implicit permission to everyone present to perpetuate it.

Eden hadn't released Glory's arm, and she now tugged again, urgent. "We need to leave *now.*"

The crowd now seethed against them, slowing their progress to a shuffle. They were shoved and wrestled aside every few feet. Glory linked elbows with Eden, desperate to stay connected. Anger had pervaded the entire crowd by now; fear had her gulping deep breaths, trying to stay calm. Glory heard raised voices, grunts, and gasps of pain. Strains of the reverend's voice floated by. *Forward*, she thought. *We have to move forward.* But the noise, the smells pressed in on her. *How were they going to escape?*

"In here." A calm, familiar voice called to Glory and Eden.

Ms. Carville reached out from the entrance of the bookshop to clutch Eden. The young woman yanked them into the shop with a swift motion and shut the door. Locking the door, she moved to draw the shutters over the windows.

Glory jumped back in fright when a table laden with books leapt off the floor and flew to the door, scattering books in its wake. It leaned itself up against the door, reinforcing the locks by providing a secondary barrier. Another table went to barricade the large windows, and the shop's interiors darkened as the natural light dimmed. Glory hadn't realized that Ms. Carville was a magician. She supposed it made sense. Who else would stock a bookshop with magical texts?

"Are you safe?" Though the question was aimed at both of them, Ms. Carville's eyes ran over Eden, clearly searching for an injury.

"Yes, we are." Eden took a deep breath. "Thank you."

Ms. Carville ushered them back away from the shopfront. The fighting continued outside. The shop walls shuddered every time someone was slammed against the exterior of the shop. Agonized grunts and shouts of fury rose and fell like a bizarre jamboree band of chaos, with arhythmic sounds of pain and suffering. Glory caught snatches of the reverend yelling, random words that punctuated the noise of the crowd. She felt disgust and worry. A supposed man of peace had caused this, had instigated a mob that harmed everyone involved. How could a person do such a thing? Another worry crowded in: Would she have to worry about similar attacks for the rest of her life? Glory shivered. *No wonder her mother and father had left this life behind.*

A soft scrape of a shoe on the floor distracted Glory, and she turned to look for the source. With a start of surprise, Glory realized that Ms. Carville had sheltered other people in the store. A young matron whose two children clutched either hand stood behind the tall desk with the cash register. A cluster of three other women, accompanied by two older gentlemen, stood opposite of the shop entrance and along the back wall. Every face wore some expression that ranged between grim and resigned. The gun safe had been emptied, and everyone save the mother with children was armed. When someone did speak, they spoke in hushed tones. Glory wondered if they were all magicians, or if Ms. Carville had simply sheltered everyone she could.

Eden and Ms. Carville spoke, heads together. "Who is that?" Eden asked. "Is he new to Denver?"

"That man is the good reverend Matthew Brown," Ms. Carville answered, her tone edged in disdain. "I believe he arrived in Denver in the late summer of last year. The Academy and the local magicians began hearing of his rallies in November or so. They weren't sermons per se but lectures on the myriad evils of magicians." Ms. Carville shook her head. "The usual ignorance, I'm afraid, parading under a guise of holiness. I heard that he insisted that we magicians have multiple affinities, supposedly in exchange for our souls to Beelzebub." She snorted, then turned serious. "We don't have any real evidence but we think he's connected to the national God's Word movement."

We? Glory thought. *Who is we?* But she didn't ask that question. "Why is he doing this?"

Both Eden and Ms. Carville glanced up at Glory. Ms. Carville answered. "Holiness. Power. Money." She eyed the makeshift barricades; they remained steady. "I believe Brown's coffers are overflowing with donations and displays like these —" she waved at the street with an impatient gesture "— only garner more followers and admirers from those who mistake mischief-making for righteousness."

A gunshot rang out. Glory froze.

Another shot, and then another. A deep voice boomed outside. "Clear this street *now*. I will shoot the next man who throws another punch."

Glory watched as Eden and Ms. Carville relaxed, both sets of shoulders sinking. She heard sighs of relief from the people behind her. At Glory's questioning look, Eden explained. "That was the sheriff."

"He is a magician himself, though he doesn't advertise it," Ms. Carville added.

Outside, the mob had started to subside. Glory heard the sullen murmurs and several curses while the sheriff continued to shout his orders for dispersal.

Ms. Carville walked to the windows and peeked past the barricades. After peering up and down the street, she must have been satisfied with their safety for the wooden tables detached themselves from the shopfront with a gentle clunk, landed with table legs on the floor, and scooted across the shop back to the original locations. A collective sigh seeped from everyone in the shop.

Through the window, Glory saw that the crowd had thinned. The participants and spectators went separate ways, and Glory saw the reverend argue with a man in a cowboy hat with a pair of six guns on each hip. *That must be the sheriff,* Glory thought.

A scuff of shoes and a swish of skirts behind Glory drew her attention away from the street, and she turned to see Ms. Carville and Eden walk through the shop, picking up the books and other items that had fallen to the floor when the tables had flown into action. Glory joined them. Soon, all the books were back where they belonged.

The bookshop patrons and erstwhile refugees exited the store in short bursts. All of them stopped to embrace or thank Ms. Carville. Finally, only Eden and Glory remained. Ms. Carville moved behind the tall desk with the register.

"Thank you for your assistance in cleaning the shop." Ms. Carville pointed at the stacks of books upon the tables which were recent barricades. "That would have taken a great deal longer without you both." She paused, looking over Glory and then Eden. "Are you ready to go back to Thornhedge? Shall I call a buggy for you?"

Eden demurred. "We can find one."

Glory and Eden gathered up their packages, and after a quick farewell and another expression of gratitude to Ms. Carville, they left the bookshop to walk to the buggy stand. After confirming their destination with the driver, they were on route back to Thornhedge. The skies had clouded over the sunny day — a fitting end for a troubled day. Eden nor Glory spoke much during the drive back.

Glory had a great deal to think about. She went over the riot, and the inflammatory demonstration that led up to it, in her mind. Growing up in a frontier town, Glory hadn't thought much about magic. Why would she have? She hadn't thought it was relevant to her. But she had known that magicians and Affinities were real, and she had understood in a vague, distant way that many people did not like nor did they approve of magic. But Glory had not realized until today that magic could be dangerous. Not necessarily to have and to wield, though Glory supposed a poorly trained magician, or one with ill intent, could be very dangerous. But Affinities were dangerous to those who had them because of the prejudice and bigotry aimed at magicians, and that same prejudice that could lead to violence. Even murder.

Until today, it hadn't occurred to Glory that she was a potential target. A fine tremor shook her hands at the thought, and she clenched them into fists. How did one carry that knowledge without it weighing down life activities and influencing choices about what to do and where to go?

A sudden thought snuck through her labyrinthine ruminations: Was this, the knowledge that magic was dangerous on many levels, why her father had hidden his life at Thornhedge from her? Refused to discuss Juliet or her work? Hidden the knowledge of her Affinity from Glory? Because magic was dangerous, and he had wanted to keep her safe? To protect her from it all?

No answers came to Glory throughout the drive back to Thornhedge. And sadly, she could never ask him about his choices. That knowledge settled over her like a heavy blanket.

Outside the buggy, the skies continued to cloud over.

INTERLUDE

He trailed after the young man, careful to keep a block or two of distance between them.

A thrill chased down his spine, and he shook his head. He had tried to maintain a sense of detachment with this one but found it near impossible: The young man in front of him, with black hair and brows, and stopped outside a men's clothing emporium on one of the busiest streets in Seattle, had an Affinity for the physical states of matter.

He shuddered in anticipation, with tremors rushing through his limbs.

He had first seen this man, a local university student named Wendell Barnum, at a lecture on physics. Barnum had offered the lecture to university students and interested laypeople alike, and had demonstrated different states of matter with his own Affinity by transforming room temperature water to ice to a mist that had wafted across the crowd. Then he demonstrated his gift again and again: A potted rosebush that had melted into a pile of liquid plant matter. A single glass reduced to fine sands.

He had watched Barnum throughout the lecture, astonished and with delight. Then came the envy, and the decision.

He had followed Barnum since the lecture two weeks ago, learning the young man's daily routines. Barnum had no wife nor a mistress nor any children. Instead, the young bachelor had a devoted mother with whom he visited each Sunday. Barnum also seemed to have limited interests outside his work: The man drank whiskey and smoked cigars at his social club, got his beard trimmed once a week, and went to the University for his work.

He was pleased by the lack of family connections. It would be some time before anyone noticed Barnum was missing — more than enough time for him to leave the city, unnoticed.

He watched Barnum pull away from the window looking into the menswear shop and continue down the sidewalks. He followed. His heart rate accelerated in anticipation.

Maybe Barnum would be the *one*.

The one that changed everything.

CHAPTER ELEVEN

Three weeks later, Glory was *exhausted*.

Her body ached from traversing across campus multiple times a day and going up flights upon flights of stairs. She had worked in the general store, so Glory had thought she was used to physical activity. But the lectures were held in different locations throughout the campus and required long walks, which had to occur during the short breaks between lectures.

The lectures were both familiar and unlike anything Glory encountered prior to attending Thornhedge. On her third lecture, she finally placed the nagging source of her familiarity: In her lessons with her father, he would sit next to the fireplace in their home in Agate Creek, and a steady stream of knowledge would issue from him in his deep and warm voice. He had asked questions to test her comprehension of the subject at hand and offer gentle correction when she and her sister had misunderstood a detail. After a week of lectures at Thornhedge, Glory knew that she and her sister had been fortunate to have their father as an erstwhile lecturer. Many of her current teachers were not so skilled in sharing knowledge.

Glory was pleased to discover that she was familiar with, or already proficient at, some of the subjects at Thornhedge. The general curriculum was composed of the usual array of liberal arts: literatures, arithmetic, and rhetoric. She had no trouble completing the work assigned during these lectures.

But the magic classes were different.

They were *hard*.

Her first class was Magical History. The subject covered the history of Affinities throughout the world, and the lecturer, a Professor Simmons, was a tall African woman with almond eyes and slender hands. Upon Glory's arrival to the large lecture hall, Simmons had almost danced in place, and her graying black curls bounced with the movement. "You are Jules' daughter, yes?"

Glory swallowed hard, feeling the eyes of every student on her back. "Uh, y-yes," she muttered. *Please, please let me sit down already.* Glory handed her a note from the Curriculum office. Simmons had scanned the paperwork. Her eyebrows flew up and Glory braced herself. She knew what was coming.

"An Affinity for metals?" Simmons looked like a child in a sweet shop: Gleeful, captivated. "You're my first student with this Affinity."

Murmurs rippled through the class like a strong wind through grass.

"*Metal*?"

"...yes, that's what Simmons said."

"D'you think she can make gold?"

"Don't be dumb."

"...daughter of the woman who wrote one our textbooks?"

Glory stared at the floor, her discomfort at the scrutiny of others acute. She clenched her hands around her satchel handle and the supplies within rattled in response. A flush stained across her cheeks, the warmth uncomfortable.

"Settle down." Simmons called the class to order with a stern gaze before turning to look to Glory. "Find a seat, Rue, and welcome. I look forward to seeing what you can do."

Glory fled from the front of the room and took the first empty seat she spotted. As she sat upon the hard wooden bench, she glanced at the young woman to her right with a small smile.

And was astonished to find the girl sneering at her.

Red curls gathered around a doll-like face with ruby lips and blue eyes. The girl wore disdain like the fine trimmings on her sage green gown: With practiced ease and long familiarity.

"You're not *that* special." The girl sniffed before she turned towards the front of the class, dismissing Glory.

Shock held Glory still. *What on earth?* What had prompted *that?* She shook her head, trying to shake off the confusion and embarrassment that suffused throughout her body. *Maybe there was a reason the seat next to her was empty*, Glory thought. She turned back to Simmons, pulling out her writing pad and pen.

She hoped the lecture didn't leave her too lost.

Since the Reverend's Riot (as the skirmish with the religious procession in Denver came to be called), Eden and Glory ate meals together. The event seemed to have solidified something between them, and the unexpected friendship was a boon to Glory.

At lunch that day, Eden quizzed her. "How was your class?"

"Good, I think?" Glory picked apart a biscuit. "Simmons was very excited to meet me, which was a little embarrassing." Glory paused, then continued. "And another girl told me I wasn't special." Glory shook her head at the memory. "I have no idea why. It was... unpleasant."

Eden sipped her tea. "What did the girl look like?"

"Red curls, nice clothing, and she wore a sneer like one wears fine jewelry."

Eden burst out laughing. A few heads turned their way at the noise.

"What's so funny?" Glory asked with a puzzled grin.

"I bet you had a run-in with Eliza Hicks." Eden swallowed her last giggle. "You described her perfectly. She's terrible. Entitled and *mean*."

"I gathered. But why? I don't even know her. What could I have done to her? It's literally my first day of classes." Glory scowled.

"I'd guess that Eliza pitched a fit for the same reason Simmons got excited: You are a metal magician."

Glory thought for a moment. "And? I don't understand."

Eden leaned forward. "Magicians can be horrific snobs. The rarer a gift, the more social cachet they're afforded in the community. Sort of bragging rights. Like when cowboys and lawmen brag about their pistols and rifles. Or ranchers about the size of their herds."

Glory shook her head. "But I didn't do anything special. I just have it, right?" *I hope I can use it.* She hadn't tried to use her gift since she left Ravesbroke's office.

Eden shrugged. "I'm not saying it makes sense. It's just the way things are. Eliza probably went positively green with envy." Eden gave a delighted cackle.

"Doesn't she have an Affinity?"

"Well, Eliza comes from the wealthy Hicks family. Full of power-house magicians, each one of them," Eden said. "She has an Affinity for gemstones, a decent gift. Between the gift and the rich family, she just *knows* she's better than everyone else." Eden rolled her eyes before continuing. "If she was awful, she's probably threatened by you."

Glory sighed. "Great. Making friends already."

Eden laughed. "Oh, you don't want her, trust me." She gave an impish smile. "Keep me instead."

Glory grinned back and offered Eden her extra cookie. "Thanks, I will."

That afternoon, Glory had had her first Fundamentals of Affinities course. Having had no magical training before her arrival at Thornhedge, she was placed in a basic course. When she arrived at the room, decorated with posters of magical principles interspersed with large windows, Glory was dismayed to discover herself to be the oldest student in the classroom. The next oldest student, a young Latino man, looked to be fourteen or fifteen.

The students stared at Glory as she stood in the doorway.

Then the whispers started.

"Rue?" A short, young white man in a crisp burgundy vest over a white shirt and dark slacks approached her.

Glory looked away from the young students. "Um, yes?"

The man gave a small smile. "Welcome. I am Professor Bader. Have a seat, anywhere you'd like."

Glory felt a trickle of shame spiral through her as she took her seat amongst the young students. She avoided the others' gazes as she sought a seat near the back, away from scrutiny. The worn, wooden seats and desk felt tight and narrow, as though built for smaller — younger — bodies. She squeezed in with some difficulty, wincing as the chair legs groaned against the polished floor. As she pulled out writing supplies from her satchel, she glanced around. Waist-high shelves lined the edges of the classroom, filled with books, crates, and writing supplies. The large posters she had spied earlier offered statements that made little sense to Glory:

"An Affinity is a Gift."

"Each Affinity is Unique to its Bearer."

"Affinities Should Serve the Community."

Glory looked away from the posters and focused on the instructor, who walked the length of the room and back as he spoke in soothing tones. Worry weighed like ballast in her gut. None of this made any sense to her.

Glory sighed inwardly. What had she gotten herself into?

If the Fundamentals of Affinities was a theory class focused on *how* magic worked, Magical Studies was the semi-tailored class on learning about each individual ability. Upon arrival to this course, Glory was relieved to discover that the students were older, closer to her own age of seventeen. They sat in tight clusters at circular tables within an enormous room, their heads nestled together over open textbooks and notebooks. The air smelled of leather, paper, and ink. Quiet murmurs burbled throughout the room like a river across stones.

Then Glory spied Eliza Hicks.

The girl eyed Glory in the doorway, then gave a sneer and a sniff before turning back to her tablemates. Glory couldn't hear what the other girl said but whatever she had shared with them caused the other three girls to look up and over at Glory. They giggled, then bent down to mutter among themselves.

At least she's consistent, Glory thought. *Consistently awful.*

A tall man with tan skin and lanky limbs, approached Glory in quick steps and even quicker speech, as though he were in a hurry to get all his words out at once. "Rue, yes? Professor Lucas Whitetail. With your Affinity for metals, I believe you're best suited to work alongside Joule and Marie. Over there. You may sit down." He pointed.

Taken aback by the swift delivery of information, Glory gave a stuttered nod. "Uh, yes. Alright."

"Good." Whitetail strode away to another corner of the room.

Glory made her way over the table in question, occupied by a boy and another girl. "Um, hello."

The young man looked up, then nodded.

The other girl smiled. "Hello."

Glory sank into a chair at the table, relieved by the simple acceptance. *At least they're not like Eliza*, she thought. "Um, what am I supposed to do?"

Joule and Marie grinned. "Whitetail can be abrupt," Joule explained. "You'll get used it."

Glory soon learned that Joule and Marie were relative newcomers to the Academy. With an Affinity for soils and sediment, Joule had been there for five months and was an exchange student from an Indian community in Washington Territory. Glory was surprised to learn that Thornhedge and the other Academies had their own treaties with the Indian tribes throughout North America, hosting exchange students and visiting faculty at their respective learning centers. Marie, the quiet one at the table, had been here for seven months and had an Affinity for water.

A shadow fell over Glory, distracting her from the other two students. Whitetail had come back. He loomed close over Glory, Marie, and Joule, and stared out a window while he talked. He seemed to avoid eye contact with everyone, Glory noticed. "The purpose of Magical Studies to learn everything there was to know about one's own abilities. By obtaining a thorough understanding of the variables that went into an Affinity, this knowledge then provides the student with insight on how to manage and expand their inborn gift."

He sounds like a manual of sorts. Glory swallowed hard. *I can study metals. That should be... do-able.*

"For example, if a student understood the propagation methods of a flora, they could replicate and speed up the process with their Botanical Affinity," Whitetail continued. He turned from the window and focused on Glory in an abrupt motion. "Your task in this course is to learn about the composition and nature of various metals. You will likely have a specific attraction to one or more of these materials. Once you understand the nature of these metals, you'll discover the limits of your ability."

"I understand." Glory did *not* understand but nodded as though she did. *I just have to practice. I can do this.* Inside, however, she shrank and wilted more with every new bit of information. Learning about metals didn't seem too bad — she could read and take notes and absorb information about the properties of different types of metals. But how would she apply knowledge to an ability she could barely access? Unless she panicked or got angry, since strong emotion had been the only way she had accessed the gift up until now?

Whitetail gave a single nod and drifted away to another small group in the classroom. When Joule and Marie had returned to their own studies, their heads bent over their notebooks, Glory barely restrained a sigh.

How on earth would she be able to do this?

CHAPTER TWELVE

Glory's most challenging course was Applied Magic. Three times a week, Glory met with a tutor to practice using her Affinity. Unfortunately, the tutor was an impatient, middle-aged white man with thin hair and a disturbingly red nose named Galvan, who gave Glory assignments to complete before each subsequent appointment.

In a pattern that already felt familiar to Glory, Galvan had been excited when he had realized that Glory was the daughter of Juliet Rue.

But as the first session wore on, Glory saw the gradual creep of confusion, then outright bafflement, before segueing into somewhat hidden frustration. At the fourth lesson, Galvan was openly frustrated. The red of his nose seemed to stretch and stain across his cheekbones, a clear flag of his irritation.

"You don't *feel* the magic, do you?"

The assignment had been to feel different metals, and to try to alter or physically change the shape. She wasn't to feel the metal through her physical senses like touch or smell but through her Affinity. Though Glory had moved and modified metal in the past, those instances had always been emergency situations. Galvan had informed Glory that the goal of these appointments was to teach her how to access her Affinity in everyday circumstances so she could use her gift whenever she wanted — not in the spectacular but dangerous fits and starts.

At first, Glory had been pleased with the no-nonsense explanation from Galvan. This was exactly the purpose of a magic school. But Glory's enthusiasm had withered under her own frustration with her lack of progress and Galvan's growing dismay at Glory's seeming inability to do this work. The simple fact was that Glory couldn't seem to access her gift unless sit was a dire emergency. She felt the wellspring of power, tucked away beneath her breastbone. Sometimes her fingers even tickled with the promise of magic but nothing came of it.

Glory bit back her own dismay. "I'm trying." *But I don't know what I'm searching for...*

"It is embodied. Your magic is a part of who you are, an essential element of your very being. You must *feel* it."

"I will try again." Glory swallowed hard. She loathed closing her eyes in front of Galvan, but she did so, determined to feel *something*.

Anything. She took a deep breath. And another. Glory cast back to the train robbery, to the moment she felt her magic course through her, to send the iron rails soaring through the air. What had happened then? Her fingers had felt ticklish, she remembered. The magic had felt warm, then too hot, like a campfire turned rogue. The power seemed to emanate from her... chest? Her gut? Glory frowned, her eyes still closed. She couldn't *remember*.

"Anything?" Galvan asked, his tone salted with irritation and fatigue.

Glory opened her eyes — and realized her mistake. She withered under Galvan's open disapproval; her insides shrank under the frank dismay in the man's gaze. She switched her eyes to the polished tile floor beneath her feet and wished the ground would open up to swallow her.

"Um, no. Nothing."

Glory muttered to herself as she sat next to Eden. Breakfast was her favorite meal at the Academy; the cooks never stinted on pastries, which were rich with sugar and butter.

But even breakfast couldn't cheer her up.

Eden's eyebrows rose. "Is everything alright?"

Glory sighed. "I have another appointment with Galvan this morning." Thus far, Applied Magic was *not* Glory's best subject. That Galvan was impatient, abrupt, and a little more than dismissive of Glory's ability did not bode well for her present or her future. Glory had come to dread these appointments.

Eden's expression turned sympathetic. "Ugh."

Glory envied Eden's Affinity. Botanical Affinities, the ability to manipulate and transform plants and other flora, were very common at Thornhedge and at the other Academies throughout the States. This meant that Thornhedge had plenty of instructors and knowledge available to the students. As far as Glory knew, she was the only student at Thornhedge with an Affinity for metals.

Eden gave a sudden, mischievous smile. "Forget Galvan. I have the perfect distraction for you."

Glory eyed the other young woman. "What?"

Eden leaned forward and lowered her voice. "I'll take you to the Corral on Friday evening."

"The what?" Glory echoed.

Eden gave a quick glance around dining hall to see if anyone could overhear, then leaned forward. "The Corral. It's just outside of Thornhedge. Students go there every Friday to show-off, to brag about what they've learned. Some even challenge one another."

"And the faculty allow this?" Doubt laced Glory's voice. Given how regimented and safety conscious Thornhedge was, Glory couldn't imagine any of the faculty supporting what sounded like a showdown. But she felt a wistful pang echoed across her chest. When would she get another opportunity to see other magicians flaunt their powers? To push beyond the safe — boring — limits of the class assignments and workshops, and truly *do* magic?

"Um. No?" Eden grinned. Her eyes sparkled with devilry. "No one has asked. If they find out and say no, better to ask forgiveness than permission, yeah?"

Glory felt an answering spark of excitement. She grinned back. "So, what, we sneak out and watch a bunch of magicians try to out-do each other? Possibly cause a little hell? Or break things?"

"Yep."

Glory bit into her pastry. "I'm in," she said, her mouth full.

Glory arrived at the studio a few minutes later and was greeted with Galvan's barely disguised scowl. *I shouldn't take this personally*, she thought. But Glory had noticed that Galvan didn't quite scowl the same way at anyone else at the Academy.

"Good morning." Glory tried to be polite.

"Yes, let's get started." *Abrupt as usual*, Glory thought. "Have you completed the assignment from our last session?"

"Um, no."

Galvan seemed unsurprised by Glory's tentative admission. "Right." He bent to write something in her notes, then looked up. "Let's start with the copper today."

Glory set her knapsack on the chair and rustled within until she pulled out the samples of various metals. Picking up the copper, she stood straight and closed her eyes. Glory tried not to feel foolish as she tried to feel the copper. Glory didn't quite know what she was supposed to search for during this process but started with the pulse of something extra within her chest. *Come on*, she wheedled within her mind. Fear trickled through her. *Please. I need to do magic. I can't stay here if I'm not a magician.*

Minutes passed in silence.

Glory could hear her own breathing in the still room; it felt loud and intrusive. Embarrassment and frustration heated her face, and she began to perspire. Glory waited and dreaded to hear Hicks' voice.

And then it came. "Well?"

Glory could hear impatience and irritation in the brusque voice. She opened her eyes — and wished she hadn't. Open frustration marred Galvan's face as Glory watched him write yet another note among the papers on the desk. Galvan looked up and sighed. "I don't think you're trying hard enough. Let's do this again, and this time, *feel* the metal. Let the copper share its secrets with you."

Glory restrained herself from sighing aloud. What did that statement even mean? Share its secrets? What secrets? Like the mystery of whether she truly had an Affinity at all? Glory took a breath, squared her shoulders, and tried again.

Glory focused her attention on the copper, and the weight and texture as it lay in her palm. She had always liked copper. It was warm, malleable, and seemed eager to partner with her. The day she had been diagnosed in Ravesbroke's lecture hall, the copper had felt like a long lost friend. It would sound silly to anyone else, Glory knew, but copper seemed to be a forgiving sort of metal. She rolled the copper between her palms, getting a feel for the texture and the weight.

Then Glory hear Galvan mutter to himself. "This is ridiculous."

Her heart stuttered in her chest.

Hurt veined through her like cracks in marble. *I'm trying my best and it's still not good enough.* Glory bit back a bitter, angry retort, her teeth tearing at her bottom lip. She set the copper down on the table in careful motions. She avoided Galvan's gaze as she gathered up her satchel and slung it over her shoulder. She walked out of the classroom.

"Wait a minute, miss." Galvan's sharp voice tugged at her. "Where do you think you're going? We aren't done here."

Glory ignored him as she continued out the door. The crowded hallway bustled with students between classes and workshops; the noise stung at her senses and Glory had to blink back tears of frustration.

I'm done. I won't — can't — do this.

Glory hadn't shared her abrupt departure from Galvan with Eden. She hadn't wanted to dampen the other girl's high spirits as they left the dining hall, and then the campus, on Friday evening.

"Glory, you will love the Corral." Eden linked elbows with Glory, tugging her along the brick path at a faster pace. She leaned into Glory with a conspiratorial tone. "I'm so excited for you."

Glory made herself smile, though the expression felt like the pulled taffy she once saw at a sweetshop in Denver. She was still upset from Galvan's thoughtless, hurtful comment. His frustration underscored her deepest fear: That she couldn't be a magician, let alone an accomplished one. For what kind of magician couldn't complete basic magical tasks? What kind of magician could only destroy and maim, rather than create? Glory's shoulders sank as she let herself be dragged along in Eden's cheerful wake.

What if I can't do this? What if I'm a failure?

Eden led them across the Academy grounds and behind the last building that lined the western edge of the campus. The sunset limned the mountaintops; the skies to east had purpled and began to dust starlight across the vast space. Glory found herself in a loose line of students, most of them older, making their way to what appeared as a pile of rocks. The air smelled of cold and manzanitas, and the darkness had deepened to the point where many of the students had lit lanterns that weaved and bobbed in the surrounding black while other students found ways to create light using their Affinities. Glory noted that these lights glowed different shades and textures — a gently pulsing white-blue or a steady green fog — than the lanterns.

As she drew closer to what she thought was a pile of rocks, Glory realized that she approached a natural amphitheater of sorts. The red rocks, made rust by the dim lantern lights, rose in a rough semi-circle around a large clearing studded with pebbles and coated in dust. The students stood at the edges of the clearing, leaving an open space in the center. Glory recognized Joule and Marie across the circle and waved. They smiled back.

"Alright, ladies and gents." A tall Latino boy stepped forward with a challenging smirk. "Who is going first?"

A boy with black hair and laughing eyes was shoved to the center by two of his friends.

"Go on," one of his friends shouted. "Show us what you can do, Stephens."

The boy made a rude gesture at his friends, who only howled in response. The boy then removed a near invisible item from his pocket. Glory squinted in the darkness. Was...was it a seed? The boy placed the small speck in the center of his palm, then closed his eyes to concentrate. He took a deep breath — and Glory gasped. Roots ripped out of a seed to weave and wrap around his arm. A thick trunk emerged from the seed, and branches dusted with leaves unfurled to stretch up into the night sky. The tree continued to grow and move, roots wrapping around the boy's torso. Soon the weight of the tree caused the young man to stagger and adjust his stance.

Then, as quickly as the tree had erupted, the tree shrank and reversed in growth. Leaves curled up before tightening into buds, then shrank back into branches. Roots shriveled away from the boy's torso and down his arm, racing towards his palm. Soon, the nut was all that remained of the display.

A loud applause broke out.

Stephens opened his eyes, grinned, and took an elaborate bow before rejoining the edges of the circle.

Eden grinned at Glory. "See?" she shouted over the applause. "It's wonderful."

Glory clapped, impressed and envious. *I wish I had that kind of control.*

Other students stepped or were nudged, like Stephens, forward. One brunette boy poured a canteen of water into the air, the drops flickering like molten gold in the lantern and magical lights that lined the Corral. Glory expected it to splash onto the ground but instead the water rose in tandem with the boy's other hand and hovered in the air. She watched as the boy tossed aside the canteen and stepped forward to greet the water with a... bow? Her brow furrowed as she watched the young man step around forward, then back, before moving from one side to another. Wherever he went, the water followed through the night air like an eager puppy, close and fast and wet.

He's dancing *with the water*, Glory realized. A grin spread across her face. Around her, the crowd yelled and hooted their approval as the boy danced faster and faster, with the water waltzing on air, as close as an embrace.

Finally the boy stopped, panting through a grin. The water rose up and erupted into a brief shower that sprinkled moisture on those nearby.

Glory laughed in delight. The boy took a bow and stepped aside, leaving the arena open for the next student. A pair of girls with matching blonde curls and rough slacks stepped forward only to pelt one another with projectiles of rock and wood. One of the girls grew a sliver of wood into a spear and hurled it at the other girl, who diverted the spear with a well-aimed flying rock before launching a volley of pebbles in return which rained upon a woven, wooden shield. As far as Glory could tell, the girls were evenly matched and only stepped down due to fatigue.

Eden leaned in to yell over the applause. "They're sisters. They fight all the time. It's kind of...adorable?"

After the applause died down, a short silence fell over the Corral.

"Anyone else?" The Latino boy who first spoke queried the attendees.

"How about a demonstration from our *famous* metal magician?"

Glory's head shot up.

She hadn't realized Eliza Hicks was here. *Ugh. This won't be good.*

Eliza emerged from the edge of the crowd across the amphitheater. She smirked at Glory in the dim light, the expression more ominous with deep shadows etched across her face. "Come on, Rue. I'm sure you're dying to show off your magic. After all, it's so *rare*." Eliza hurled the last word like an epithet, her porcelain face wrought into an ugly mask.

Glory felt the weight of multiple stares. Whispers rustled through the circle.

"Uh, no, thanks," Glory said. She swallowed hard. "I'd rather watch the others this time."

"Oh?" Eliza quirked an eyebrow. "You're not shy, are you?"

"No," Glory gritted out. *Please stop talking. Just go away.*

"Or perhaps you're just scared?"

A murmur rippled around the circle. Eden grabbed Glory's arm, in support or to restrain her, Glory couldn't tell. Glory shook her head, then gave a weak laugh. "I don't feel like it, Hicks." *I can barely do magic — I can't let them know that.*

The whispers grew. Glory could see the other students lean into one another, cast dubious looks her way. Frustration and fear simmered and bubbled within her. How was she going to get out of this mess?

"I think you're scared," Eliza mused aloud. The other girl's cheerful calm did nothing to hide the malicious glee that emanated from her eyes, from the smirk that marred her mouth. "Definitely scared. Or maybe — maybe you just can't do it."

Fear swamped Glory like a sudden thunderstorm. *What did Eliza know? How?* Glory could taste something metallic on her tongue. She shivered in the cold air, feeling exposed. Raw. *They are going to know,* she thought numbly. *They are going to know I'm a fraud.*

"Maybe you aren't that special after all," Eliza sneered. The other girl's voice rang with victory.

Anger ripped through Glory. How dare Eliza? She was new to the magical world and to her own ability. Of course she would struggle with this new skill — any student would. The unfairness of Eliza's insensitive, mean cattiness chafed at Glory. She also remembered Galvan's disbelief and frustration, and the wound was salted anew. She *was* a magician, damn it. Her hands tremored with her fury; the back of her throat tasted of bile and upset. Glory shivered in the cool night air, as hot anger twisted through her body.

Her fingertips trickled. Her palms itched.

A sharp jolt shuddered through Glory and her body blazed with fire. She staggered sideways from the force, stumbling to stay upright. *CRACK.*

Glory opened her eyes. What had happened?

And her jaw dropped.

A twisted spike of copper and silver rose from the center of the clearing. The contrasting metals gleamed in the lantern and magical light, spirals chasing each other up into the sky. Glory stared up at the top of the spike, which topped her by a foot. The top of the spike splayed outwards from the twisted spirals like rose petals cast in metal. Glory followed the spike down to the ground and saw that the red rock ground had split asunder to permit the metal intrusion. Sharp shards stuck out from the metal spirals, not quite thorns but sending the same message: *Dangerous. Keep away.*

The others had leapt back with yells of fright and gasps of awe. Several other students had backed away, giving Glory a wide berth while they watched her with wary eyes or admiring faces. Glory searched the crowd in a quick sweep. No one seemed injured or hurt.

Thank goodness.

Eden stepped forward. "Glory? Are you alright?"

Fear trickled across her scalp. Glory shivered. *I really could have hurt someone.*

Eliza found her voice at last. "What were you thinking? You could have injured me — us — very badly!" she shouted. Glory winced. The voice ricocheted and echoed through amphitheater; the sharp notes hurt her ears. "You are a danger to everyone here." Eliza gathered herself up and stood tall. "My father is good friends with Provost Burst and when he hears of this — this assault, you will be gone like that." Eliza snapped her fingers, her words were glazed with vicious satisfaction.

Eliza stomped through the clearing and past Glory.

At any other time, Glory would have enjoyed seeing the bully, her unwanted and unwarranted nemesis, so flustered and in such angry disarray. But now she only felt trepidation: *What will happen to me? Will I be kicked out of the Academy?* A sense of suffocation swamped her and Glory struggled to take a deep breath. She didn't want to leave Thornhedge; she had just arrived — and she had nowhere else to go. She had barely learned about the world of Affinities. The very existence of magic had made the world seem bigger and richer to Glory.

Eden. Glory felt a pang at the thought of leaving her newfound friend behind. And Seth and Gareth. Though Glory still felt hurt from how they had deposited her at Thornhedge and then simply left, Glory found that she still missed them.

But what if she never saw them again?

EXCERPT

Research Notes, J. Rue

July 27, 1878

Hickory, Missouri

I

n contrast to my efforts with C. and the other, more contrary participants in my field research, R. found me *in Hickory rather than the other way around an hour after I had arrived by stagecoach.*

Short, with a wiry frame and an angular face beneath a wispy gray halo of hair, the woman marched up to me and asked if I was the "...magical research lady." Usually, I demur or inquire who's asking before I confirm this bit of information; you see, I've been run out of too many towns at the wrong end of a rifle or a pitchfork. But with her open gaze and cheerful grin, I found myself answering the affirmative before I could stop myself.

"I want you to take down my details, record my gift," she announced just outside the entrance to a saloon. "I've been using it for five decades now and it's served this community well."

I nodded my assent hastily and followed her as she led the way to a nearby buggy. She waved away my offer of assistance, and stepped up into the seat with little trouble. The woman then stared down at me. "Well? Are you coming?"

I could hardly decline.

I jumped into the buggy, clutching my luggage to my chest, and we clattered away from town and into the country. It was a beautiful day, though the heat and humidity had set in by late morning and my clothes were damper than I liked. In no time at all we were approaching the woman's home, and as we crested a hill that stood sentry to her property, I had gasped aloud.

The old woman, who still hadn't shared her name, chuckled. "It's a sight, ain't it?"

I had only nodded, feasting my eyes on the majestic concoction of a house before. No, the word 'house' was too humble a word for this abode. Out of every material possible, it had been crafted and wended and molded from multiple materials. The roof draped over a multi-story home like a duvet on a bed, with folds and curls. The windows were round, square, rectangular — I even saw a triangular window on the facade of the house. The wooden trim around the entrances and windows were fashioned to wrap around the home like ivy and climbing flowers. A stone patio reached out from the base of the home to form a courtyard of sorts, speckled with golden and grey and rust red stones.

The effect was stunning.

I looked at the woman besides me. "I don't believe I caught your name."

She grinned up at me. "It's R. I have a gift for building."

Throughout our subsequent conversations, it emerged that she more correctly had an Affinity for architecture, though 'building' would suffice for most people. R. had built this home through two husbands, both of whom have passed on, and six children, four of whom have an Affinity (culinary, two with a healing Affinity, and botanical). In the last five decades, R. had been to nearly every barn raising and consulted on most homestead plans. The only ones she had missed were earlier in her life, due to childbirth or infrequent illness.

What was truly remarkable about this recital was an absence of prejudice and fear from the locals without Affinities. When I carefully inquired about the social climate with regards to magical abilities — particularly during the era when magic hadn't yet been legalized — R. snorted and waved off the question.

"I was useful, see," she retorted. "Every home I built or contributed to has stayed standing, unless it was a fire. Or a tornado," she added as an afterthought. "Sure, I heard harsh nonsense about being an instrument of the devil from the townsfolk from time to time but that didn't stop them from knocking on my door when they needed my help." She shook her head. "No, they needed me."

Reflecting on some of the more horrific stories I had heard from other magicians, I thought it was fortunate that R. had been largely embraced by her town. Too many of us hadn't, and suffered for it.

In summary, the ability manifested around fifteen for R. and it took some convincing of her father that she had a gift and further convincing to allow her to attend and contribute to barn and home buildings. R. describes the gift as a knowing: When looking over a plot of land or building plans, she knows *what is right and true for the space and the proposed function. Then she draws up or modifies the plans to improve them. She also joins in on the building, often redirecting efforts when necessary to avoid mistakes and near disasters.*

After two days of interviews with R. and her family, and some of the best cornbread I've ever had the opportunity to eat, I took my leave. As R. drove me herself, manning the horse and buggy, to the stagecoach pick up point (she had insisted on it), we talked about the future generations of those with magical gifts. What new abilities would emerge? How would these future generations use these gifts to shape the world around them? We didn't have any answers, of course, but it was a pleasant way to take leave of an extraordinary individual.

—J. Rue

CHAPTER THIRTEEN

G lory worried all weekend.

The rumors had run rampant. Heads had swiveled every time Glory had entered the dining halls and by Sunday morning, Glory had overheard rumors of Eliza being sent to the infirmary after Glory's supposed, unprovoked, and horrific abuse of her magic.

Eden had tried to console her. "It's just nonsense," the other girl had said with worried eyes. "It'll die down."

Glory couldn't sleep on Sunday night.

Then, at her Monday morning lecture, a History of Magic course led by Professor Simmons, the summons came.

A student entered the room mid-lecture. Simmons paused to send an inquiring look at the young man. "Yes?"

"Um, pardon the interruption," the young man began. He checked the piece of paper in his hand. "I'm here to escort Gloriana Rue to the Provost's office."

Murmurs swept through the hall. Inquisitive students craned necks to see where she sat. Glory stayed still, hoping the message was a mistake. That Eliza hadn't carried out her threat. Fear spread through Glory's body, and her fingers tingled. She would be thrown out of Thornhedge today. Glory wondered if she would have to leave today, or if she'd get to stay a few days, to figure out her next step.

She hoped she got to say goodbye to Eden. She would miss the Brothers Hill. Maybe she could leave a farewell note for Seth and Gareth.

"Miss Rue?" Simmons' voice intruded on Glory's thoughts. Glory looked up to see Simmons' concerned face. "Please accompany Peters to the Provost's Office," she said in a gentle voice.

Glory nodded. Feeling numb, she stepped forward. She ignored the scattered mutters all around her, speculative and prying, and made her way to the door.

"This way." Peters ushered Glory from the lecture hall and closed the door. Glory could hear Simmons resume the lecture. Peters led Glory into another building to the east of campus, and up a flight of stairs. It was sunny outside and a bit too warm. *An odd day to get kicked out of school*, Glory thought.

At last, they arrived at a set of double doors with expensive glass panels inlaid the frames. The oak gleamed with polish and the brass knobs were shiny from frequent use. Peters led them inside the room and conferred with an assistant sitting at a nearby desk. "Miss Rue is here."

The assistant smiled at first Peters, then Glory. "Wonderful. Thank you, Peters. I will let them know." She turned to Glory. "Please have a seat."

Glory sat in a chair and waited. She looked around the office, and saw the room was filled with grand embellishments to the furniture and textiles: Lush, patterned rugs lined the length of the wooden floor. The desks had floral motifs carved into the polished surfaces. The walls were lined with expensive, high quality wallpaper. *This room was design to impress,* Glory thought.

"Miss Rue?" Glory looked up. "They are ready for you."

Glory stood. *They?* Would she be kicked out by a group of magicians, rather than one? Entering the room, Glory saw a man and a woman conversing in low tones. They paused as she entered, then the man spread his arms wide and a smile lit his face. He strode up, and Glory noticed his well-trimmed beard, strong nose, and prominent cheekbones. Blue twinkling eyes and white hair completed his appearance.

"Welcome, Miss Rue! It's a great pleasure to meet you. Allow me to introduce myself: I am Howard Burst, the Provost of the Thornhedge Academy."

Confusion rippled through her. *Why is he so happy to see me?* Glory offered a weak smile. "How do you do, sir?"

Burst beamed at Glory, as though she had accomplished a great feat rather than a simple greeting. "Wonderful! Quite well, in fact. Sit down, sit down. We can discuss the matter of your schooling in comfort." Burst waved Glory and the other woman to a pair of couches appointed in lush fabrics.

Glory paused. If she were expelled from Thornhedge, she'd rather it know it now — rather than drag it out over afternoon tea. She stood still and straight, despite the mad racing of her heart, and made herself ask the question. "Sir, am I being expelled from Thornhedge?"

Burst and the woman paused in mid-seating.

"Expelled?" echoed the older woman. Crowned in iron grey hair and with black eyes that missed nothing, she stared at Glory. "Not unless you pull another stunt like Friday's nonsense."

Glory swallowed hard. "It was an accident, I swear. I didn't mean to."

The woman snorted, and Glory saw that Provost Burst hid a smile behind a hand. The other woman continued. "Accidents can still grievously injure others. You need better training, and fast."

Burst leaned forward. "Miss Rue, let me make introductions. This is Jacinda Eldredge, one of our professors at Thornhedge. She's been here... how long?" Burst turned to Jacinda.

"Much longer than you," Jacinda smiled despite the bite in her words. It was clear that they both shared affection for each other.

Burst almost rolled his eyes. "Yes, longer than me."

Glory studied Jacinda. The older woman's black eyes were opaque and she examined Glory as though she could dissect with her gaze. Very tan skin, speckled with age spots, made Glory think she traveled a great deal. Or had spent a lot of time out of doors. She looked to be in her sixties.

Glory realized that she had been staring. "Pleased to meet you."

"Likewise," Jacinda nodded. No smile, Glory noted, but it didn't seem that the older woman was much bothered by social frivolities.

"Miss Rue," Burst began. "You are here because I feel Jacinda is a better match for you than Galvan."

"Oh." Glory was relieved. Then confusion set in. Did the Provost often take such a personal interest in students at Thornhedge? To the extent of matching them with new tutors? Some of Glory's confusion must have shown on her face, and Jacinda laughed outright.

"You're not fooling her, you know. She's too sharp for that." Satisfaction gleamed through her words like sunlight through glass. "Burst wanted to see you in person, our famous metal magician," Jacinda explained. "We only know of two on the East Coast." The woman smiled now, kindness filtering across her face. "Burst wanted to meet our local rare bird, you see."

Glory gave a tentative smile, charmed by the honest humor.

"And the daughter of Jules, too." Burst beamed at Glory. "She worked with us before she passed. Both of them did, prior to her death and his move back East."

Glory's smile fell off her face. She hadn't known her mother had worked at Thornhedge, much less died here. Her father had rarely spoken about her mother, even to her sister or to Glory.

"But we're not here for a trip down memory lane." Jacinda's smooth voice interrupted Glory's thoughts. "After Friday evening's demonstration, you clearly need a new instructional approach."

Glory gave a slow nod. "I guess I do." She darted a look between Burst and Jacinda, then swallowed. "You know about the Corral?"

Jacinda snorted. "Of course we do. We started the tradition. If no one gets hurt, we turn a blind eye." The older woman studied Glory for a moment. "Do you *want* to keep working with Galvan?" she asked, doubt clear in her voice.

Glory shook her head. "No. I simply didn't realize I had a choice," she admitted.

"You always have a choice — at Thornhedge or anywhere else." Jacinda met her eyes. "And if our partnership doesn't work for you, we will find you another tutor. You have a place at Thornhedge, I assure you. As long as you put in the work."

Glory's shoulders relaxed, and a sigh of relief escaped her before she could stifle the emission. *I get to stay*, she thought. *Thank goodness.*

Burst beamed again, as though he had solved the problem, and not Jacinda. "Excellent. This is the perfect match, I'm sure of it."

"We'll see, Burst. One day at a time," Jacinda said. "Glory, would you be willing to meet with me tomorrow? I'd like to understand where you are in your education before I develop our further studies."

Surprise flickered through her. Could it be? At last, someone seemed ready to meet her where she was. She felt...hopeful since the first week she had arrived at Thornhedge.

A small smile crept across her face. "Yes, I can do that."

The next morning, Glory found herself in Jacinda's study. The older woman's apartments were bare and bespoke of a single person's quarters: Worn rugs and cushions in the sitting area, with a wobbly table with one leg steadied by a short stack of books. The shelves housed more books and scrolls and artifacts, all nestled into each other. A long work desk cut across the middle of the room.

"Welcome." Jacinda smiled. Much more reserved than the effusive Provost, the woman wore calm like a cloak. "This is my library and studio. After today's evaluation we'll meet in your new studio. Let's get started. How much do you understand about Affinities? About how they work?"

Glory blinked. "Um…" She struggled to recall the words she had tried to memorize from her textbooks. "Wait. Studio?" *What did that mean?*

Jacinda gave a single nod. "Your response explains a great deal."

Glory flushed. "I'm sorry."

"Don't be. No one is born knowing magic or even how to learn. It's irrational to believe or expect that of yourself."

Glory gave a cautious nod.

"I could provide a long lecture about the nature of magic, how magic — even those with similar Affinities — is unique to the individual who bears it, etc., etc." Jacinda shook her head. "But you will have enough of theory in your coursework here at Thornhedge. I want you to learn how your own magic feels to you."

"Feel the magic?" Glory echoed Galvan's words, dismay settling on her chest. Would she never escape that dreaded admonition?

Jacinda gave a dark chuckle. "I hate that phrase." She picked up an ornate silver candlestick from her work desk. Glory watched her remove the tapered candle and place it upon the table. "Galvan has it partly right: By learning how your magic feels to *you*, you can train yourself to call upon it whenever you wish. You can avoid repeats of what happened in the Corral. But with Galvan's impatience and poor communication skills, you probably didn't get that from your appointments with her."

Jacinda transferred the candlestick from one hand to the other — and threw it at Glory. "Catch."

"Stop."

The candlestick stopped in mid-air, two feet from Glory.

The silver quivered in the air. Light bounced off the metal as Glory realized in rapid order what had happened.

Jacinda smiled. "Now think: How did you do that?"

"What on earth? Y-you threw a candlestick at me." Glory could barely get the words out. Her cheeks prickled with heat; chills pebbled her skin. "What if I hadn't stopped it?"

Jacinda walked forward. "Then you'd take a quick trip to the infirmary. Take a moment, if you please. Focus on the candlestick —not me. You stopped it, and you're still holding it. Listen to your body. Where is the effort coming from?"

Glory frowned, still miffed. But she did as he asked: Closing her eyes in order to concentrate, she got to work.

After the first appointment in Jacinda's studio, they began to meet in Glory's new workshop. To Glory's relief, Jacinda threw no more candlesticks at her. Instead she brought a blacksmith's toolset and additional texts about chemistry and metals to supplement Glory's Applied Magic lessons. Sometimes the tools were useful, such as forceps for picking up metal slivers; other times, Jacinda used the tools as instructional metaphors. Once Jacinda brought an antique brass protractor to a lesson and encouraged Glory to think of expanding the reach of her powers by casting a wider and wider circle. Often, Jacinda encouraged Glory to use the hammers, pliers, and other tools in tandem with her magic, to have a physical tool through which to channel her magic.

That did the trick.

By focusing her magic through the blacksmith tools, Glory found a way forward in her magical studies. She no longer struggled to imagine how she could shape, enlarge, or reduce metal — she could practice with a combination of magic and the tools, until she no longer needed them.

Over the next month, Glory learned about the physical and magical properties of various metals: Silver for protection, copper for everyday use, iron for battle, gold for healing and ornamentation. Glory learned to transform the shape of each metal, while growing her own understanding of how each metal required a different technique, a different partnership between herself and the medium. She also learned to find metal in any object, and then to manipulate the metal *within* the object.

The first thing she mastered was extraction.

Jacinda had placed a block of wood, studded with iron nails, on the worktable in front of Glory. "Pull these nails out."

Glory reached for a small pry bar.

"With magic."

Glory groaned. She knew she sounded petulant but couldn't bring herself to care.

"You have to learn this." Jacinda's tone brooked no argument. "The tools are a vehicle, not a replacement."

Glory sighed, then closed her eyes. She held the block of wood in her hands, feeling the scratch of the rough wood against her palms, the chill of the iron that warmed at her touch. Her magic, which had seemed so remote — even absent — before rustled and shifted within her chest like a cat uncurling from a nap. She felt the differences between the metal and wood, friend and unknown, and reached out to the metal. She wrapped her magic around one nail, traced the dull edges with warmth.

"Move."

Rrrrrip.

A clamor rumbled through the room, a rumble in several different corners of the space. Something slammed on her toes. "Ouch!"

Glory leapt back, flung open her eyes.

She stilled, stunned.

She *had* moved the nail from the wood block.

But she also removed every other nail within the room. The nails in the worktable. And the chairs. And the toolbox. Everywhere she looked, she found piles of wooden debris, slats and legs, and odd pieces, cast down like discarded toys from a child's empty treasure chest.

Iron nails shimmered in mid-air like raindrops.

"Goddamnit," Jacinda cursed, her eyes wide.

Glory jumped as the door flung open. A young man stumbled into the room. "Aunt Jacinda, are you alright?"

Jacinda waved away his concern. "Jason, we're fine. Glory carried out my instructions a little too well."

Jason stared at the shambles of the room, his eyes wide and his mouth agape. Tall and lanky save for a small belly that hung over his loose pants, the young man had dark circles under his eyes. Pale skin and thin hair reminded Glory of a church elder she knew back in Agate Creek; his clothes were respectable but clearly patched over time and again.

"Jason, don't worry," Jacinda repeated.

The young man straightened, looking from the piles of wood to Glory. He visibly swallowed, looking anxious. "If you're s-sure," he stuttered.

"Yes." Jacinda's tone gentled. "I'll meet you in my study."

The young man swallowed again, then nodded. He left a moment later, shutting the door behind him with a gentle thump. At the quiet noise, the nails rained down onto the floor. Glory winced as they pinged against and bounced off of the mess.

"Who was that?" Glory asked, hoping to distract Jacinda from the disaster she had made of the studio.

"My secretary," Jacinda replied. "My nephew, too, for that matter. He conducts research on my behalf at other institutions and keeps everything organized." Jacinda glanced around the room, then shot Glory a meaningful look. "This is quite the mess. Good thing you can put it back together. What a great learning opportunity." The older woman grinned at Glory.

Ugh. I hope she is joking.

Jacinda was not joking. The older woman made her put the nails back into the desk, using magic and persistence, one by one. Two hours later, Glory sagged against the wall outside the studio. Perspiration dripped from her hairline and down her back, and she winced at her own scent. *I'll have to go back to the residence hall to change my dress before my next class.* After a moment, Glory grinned to herself. *But at least I'm using my magic.*

Chapter Fourteen

G lory adored her new magician's studio.

The space was outfitted as a smith's shop, furnished with a long workbench, a wall hung with gently worn but serviceable tools, and a small, portable blacksmith's forge. She was awkward with many of the tools at first but grew better and more proficient by the day.

Glory worked long into the evenings, well past the end of her classes. She came to love the feeling of being surrounded by scraps of different metals: gold, silver, copper, and iron. It felt like being surrounded by friends, or family. It was hard for Glory to describe but she felt that each metal had a different personality.

Glory thrived under Jacinda's tutelage. She went on to master a series of ever-challenging tasks she had set before her: Molding new shapes, melding metals together, and extracting the elements. Soon each new task seemed easier than the last.

In a recent conversation, Jacinda had warned Glory these new skills were among the easiest for a magician. True transformation of physical properties was much harder, and in some cases, impossible without several years of further study.

"Lead to gold?" Glory had asked, skepticism and humor in her voice. She remembered reading such silly tales among her father's library.

Jacinda had chuckled. "Not quite. You're bound by the chemical properties of the source material. But with study and practice, who knows what's possible? The magical properties of metal are vastly understudied and largely composed of myths and legends about alchemy. And because there are so few metal magicians, we still don't know what they — you — are capable of."

Glory had filed that information away for another time. She enjoyed the tasks Jacinda set before her. The challenge caused a frustration that quickly turned to triumph when she succeeded. Jacinda merely smiled when Glory succeeded, and then set before her another task. Outside of the appointments with Jacinda, Glory practiced her newfound skills in between lectures. She still felt behind compared to the other students at Thornhedge.

Glory often left her workshop sessions smelly, dirty, and sweaty. Use of her magic felt like the physical exertions like her work at the general store in Agate Creek. Glory's limbs would ache with sore muscles, she often sweated through her clothes, and without fail after every single session with Jacinda, she experienced profound hunger.

One of the first magical tasks involved the reshaping of a copper ingot, and Glory had been surprised and then embarrassed by the loud grumble of her stomach pangs. Without a word, Jacinda had reached into her knapsack to retrieve a napkin-wrapped sandwich. She handed it to Glory, explaining that the use of magic depleted a magician's physical reserves. Glory would have to rest and feed herself often to maintain her abilities, or face severe limitations in using her magic. Glory had nodded, a little embarrassed by how quickly she had inhaled the sandwich. After that episode, Glory always brought a snack to the Applied Magic lessons.

Because Glory often returned to her room sweaty and dirty — metal was never clean — her roommate took exception to the mess and the smell. Glory bathed often, but a metalsmith simply couldn't stay perfectly clean. Glory had learned to ignore Franny's disdainful sniffs and pointed stares. Franny was very ladylike, with an already established group of friends, and thus their entire relationship consisted of a series of short greetings or requests:

"May I open the window?"

"Yes."

"Thank you."

So when Eden asked Glory if she wanted to be roommates at the start of the next semester, Glory replied an affirmative so quickly that she had almost bit her tongue. Within a week, Glory moved into Eden's room, a bigger space with a sitting room as a bonus.

For the first time since she had arrived at Thornhedge, Glory felt like she had come home.

Glory had reshaped the iron nails into an ornament of sorts by the time Jacinda had arrived that morning.

"You've been busy, I see." Jacinda smiled.

Glory gestured with the object. "Yes. But I'm not quite sure what this is supposed to be."

Jacinda hefted the book she carried, capturing Glory's attention. "I brought this to supplement your knowledge on the origin of magics."

Glory read the title and stilled. *An Inventory of Magics* by Juliet I. Rue.

Jacinda cleared her throat in the sudden silence. "Simmons tells me that you don't know much about Jules' background? Her past at Thornhedge, or even her Affinity?"

"No." She stared at the cover of the book without seeing it, and avoided the older woman's gaze. She didn't want the instructor's pity.

"Ah." Jacinda's voice was thoughtful when she spoke again. "Did I tell you that I knew your parents?"

Surprised, Glory gave her a sharp look. "No."

"I'll explain that in a moment," Jacinda continued. "But first: Juliet was a decent magician but not a spectacular one. No, magic was simply a bonus to her. Where Jules truly shone was as a scholar. Her ability to conduct fieldwork and use of that data to transform our community's understanding of how magic is inherited is a gift of a different kind of magic."

Glory said nothing but remembered that Simmons had said something similar during a lecture.

"Jules loved her fieldwork." Jacinda chuckled. "You have to understand that your mother conducted her work even before the Falstead Act was enacted. People — magicians, and many of them — didn't trust the federal government's promise to legalize the citizenship of magicians and the open practice of Affinities. Add that distrust to centuries of hiding magic from others, of surviving witch hunts, and Jules often had her work cut out for her, trying to convince other magicians to participate in her survey for the sake of knowledge."

Jacinda shook her head, a fond smile on her face. "Magicians were right to distrust strangers who pried into their business. It had never ended well for any of us when that had happened in the past. But Jules had persisted with charm, placation, and even bribes in some instances. She was shot at, attacked through magical means, and spit on. But she carried on — and eventually had a large enough sample size to publish this volume. Your father stayed at home with you and Lily." Jacinda waved the text she held. "That's how she met Abraham, you know. He was the son of a magician Jules had interviewed, and then an eventual subject of the survey. Jules swore she knew when she first met Abraham: He was the love of her life. She first proposed to Abraham after he had informed her that a question in the survey needed to be rewritten to gather more objective data."

Jacinda gave Glory a sad smile. "After they married in Agate Creek, they came to Thornhedge — which is how I met them. Abraham taught History of Magic while Jules conducted her research. They were so very happy."

Tears slid down Glory's face. She hadn't known any of this. Glory wiped at the tears away with an impatient hand.

"I don't tell you this to make you sad," Jacinda said. "Rather, I hope you'll better understand Abraham's decisions, and perhaps even forgive him for withholding so much about your mother. Jules was so very special."

Glory let out a wet, skeptical snort.

Jacinda smiled again. "You look so much like Jules. And you have her impatience, too." She paused. "Your parents were very happy, and in short order, you, then Lily, arrived. Jules had published the monograph to great acclaim, here in the States and in Europe, too. She was feted by scholars and went on a speaking tour shortly after Lily's birth. Jules was reluctant to go at first, but Abraham urged her on," Jacinda explained. "But he wanted Jules to enjoy her success."

"Then Jules died."

Though Glory had been expecting them, the words felt like a punch to the chest. More tears slipped down her cheeks. "H-how?"

Jacinda reach out and took hold of Glory's hand. "An aneurysm. In the gardens of the Avamere Academy in Chicago. A student found her, and a healer confirmed her cause of death."

Jacinda paused, as if to gather her thoughts. "Abraham was devastated. When they told him, I'd never heard a man make a noise like that. I hope I never hear it again." Her voice broke, and Glory squeezed the dry and rough hand she still held. Jacinda squeezed back, then cleared her throat.

"He gathered you and Lily, and moved to Agate Creek. But he didn't just leave Thornhedge behind — he also gave up magic. He never told me why, but I suspect he blamed himself for Jules' death. Had he been here, I think he felt that he could have prevented her death." Jacinda cleared her throat. "So my challenge to you, though not to be completed today or any time soon, really, is to understand your father's decisions. You don't have to forgive him, now or ever. But to understand that his choices stemmed from love and were shaped by grief."

Jacinda stepped forward and offered Glory a handkerchief. "I'm so sorry that I made you cry." She shook her head, brow knitted. "I got caught up in my own memories."

Glory wiped her tears and crumbled the cloth between her hands. Emotions assailed her. Grief for her losses. Anger at never really knowing either of her parents. Resentment at Jacinda for having seen her vulnerable. But excitement, too: Here is someone who knew, or had known, her parents. She could know more about them. Her parents and her sister may be gone but here stood someone who knew them — not only as the scholar of magics and her magician husband but as humans, too.

Glory cleared her throat. "I'll be alright." A pause. "I miss them. Every day."

Sadness deepened the wrinkles on Jacinda's face. "I understand that both Abraham and Lily passed within the last two years?"

Glory nodded.

"If I had to speculate, that's possibly why your gift manifested so late into your life," Jacinda said with a sad smile. "Grief is hard on a person. Please, let us sit while I call for some tea."

Glory sat on a stool to the side of the work desk and took deep breaths to calm herself. Jacinda busied herself with arrangements and returned to sit on the stool opposite of Glory. Jacinda gave a cough. The older woman the placed several books into a neat stack before sorting the papers into a tidy pile. All the while avoiding Glory's gaze and giving her time to regain her composure.

Glory watched her sort the papers, then spoke. "You know a great deal about my family, but I know so little about you."

Jacinda smiled. "That is an easily solved. Ask me your questions."

Glory smiled in return, relieved to change the focus from her. "Do you have family? Here, at Thornhedge, or otherwise?"

Jacinda gave a rueful chuckle. "The hardest one, right out of the gate." Glory started to stammer an apology, but she held up a hand. "No, no. Fair is fair." She sighed. "I have a nephew, Jason. You met him during your first lesson, remember? He grew up in the San Francisco community, where I taught before I transferred here. He..." Jacinda paused. The corners of her mouth turned down, and the woman turned to stare out of the nearest window. "He doesn't have an Affinity."

"Is that... unusual?" Glory asked in careful tones. She twisted her hands in her lap, nervous. This was clearly a sensitive topic for Jacinda.

"In the Eldredge family? Very." Jacinda shook her head. "We haven't had a mundane child in generations. We watched him grow older and older, waiting for a sign — and nothing." Jacinda met Glory's gaze with a pained grimace. "I thought my sister would disown him. She practically has."

Glory berated herself in silence. What should she say? "I'm sorry."

"I'm sorry, too. I feel for the lad. He never had a fair shake, having been born a mundane in our family. He's struggled to find employment, so I took him on as my secretary." Jacinda sighed. "I worry about him. I want him to be happy but..." Jacinda gestured at the surrounding studio. "Could you be happy, working in an environment that reminds you daily of what you are not?"

Glory regretted asking the question now. Jacinda seemed so unhappy.

A knock echoed at the door. Glory jumped at the noise.

The tea had arrived, offering a welcome interruption. Glory nibbled on a teacake and listened to Jacinda describe the various locales in which she lived and taught: Chicago, San Francisco, Montana Territory, and then Denver. Glory listened and smiled and nodded at the appropriate times, even asked a few questions. But her mind revolved around the newfound and precious knowledge of her own family. Glory hadn't realized until that day how few pieces of her past she had possessed. Jacinda's words lit a fire in her: Glory wanted to know more. But how?

Chapter Fifteen

"I need to go into Denver this afternoon." Eden had already gotten out of bed, and into her usual cotton blouse and skirt ensemble. "Did you want to go with me?"

Glory groaned. She wasn't *not* a morning person but between the general curriculum and her magic lessons with Jacinda, she was exhausted. "Yes?" She closed her eyes again and buried her head beneath the quilt.

Glory heard the amusement in the other young woman's voice. "Then I'll meet you at the taxi stand after the last lecture?" Glory groaned another affirmative and heard Eden chuckle as the girl left the room. Eden had accepted another ambassadorship for a new student, a young man with an Affinity for insects and was on her way to greet him on his first day during classes. Glory had wondered why Eden volunteered so much but hesitated to ask. She took on ambassadorships for newly arrived students, and even set up exam halls. The other young woman was determined to be involved, to give her time and energy to Thornhedge.

Glory wrestled herself out of bed and stumbled through breakfast and into her first lesson. The rest of the day was uneventful save for a young woman setting fire to the studio adjacent to Glory's. Glory and Jacinda had rushed to put out the flames. The young woman didn't even have an Affinity for fire — she had simply added too much fuel to her little stove, due to a severe cold snap that had struck Denver the night before. Jacinda had alternated between being disgruntled and amused, muttering under her breath.

At the day's end, Glory greeted Eden at the taxi stand with a quick hug. The weather had shifted throughout the morning and early afternoon. Sunlight warmed their faces as they pinned their traveling bonnets on. Yesterday's cold snap was a distant memory.

"Why do you need to go into Denver?" Glory asked, as she settled herself on the taxi seat. The driver snapped the reins and whistled, and a pair of bay horses moved forward at an easy amble.

"Mostly errands." A shadow crossed over Eden's face. "I also need to send a reply telegram."

"Oh?" Glory was surprised. She hadn't realized that Eden had received a message from out of town.

"Family matters." Eden's reply was short and pained.

"Oh." Glory didn't pry further but her heart hurt for Eden. Glory suspected that Eden's family history was not a happy one. The other girl had rarely mentioned anyone over the last few months. Glory turned to look out to the buggy window. *At least my family had loved each other.*

The rest of the trip into town was smooth. Glory begged for a quick stop at a specialty smith's supply shop to purchase a set of small jeweler's tools. Though she could manipulate metal with her bare hands now, and even multiple types of metal all at once, Glory couldn't stop the habit of working with tools in her magic craft. The tools afforded her a sense of control and focus.

Glory and Eden left the smith's shop and walked down the worn wooden boardwalk. Cowboys, travelers, miners, and businessmen lined the streets. Bright daylight and clear skies were laden with the scents of animals, oil, and food.

Eden gasped, then stopped.

Glory grasped Eden's arm. "What is it?" She followed the other woman's gaze to a shopfront. It seemed normal enough: Advertising linens, sheets, and other clothing goods through the window. However, ugly gouges littered the wooden door front. The symbol of a Christian cross was slashed into the wood in deep strokes. Red paint splattered across the doors, and the lintel of the doors were plastered with pamphlets.

"Magicians are sinners," read one.

"Are you ascending to the Promised Land?"

"Witchcraft is consorting with the devil."

Someone jostled Glory from behind. She realized that a small crowd had gathered a small shop front. Murmurs rustled through the crowd like wind through wheat stalks.

"This is the third incident..."

"...goddamn Reverend and his cronies..."

"...intimidating and harassing the magicians all over the city. They burned down Foster's farm..."

Eden grasped Glory's hand. "Let's go."

Together, they pushed past the crowd. As they stepped away, Glory saw the Sheriff ride up, a grim countenance upon his face as he looked over the scene.

"I hadn't realized this was still happening," Eden murmured.

"Still?" Glory echoed.

Eden's brow furrowed. "Haven't you heard? Well, I guess you're still new to Denver," she muttered to herself. Eden leaned closer. "Over the past six or seven months, many of the magicians' shops and studios have been vandalized. Broken windows, pamphlets, graffiti — and it's occurred often. At least once per month."

"Is it the God's Word movement?" Glory asked. "Or someone else?"

Anger darkened Eden's face. "It's very likely the Reverend and his devout flock." Disdain coated her words. "Who else would it be? He has the most radical church in town."

Glory thought for a moment. "Surely something can be done. These aren't merely scare tactics. Damage has been done to these businesses."

Eden looked dubious. "I'm not sure." She sighed. "Though it's much better than the small, rural towns, prejudice against magic is still strong in the cities. Let's visit Ms. Carville. Maybe she will know something."

The telegram cost Eden more than she had expected. Glory paid the remainder and ignored Eden's embarrassed gratitude. As Eden handed over the slip that bore her message to its recipient, Glory read the words in a flash:

CANNOT COME. STOP. APOLOGIES. STOP.

Glory averted her gaze, and a guilt skittered through her. While Glory didn't want to intrude, she wished she could something for Eden.

"That's done." Eden forced a smile. "Let's go to Ms. Carville's."

Ms. Carville's shop was busy when they arrived. Glory had to dodge two children who streamed out the front door, followed by stern nanny who spoke loud German at their retreating backs with little effect. Inside, the din subsided into quiet murmurs. Still, a line at the register told Glory that it would be some time before they would be able to speak to the owner.

"I'll let her know we're here," Eden said. A bright smile lit her up from within as she made her way to the bookseller. When Ms. Carville looked up to see Eden, an answering smile unfolded across her face and her expression turned... tender? Affectionate? Ms. Carville then shuttered the emotion with a neutral smile of welcome. She nodded to Eden and Glory before turning back to the customer in front of her. Glory hid her own gleeful smile. *There is definitely something between those two.*

Finally the shop cleared, and Ms. Carville came over to Eden and Glory. "Good afternoon."

"Hello." Eden smiled.

"What brings you two into town?"

"A telegram," Eden replied. "Family matters."

"Oh." Understanding crossed Ms. Carville's face. "It will be fine, I promise."

Eden smiled again but didn't nod. Her eyes looked bleak.

Glory watched the exchange and felt a twinge of loneliness. Ms. Carville clearly knew of Eden's family issues. She wondered when, or if, Eden would trust her enough to share.

Eden frowned. "We saw more vandalism on one of the shops this afternoon," she said. "Is it increasing? Has it gone beyond vandalism?"

"It's a bit worse than that." Ms. Carville sighed. "The vandalism is merely petty. Costly nonsense but still petty. It's the work of small-minded people with little else to occupy their time. No, the real problem is the spike of suspicious deaths."

Ms. Carville's matter of fact tone threw Glory. It took her a moment to comprehend what she had heard. "What?"

"Hush." Ms. Carville reached beneath the counter to pull out a stack of worn newspapers. "San Francisco, Portland, and Seattle have all had a string of murders in the last year. The police have done a cursory investigation and offered a reward for information but..." The woman shook her head, her spectacles flashing reflected daylight. "No one wants to get involved with magicians."

"So what does that have to do with the vandalism in Denver?" Glory asked.

"These murders —" Ms. Carville paused, as if seeking the right words "— they seem magically motivated. The killer is hunting magicians, hurting them in terrible ways. We think the God's Word movement is behind these deaths." A grim look marred her face.

"We?" Glory echoed.

Ms. Carville looked irritated at her own slip. "Never mind that. Merely a group of concerned magicians."

Glory looked from Ms. Carville to Eden and back. *Horseshit.* She remembered how Eden had talked of a whisper network that had assisted her to Thornhedge. "Right," she drawled.

Ms. Carville shook her head. "Regardless, magicians are being singled out, killed."

Glory frowned. "But... wouldn't magicians defend themselves? That's an entire course at Thornhedge — defensive magic." The course was a discreet remnant of the recent years when magic was still illegal, and magicians needed to protect themselves. She was scheduled to take the course next fall. She now wished she were enrolled in the class this semester.

"A magician can be overwhelmed." Ms. Carville's voice grew quiet. "Especially if there were several attackers. But there's no denying a pattern. It gets worse: Some sort of dissection was performed on them—"

"What?" Eden looked ill. Glory swallowed back her own nausea and shivered.

"Yes." Ms. Carville winced. "The descriptions are awful. The murders are bad enough but the desecration of the bodies? It's sick. An abomination." She gave a slight shudder. Eden reached out to grasp the older woman's hand, offering comfort.

Ms. Carville kept hold of Eden's hand as she continued. "The murders are occurring up and down the Coast. Most of the papers are fixated on the butchered remains of these poor people rather than the fact that they were murdered for being magicians." Ms. Carville shook her head. "They go after the most sensational angle, of course. Anything for headlines."

Glory thought for a moment. "Seattle, Portland, San Francisco. So the killer is traveling from city to city? To kill magicians?"

Ms. Carville nodded. "We — I think so."

A theatrical throat clearing occurred behind them, and Glory turned to see an older man with a stack of books in his arms and a glare. "Hmph." The man was not appeased.

Ms. Carville turned back to Eden and Glory. "Duty calls." She released Eden's hand to gather up the newspapers on the counter.

"May I borrow these?" Glory asked. She felt Eden's jolt of surprise next to her.

Ms. Carville's eyebrows flew up. "A little light reading?" Despite the lighthearted query, Glory could hear her puzzlement.

"I'm..." Glory didn't know how to explain herself. "I'm worried," Glory said at last.

Ms. Carville wrapped the papers into a neat roll with swift motions before handing them to Glory. "Stay safe. Head back to the Academy before it gets dark." With a final smile for Eden, she stepped away to deal with the irritated man next in line.

Glory clutched the roll of papers under her arm as they exited the bookshop and made their way to the taxi stand. Then Eden spoke.

"We'll be safe, you know." At Glory's questioning glance, Eden clarified. "At the Academy. Thornhedge has never been attacked."

"Oh." Glory felt a stab of guilt for not sharing what she knew with Eden. "I understand. I'm not worried about my safety. I just... want to know more."

"Right."

The ride back to Thornhedge was quiet.

Chapter Sixteen

Back at their room, Glory unpinned her hat and set it on her desk, where it brushed against an envelope of good quality paper, addressed to her, resting upon her desk. Puzzled, Glory picked it up. *Who could it be from?* She opened the envelope and pulled out a single piece of paper. The scent of sandalwood rose from the sheet. She scanned the signature and froze.

It was from Seth Hill.

Dear Miss Rue,

May I meet with you at your earliest convenience?

Very sincerely,

Seth Hill

Glory stared at the paper, unseeing.

The Brothers were back at the Academy. She would like to see them, Glory decided with a smile. She had felt some residual hurt from their precipitous departure but had decided to set it aside. The Brothers had lives and commitments beyond her.

"Glory?" Eden's voice drew her out of her reverie. "Who is it?"

Glory smiled. "A friend."

Glory arranged to meet the Brothers later that afternoon. At the appointed hour, she arrived at one of the many faculty studios at the main library. With a sudden hesitance that she couldn't explain to herself, Glory paused to smooth her skirts and pat away errant wisps of hair into place. Nerves ate away at her insides and a flush warmed her face.

Silly, she scolded herself. *It's just the Brothers.*

Glory knocked on the door — and it flew open almost before she had finished knocking.

Seth stood at the threshold, a welcoming grin frozen on his face. As she watched, the smile froze then began to fade. His eyes darted across her face and he seemed stunned at her appearance. Glory wondered if she had missed a spot of soot from her work in her smith's studio.

"Hello," Glory said.

"Miss Rue! What a delight to see you again." Glory heard his voice before she watched Gareth shoulder Seth aside. He reached out to draw Glory into the small studio. "You look marvelous. Thornhedge truly agrees with you."

Glory smiled and relaxed as Gareth drew her into the study. A quick glance around the room told her that someone with wealth enjoyed this room: Rich, polished wooden shelves shone with wax above tiled floors. Housed in glass domes, several entomological and botanical specimens were dust-free and resplendent. The furnishings were comfortable with pillows and thick cushions, and she could smell lamp oil and tea. Glory took a seat by the room's only window.

Gareth sat opposite of Glory. Seth stood near the door and watched Glory with a steady gaze. His handsome face remained the same as she remembered but without its customary grin. He seemed taller, or perhaps more remote. His mouth turned down at the corners, giving his countenance a grim cast. *What is wrong with him?* Glory wondered.

"It bears repeating, Miss Rue." Gareth beamed at her. "You look wonderful — hale and hearty. And you have an Affinity for metals? Well, we knew that but an official diagnosis is best."

"Call me, Glory, please. Yes, it's true." Glory smiled. She couldn't help herself. It she had ever had a brother, she would have wished for someone like Gareth. Warm, concerned, and so kind.

"With whom are you studying?" Gareth asked.

"Jacinda Eldredge."

Seth whistled. The frozen countenance from a moment ago lightened and shifted to awe. "Lucky," he murmured, impressed.

Gareth slapped his knee. "There is no better tutor. She is stern, yes, but brilliant." He grinned at Glory. "You will learn so much from her."

"I already have," Glory reassured him. "Sometimes she lets me learn the hard way," she admitted with a rueful grin.

Gareth snorted. "Yes, that sounds very like her. And have you made friends? Have you been happy?"

Glory chuckled. "Yes, Uncle Gareth," she teased.

He laughed outright. "We hated to leave you so soon after your arrival but, well, we were called away." Gareth cleared his throat, then looked at Seth. "We're still working on the same... inquiry, I'm afraid."

Glory raised her brows. "Inquiry?"

"Yes." Seth's voice was hard. Glory studied him for a moment. *He looks worried and upset,* she thought. *Angry even.*

"Which brings me to our purpose for visiting. I'm afraid today's visit isn't a pleasure call." Gareth's tone was apologetic and gentle. His brows knitted together as regret flitted across his features.

Glory drew back as disappointment filtered through her. *There not here for me?* "I don't understand."

The Brothers exchanged a grim look. "What we're about to share is strictly confidential and we ask that you keep this to yourself," Seth said, his voice and mien grave and somber.

A chill chased down Glory's spine. She studied Seth, then Gareth, before looking back to Seth. "All right." She gave a nod.

"We have been asked by a group of Academy authorities to look into a matter of grave importance to the magic community," Gareth began. Seth began to pace along the confines of the study. "Discretion is important for many reasons: We don't wish to alarm the magical or the mundane folk until necessary." He exchanged a quick look with Seth before forging on. "We have reached a dead end —" Gareth winced at his words "—and are seeking new leads for our inquiry. We had hoped to ask your permission to look at your mother's journals."

Glory frowned. "My mother's journals?"

Gareth nodded. "Yes."

Seth came to a standstill and watched Glory.

Glory shook her head. "Why would her old journals be useful to you?" She looked from Seth to Gareth. "Some of them are decades old."

Gareth leaned forward. "We — well, Seth — believes that there may be some clue within her journals and notes that's relevant to our inquiry. Unfortunately, those notes may be our best lead. We have no others. We're grasping at straws right now."

Glory thought for a moment. She spoke slowly, to tease out her thoughts in a coherent manner. "She was a social scientist who interviewed hundreds of magicians in order to catalog their abilities." Glory looked up. "You're searching for the subjects? That's it, isn't it? You need to find someone, or several people, and you think you will find them in my mother's journals?"

Seth gave a humorless laugh. "Told you she'd figure it out." He began to pace.

Gareth shook his head, chagrin on his face. He sighed. "We're looking for several people of mutual... interests."

Glory frowned at Gareth. "That's... not clear at all."

Seth paused. "We're under an obligation to keep this inquiry private."

"I see." Glory thought fast. She didn't know what exactly the Brothers sought. But she knew that she had her own mystery to solve: Why had her father abandoned the magical community so thoroughly after her mother's passing? Had it been grief? Or something more? How had her mother died? If she spent time reading her father's journals with Gareth and Seth, would she get to know more of his secret life? Would she be able to make sense of the magical community? Perhaps find a role in this still-foreign world?

Glory made her decision.

"Yes, you may use my mother's journals — but only if I can help. I have my own reasons for going through her journals."

"What?" Seth's voice had almost emerged as a shout. Glory winced as he strode forward. "No. Absolutely not."

"Seth —" Gareth started but Seth interrupted him.

"No. You've *seen* the bodies. How could you even countenance this?" Seth shook his head. "No. It's too dangerous."

"Bodies?" Glory echoed. Her heart skipped a beat, and she wrapped her arms around herself. "Did you say bodies?"

Gareth groaned, and sank his head into his hands.

Seth stopped his pacing and turned to her. His eyes roved over Glory's face. "Discretion be damned," he muttered before raising his voice. "We are chasing murderers. Twisted bastards who will kill again and again unless they are stopped." Seth shook his head. "It's too dangerous."

Glory remembered her conversation with Ms. Carville at the bookstore. "Wait, are you investigating the murders of the magicians in San Francisco? In Seattle?" She looked from Gareth to Seth and hid her trembling hands in her skirts. "Someone mentioned those to me only a day ago." She paused. "You think my mother's journals will help you find this killer?" Her doubt was clear in her voice.

"Not the killers," Seth corrected, "but perhaps his potential victims. We believe the God's Word movement is responsible. We want to identify the subjects, warn them to stay safe. We need more information, though."

"We want to warn those individuals that they could be targets," Gareth added. "If they're still alive," he muttered to himself.

Glory sat back in her seat, eyes wide. Her heartbeat echoed in her ears. Of all the outcomes she had anticipated in seeing the Brothers again, searching for a killer was not on the list.

Seth continued to pace in the narrow room. His rapid movement nettled Glory, and she clenched her hands together to contain her anxiety. "We should not involve her," Seth gritted out to Gareth.

Glory thought she understood his objections at last. "I'm not proposing that I chase after murderers. I'm not crazy." She glanced between the Brothers. "Nor am I interested in being injured or killed. But I have my own answers to find, and I think they might reside in my mother's journals. With my approach, we can conduct parallel investigations — but with very different quarry."

Gareth nodded. "That is very reasonable, Glory." Glory smiled at him for the use of her given name. Gareth looked at Seth, then back to Glory. "It will be good to have fresh eyes on this investigation." His face turned serious. "We must impress upon you the need for confidentiality. It's a matter of life and death that the information we uncover doesn't leave this study."

Glory nodded.

"And you will have to excuse Seth. We've been under a great deal of recent stress."

Glory saw Seth grimace, then glance out the window. He was frustrated and seemed worried to boot. Was he upset because he was forced to work with her? Or was it something else? Just what had he encountered on his travels? Glory dragged her gaze back to Gareth.

"When do we start?"

CHAPTER SEVENTEEN

G lory was distracted all afternoon.

She dribbled tea at lunch and knocked over tools during her workshop time. She thought about her mother, and her journals, and wondered what they would find. She thought about the murders, up and down the West Coast, which felt far away and somewhat abstract to her, but for Ms. Carville's newspapers and the Brothers' investigation. She knew they hoped to find clues that would identify a killer, or perhaps save a few prospective victims. But what did she want to discover? She still didn't quite believe that the murders were tied to her mother's scholarly work. Goodness, how could they be? After all, they were only anonymous profiles of magicians.

At last the appointed hour arrived, and Glory stood before the Brothers' study. She had agreed to have the journals delivered there because the Brother's studio had more space. Besides, it was cleaner than the metal smithy. Most importantly, their doors had magical locks. Magical and physical, Gareth had assured her. After she had moved into Eden's room, she hadn't bothered hiding them again, not like she had in Franny's space.

Glory had just knocked again when door flew open. Seth stood before her, hair askew and red splotches on his cheeks. The top button on his shirt was undone, and he had shed his jacket but kept the vest and rolled up his sleeves. A finger bled and trickled over his knuckles.

"You're bleeding."

He shook his head. "It's nothing." He stepped aside.

Glory moved further into the room and saw her locked trunk on a table within the room.

Seth closed the door behind her, then walked to a nearby table. He wrapped a handkerchief around his bloody finger.

"Where is Gareth?" Glory asked. The room seemed smaller somehow, with just the two of them. She felt a flush stain across her cheeks and hoped it didn't show too brightly against the lamplight.

Seth cast her a sharp glance. "He'll be here shortly."

Glory met his dark eyes, focused on her. She felt short of breath but managed a nod. *Get ahold of yourself,* she scolded herself. *It's just Seth.*

Seth looked away, then shifted from one foot to the other. "Look, I owe you an apology."

Glory blinked. "You do?"

"Earlier today. My outburst about you helping us comb through the journals." Seth rubbed his forehead with the non-bandaged hand with a rueful expression. "I shouldn't have lost my temper. I have no right to decide what was best for you."

Glory nodded. "Thank you." When was the last time someone had apologized to her? She couldn't remember. Glory felt a small smile unfurled across her face.

Seth exhaled in relief. "Thank you. I...was worried and I handled it badly."

Glory took a step closer. "Why were you worried? I have no intention of seeking out killers. Of any kind."

A bleak, shuttered look fell across Seth's features. The corners of his mouth turned down. "My cousin, Jeremy, had an Affinity for soils. Like me," Seth began. "He was a few years younger, stronger than me with his gift — and I'm not slouch. He was smarter, too, but I never let him know that. Had to tease him, keep him humble, you know?" Seth offered a tight smile. The expression jarred with the pain in his eyes.

"Was?" Glory prompted, her tone gentle. She knew how much it hurt to lose family.

"Was." Seth confirmed. "Jeremy's side of the family is based in San Francisco. He was murdered nine months ago."

Glory gasped. Seth's simple statement hit her like an avalanche, cold and overwhelming in its horror. She had lost Lily and her father, true, but she took refuge in the fact that their last moments hadn't been filled with terror. She refocused on Seth, who studied the floor with a determined gaze. Her heart turned over in her chest. *Oh, Seth.*

Glory stepped forward and offered her hand in a tentative motion. She wanted to offer some kind of comfort. "I'm so sorry."

Seth stared at her hand, then lifted his intent gaze to her face. He paused for a moment too long, and embarrassed, flushed, Glory began to drop it.

He caught her hand, a half-smile carved on his face.

He cleared his throat. "We've never caught the killer. Or killers. We do believe it's the work of the God's Word movement, but we don't have enough evidence to present to the feds." Seth gave a hard laugh. "Not that they'd do much." He shook his head, frustrated. "There have been seven more murders since Jeremy."

Glory squeezed his hand. "I'm sorry," she repeated. "I didn't know."

"How could you?" Seth replied. "You had no way of knowing what you had volunteered for earlier today. But when I thought of you, one of the most courageous and forthright people I've met, at the mercy of those vile killers...I lost my composure. I shouldn't have," Seth finished.

"Courageous?" Glory echoed.

"And scrappy," Seth teased. "Of course you're brave. You left your only home for a brand new life. Fended off bandits during a train robbery with an unknown, untested Affinity before tending to the wounded." The half-smile was back. "You're definitely brave."

Glory felt a flutter in her chest and an answering warmth in her belly. She stared up into Seth's face, uncertain what to say.

Seth's smile slid off his face, his features made more handsome by his solemnity. He held her hand tightly as he stared down at her.

"Oh, you're both here — oops."

Gareth had arrived. His words felt like a pitcher of water had been poured over Glory.

Seth dropped her hand and stepped away.

"Are we ready to start?" Gareth asked. He glanced at Seth and Glory with an expectant look, a twinkle deep in his eyes.

"Uh, yes." Glory took a deep breath.

Seth spoke without looking at either of them. "How do you want to do this?" He gestured at the trunk with his bandaged hand, his voice gruff.

"One volume at a time?" she ventured.

"Do you know which journals are in this trunk? Or what's inside any of the volumes?" Gareth asked, with a gentle tone.

Glory shook her head. "I meant to go through these earlier this year," she admitted. "But I've been so busy."

Gareth spoke. "Do you have a key? They are locked."

"Oh." Glory thought for a moment. "No. But I have something better." Glory turned to the trunk, and focused. Breathing deep, she spoke. "**Open**."

The lock mechanism tumbled just so, and the latches popped open. The padlock slid and fell to the ground, a soft thump onto the rug beneath. Glory shivered. It felt so... easy. It scared her, a bit. The sessions with Jacinda were working.

Gareth and Seth stared at her, surprised.

"What?" Glory asked, suddenly self-conscious.

Seth grinned. "That's a very handy skill for our line of work."

"Which is...?"

"Various pursuits." Seth offered a cheeky grin at his non-answer.

Glory snorted. *One day I'll get a real answer.*

They each picked a handful of volumes and began sorting through the contents. Glory quickly realized the process of sifting through the volumes would take a tremendous of time and attention. She sighed.

The journals themselves were a mess: Some were clearly dated; others were only had titles like, "Part II" and "Part III." Many of the volumes had personal notes scribed into the margins, often indecipherable through age and the well-thumbed nature of the pages. Diagrams and shopping lists interrupted scholarly field notes; Glory even found doodles drawn throughout the pages across her stack of journals. There were also bits of paper littered throughout the trunk, stacks of letters, handbills, pieces of ribbon — Glory even found a bag of rock crystal candy, dusty but still holding its familiar shape. But despite the disorder, Glory found a rough semblance of progression. She stacked the journals from oldest to newest.

"This may take a while," she muttered to herself. She glanced up. "What are you two looking for among all of this?"

Seth looked up; Gareth continued to scribble notes with a quick hand in a notebook. "We're searching for notes on individuals she interviewed for her Inventory. Notes, parts of conversation, information — anything like that."

"Do you have a date range? A specific time you're searching for?" Glory asked. She settled a journal on her lap and frowned down at the page, her finger tracing the edges.

Gareth cast a sheepish glance at Glory. "I mean this in the kindest possible way but your mother was... scattered. I'm seeing a new side of the famed scholar." He offered a gentle smile to soften his teasing words.

Glory laughed. "So, a date range?" She repeated.

"I would venture that anything written before 1876 is fair game," Gareth said. "She published the inventory in 1877."

They continued to work, stacking journals by date and by region. Glory's mother had traveled the States and the Territories in a scattered, haphazard way. It seemed that he chased rumors and stories about unusual Affinities in effort to capture the prospective new ability as soon as he had heard about them, rather than following a plan of any kind. Once Glory had a stack of Affinities found in the Colorado Territories, she had organized them by date.

Glory looked up. "Are you looking for specific abilities? Or simply anything before 1876?"

Seth and Gareth exchanged a look. "Let me tell her," Seth begged.

Gareth sighed. "Fine. Mind, it's only a hypothesis. Pure speculation."

Glory at Seth, puzzled. "What is?"

"I believe that the God's Word folks are hunting down those with rare Affinities." Seth leaned forward, his voice gravelly and agitated. "If they know anything about our community, they know that we celebrate rare abilities. I think they are targeting them to send a message, that they know us."

"That's...sick." Glory rubbed her arms, trying to chase away the chill.

"But it makes sense. High profile murders would get more attention, strike more terror into our community."

"May I remind you that we don't have evidence for this conjecture?" Gareth shook his head, his eyes sad. "They've never been choosy about their victims before this. Why start now?"

"I don't know," Seth gritted out. It was clearly an old argument between the brothers.

A tense silence encased the room like a thick smoke.

Finally, Glory spoke. "Should I start noting unusual abilities?" She hefted a journal in her hand. "Just in case?"

Gareth seemed relieved at this suggestion. "Yes. It can't hurt."

When Glory let herself look at Seth, he thanked her with his eyes, his gaze warm and appreciative. She smiled, and looked down at the volume in her hand. They worked in silence for a short time and in a distant way, like hearing water flowing through a nearby creek, Glory noticed that the daylight dimmed through the windows. At some point during their work, Seth came over and sat down next to Glory. She looked up, expectant.

"I think we have a plan." Gareth's voice interrupted her thoughts. "We'll go to Ellison Rote first."

"Ellison Rote?" Seth echoed. "Why him?"

Gareth handed a single volume over to Seth. "Rote worked with Juliet as a student and accompanied her on some of her field studies. He may have a better sense of which magicians to start with — and he's just returned from his lecture tour."

"Huh." Seth scanned a page within the journal he held, his finger tracing a line. "So when should we talk with Rote?" Seth asked.

"Tomorrow."

INTERLUDE

He dropped his head into his hands, not caring that the blood and viscera from the old man stretched out before him stained his scalp.

Another failure.

After a moment, he let loose a muffled roar into his palms. Lifting his head, he administered stinging slaps across his face with both hands, one after another. He welcomed the physical pain, as though he could beat the failure and the frustration and the anger out of himself. He kept on, and on, until his own blood ran down the gaunt planes of his face and dripped down onto his collarbones.

Finally, he ceased.

He stared down at the old man. After the failure with Wendell Barnum, he had to leave Seattle quickly: The mother had reported her son's disappearance sooner than he had expected. After the autopsy, he had reviewed his notes: The Affinity wasn't located in the heart or the circulatory system. It certainly wasn't present in any of the other organs. The skin wasn't an anchor for one's magical ability. That only left the brain. But where in the brain did the Affinity reside? If he knew, he could proceed to the next step of his plan.

Then in Tucson, within the Arizona territory, he had discovered an old man with an Affinity for horses. While he didn't especially want this gift and thought that horses were large and smelly beasts, the old man's gift had been a lucrative one: The man owned and operated the best stud farm and stable in the Four Corners territory.

Money and prestige were acceptable trade-offs for having to deal with livestock.

But this man hadn't yielded his secrets anymore than the others had. He was no closer to his goal than he was three years ago, when he had first started this journey. He looked at the body in front of him: The cap of the man's skull was gone, his brain separated into a series of apothecary jars on a nearby table.

Rage shimmered through him. He grabbed the edges of the impromptu operating table and heaved it onto the floor. He panted at the exertion, staring at the body. Drawing a foot back, he aimed a kick at the ribcage. Then he did again. And again. The crunch of bone soothed the raw anger within. He kept kicking.

Soon, too soon, he checked himself: He was making too much noise. The shack he worked in wasn't that far from town. He needed to leave. He gathered his bloody tools and dumped them into the satchel, not caring what the drying gelatinous fluid would do the paperwork and leather inside. He ripped off the apron, dropped it to the floor. He grabbed his satchel in a rough motion and strode out the door. He gave himself the satisfaction of slamming it against the rickety frame despite the noise it caused.

He mounted his horse and struck north.

Something would come his way.

He knew it.

Chapter Eighteen

Ellison Rote was an enormous man.

He stood a full head and shoulders over Glory, and his tailored suit, complete with a floral fabric vest, couldn't conceal the thick muscle that lined his frame. His size may have been intimidating had not his demeanor been so friendly: His full beard split into a welcoming smile as he greeted them. He smiled so wide that he nearly dislodged the glasses perched upon his nose.

"Welcome, welcome." Rote beamed at them and spoke in a booming voice. "Come in and make yourselves comfortable. I ordered tea and whiskey for us."

They filed into the room, which was dominated by multiple desks. Each desk had a similar pile of artifacts, journals, and notes. Wooden chairs, presumably for the desks, were scattered throughout the room.

Rote saw Glory and froze. "Are you Gloriana Rue? Jules' and Abraham's daughter?"

"Uh, y-yes." Glory was startled by his recognition. *How does he know me?*

"Oh my." Rote strode forward and swept Glory into a hug. "It is delightful to see you again. You have grown up so much."

Glory tried to speak but her voice was muffled by Rote's vest.

"Oh, apologies. I forgot that you haven't seen me since you were a child." Rote beamed at her again. That seemed to be his default expression. He looked around. "Where is Lily? Is she here at Thornhedge, as well?"

Glory shook her head. Grief tightened her throat, and she cleared it before she spoke. "No, Lily passed a little over a year ago. Back home, in Agate Creek."

Sadness filled Rote's face, and he winced, shaking his head. "I had heard that Abraham had passed during this last year but I didn't realize that Lily was also gone." Rote studied Glory for a moment. "So much loss in your life. I'm sorry to hear that."

Glory gave a quick nod, unable to speak. She studied the floor, trying to regain her composure.

Seth came to her rescue. "I take it that you knew Glory as a child?"

"Yes," Rote replied. He ushered Glory to a nearby chair. "I studied with Jules for a spell and I was close with both her and Abraham. They truly welcomed me into their home. My own family meant well but they were farmers. Though I looked the part of a farmer, I read far too much. They didn't know quite what to do with me." Rote chuckled again. "So I lived with them when Glory and then Lily were born." Rote looked at Glory and grinned. "Lily was a happy child. You were... not. Stubborn, more like."

Glory smiled, charmed by the warm memories and obvious affection. "That hasn't changed much," she replied.

The Hill Brothers chuckled at this.

"Sit, sit." As they gathered the scattered chairs and then sat down, Rote settled a tray of food onto one of the nearby desks. "What brings you to my study today?"

"Well, we understand that you've just returned from your lecture tour —" Gareth began.

"Yes, it was marvelous!" Rote beamed.

Glory grinned. She had seen the same look on Jacinda Jacinda's face whenever she discussed her own work.

"— and given Glory's recent arrival, we wanted to inquire about your work with Juliet Rue." Gareth continued.

Rote looked at Glory. "I thought Abraham had ceased his studies after she passed?"

"He did." Glory said.

Rote shifted in his chair, clear discomfort on his face. "You have to understand, see: After Jules' death Abraham was... devastated. He was determined to protect you and Lily." Rote now looked unhappy. "The doctor told us that Jules died from an aneurysm, and with his Healing Affinity, he would known if something else had been the cause." Rote sighed, and his brow cleared. "After the funeral, he gathered up you girls up and moved to Agate Creek."

Seth cleared his throat. "I think we're especially interested in your work with Jules, when she still pursued her studies."

"Er, yes." Rote looked uncomfortable and shifted from one foot to another. "Gareth tells me you're still new to our world so you might not know this yet but... well, we're snobs about magic."

Seth snorted. Gareth nodded. Neither of them looked surprised or upset.

"Meaning?" Glory didn't quite understand.

"Meaning that our community assigns value to its members based on the absolutely arbitrary inheritance of magical abilities," Rote said. "Those with rare or unique abilities are given a certain cultural cache in the magical pecking order. It's nonsense, of course. No magician has any control over which magical ability they are born with; thus, any resulting social favor or privilege is assigned in an illogical fashion."

Glory frowned and looked back at Rote. "But what does all of this have to do with my mother?"

"Juliet disliked the social fixation on rare abilities," Rote explained. "She felt that feting rare abilities only led to more social segregation within our community and felt that instead we should be studying why the anomalies occurred in the first place. The mainstream magical abilities — botanical or agricultural, husbandry, et cetera — these all made sense to Jules. To her, these abilities enhanced the survival and well-being of the human population. The rare ones, especially some of the ones that have presented themselves over the last few decades? These either weren't present at all or simply weren't recorded via oral or literate means."

Rote smiled. "She was fascinated by the seeming newness of these abilities and wondered at the causes. Were these caused by environmental or cultural changes? Or simply the result of more mutations?" Rote shook his head. "Jules hoped to find evidence for a theory that explained the manifestation of magical abilities. She wanted to use that information to combat what she saw as social evils, which were both the prioritization of rare magical abilities at the expense of others and the ostracization of non-magical people within magical families."

Glory remembered Jacinda's pained confession about Jason and felt a twinge of sympathy for Jason, the poor man. "That's awful."

Rote cleared his throat. "Your mother thought the same thing, which is one of the many reasons she was so committed to her work." A faint look of puzzlement crossed Rote's face. "Are you interested in continuing her studies? Is that why you're here today? Not that it isn't a pleasure to see you." Rote beamed at her again.

Glory paused. She knew the Brothers wanted to keep the investigation as quiet as possible so she decided to go with a partial truth. "As you know, I'm new to this community. My father didn't speak of her or her work. He didn't even speak of his time as a practicing magician. So I want to know more about her life and her work, who she last worked with and what they thought of her."

A soft smile crossed Rote's face. "I believe I understand." He paused, taking a moment to think. "I can take a look through my notes and journals from that time and see if I can put together a list of folks you can speak with."

The next week fell into a pattern: Classes in the morning, magical workshops in the afternoon, and reviewing her mother's journals in the evening with the Hill Brothers in their study. Glory enjoyed the companionship she found with the Brothers, especially the tart affection and quick repartee Gareth and Seth fired at each other with regular precision. Beneath the banter, though, Glory sensed a deep trust and loyalty between the two men. They often seemed to speak in a shorthand of sorts, with dangling sentences finished by shrugs or nods.

Glory also enjoyed reading her mother's journals. Every time she read an entry, she heard a no-nonsense voice in her head, a calm recital colored by personal observations. In the later entries, penned after she and Lily had been born, Jules often commented on her hopes for her daughters and of her own curiosity and speculation about their future gifts. She had even tucked in drawings — scribbles, really — completed by Glory and Lily as children in between the pages of the journals. Jules had clearly loved her daughters, and Abraham. She wrote often of him, and even addressed some entries to her husband, commenting on sunsets that he would have loved to have seen.

The evenings with the Brothers had one drawback: Due to the confidential nature of the investigation, Glory couldn't invite Eden to join them nor could she share the details of what she was doing to the other young woman.

"Where are you going?" Eden had asked one night as Glory gathered up a pen and a notebook.

Glory had paused. What could she say? "I'm looking over my mother's journals again."

"Oh." Eden paused. "Would you like some help?"

"Uh, no, I can do this," Glory said. "But thank you." She tacked on the courtesy a little too late.

"All right. Good evening." Eden's voice was distant and cool. She turned her attention back to her books, ignoring Glory.

Glory winced and hurried from the room to descend the stairs. Having shared confidences and chores and all manner of life activities with one another, it was clear that Eden had been puzzled and hurt by Glory's refusal of her help. But Glory couldn't share too much about the investigation without the Brothers' consent and support — and she was unlikely to obtain it, given how strongly they objected to even Glory knowing of the matter.

Glory gave a miserable sigh. She didn't want to alienate her friend, her only confidant at Thornhedge.

What could she do?

A few days later, the hurt silence and the unspoken discord between the young women came to an abrupt end.

Glory had returned to the women's residence hall from her Applied Magic workshop, during which Jacinda had had Glory juggle copper, silver, and iron with magic. Exhausting and somewhat foolish in appearance, the task was supposed to prompt control and finesse in handling different metals simultaneously. But every time Glory had dropped something, Jacinda made her start over again. And again. And again.

An anxious man had shifted from foot to foot near the door.

"I'm so sorry, Aunt Jacinda," he said.

"Nonsense." Jacinda had smiled at him. "Come in, come in. Glory, you can stop that. For now."

Glory had stopped, grateful for the interruption. Glory felt she would hate juggling for the rest of her life. She had never been so happy to see Jason and cast a beaming smile at him. He had looked startled at first, then wary. Glory chuckled at the memory.

At the top of the stairs, and down the hall from her shared room with Eden, Glory paused.

The door to their room was ajar.

Glory frowned. She knew Eden was in class at that moment. Glory quickened her pace down the hall and came to a stop outside the entrance.

Her heartbeat tripled in her chest. A gasp escaped her mouth before she could contain it.

The room had been ransacked.

The quilts were ripped from the beds and torn apart. Pillow seams were split, leaving a goose feather coating upon every surface. Books were scattered across the floor; journals and notepads were torn at the spines, with loose pages that dappled the floor. Clothing — dresses, skirts, even unmentionables — were upended from the neat dressers on either side of the room, ripped and stained with mud, as though someone had walked across them. The dressers themselves were tipped over onto the floor, each with a few broken drawers and split wood.

Shock splashed over her, and Glory stared at the mess before her, eyes unseeing. *What on earth had happened? Who would do this?*

Glory heard a gasp behind her — and whirled around.

It was Eden, just arrived from class. Glory watched Eden scan the disarray within the room, with myriad emotions crossing her face: Shock, despair, uneasiness, and anger.

Eden turned to Glory. "What happened?"

Glory shook her head. "I don't know. I arrived only a few moments before you did." She looked at the mess again. "Who would do this? Is this a prank of some sort?"

Eden stepped into the room with care, doubt on her face. "This is… thorough for a prank." She bent to pick up a torn journal. "Have you angered anyone lately?"

Glory shook her head. "Only Eliza — and she wouldn't do this."

"No." Eden agreed.

Glory wrapped her arms around herself. "What should we do? We have to tell someone, right?"

For the first time since Glory had known Eden, the other young woman seemed to be at a loss for words. "I guess."

Glory surveyed the damage again and she shook her head. Her eyes smarted with tears. This room was the first place she had felt at home while at Thornhedge — and now it had been ransacked. Destroyed. Upended. The intrusion made her uneasy, scared. Someone knew where she and Eden lived, had come to their home, and forced their way through a locked door to destroy their personal possessions. Who cared about the belongings of two young magicians with little fortune and no renown? After that thought, Glory stepped away from their room, ignoring Eden's questioning glance, and peered down the hallway at the other rooms within the dormitory. No other doors stood ajar. Glory stepped back into her room and swept the space with new eyes.

So why had they been targeted?

CHAPTER NINETEEN

They finally decided to tell the residence hall matron of the ransacking who, upon seeing the room, gasped aloud before becoming quite angry. The matron had left the room in a huff and returned with reinforcements: Two maids with cleaning supplies and spare handkerchiefs. Everyone rolled up their sleeves and got to work on some area of the room.

Glory had made some progress in picking up the torn books and journals when a motion at the doorway caught her eye. Turning to look, she paused when she saw the Hill Brothers standing at the doorway. Gareth and Seth had leaned in to scan the room, their faces grim. Seth looked furious.

Glory was comforted by their presence but surprised. "What are you doing here?" She saw Eden look up at her query, then glance at the Brothers. Glory took a step forward. "This is a women's residence hall," she said in a quiet voice.

Gareth and Seth exchanged a glance, then looked at Glory. "We should talk."

Irritation, chased by fatigue, rippled through Glory. "Can it wait? We have a great deal to do here." She gestured between Eden and herself.

Gareth shook his head. "Unfortunately, no." He paused. "We believe this –" he swept a hand across the room "– is related to our *shared* inquiry. I believe there is a drawing room on the first floor of this building. Will you meet with us there?"

Glory shook her head in frustration. "Very well — but only if Eden comes."

Seth stiffened. Gareth opened his mouth to speak.

A guarded glance came over Eden's face. "Do you wish me to join you?"

Glory felt a pang of sadness. She was tired of the secret and the burden it had imposed upon Eden. She wasn't keeping anything from Eden again.

Glory gestured around the room. "This affects both of us. I do wish you would join us."

Eden offered a small smile. "Then I will."

A weight lifted from her shoulders. Glory took a deep breath. Finally, they could get back to normal. She turned to face the Brothers.

They were not pleased.

Seth strode down the stairs ahead of Gareth, who looked disappointed and miffed at the same time. Glory followed at a distance, having linked elbows with Eden.

"Why are they angry?" Eden asked in a quiet murmur.

"I'm not supposed to discuss our... project," Glory responded. "But I'm tired of hiding it from you."

The large drawing room on the first floor of the residence hall was empty, not unusual in the mid-afternoon of the middle of the week. Intended for socializing rather than studying, the room was often packed with young women in the evenings and weekends. Built in bookcases lined the two of the walls. Paintings and windows graced the remaining walls. Gareth and Seth stood near the windows while Eden settled herself into an upholstered chair with delicate legs decorated in ornate gold filigree. Glory remained standing. She felt too restless to sit.

Seth pointed at Eden. "You know we need to keep our investigation quiet," he said to Glory.

"She is my closest friend at Thornhedge and she was affected by the break-in. Whatever you have to share, you should share with her, too," Glory argued.

Seth gave an irritable sigh, then sat on a matching chair. He started without ceremony, looking at Glory. "We believe the vandalism in your room is associated with the investigation. We think that someone is looking for your mother's journals. Again."

Glory stilled. "What?"

Seth gentled his tone. "Where better to search for magicians than through Juliet Rue's journals? The very woman who had created the Inventory? He had the same idea Gareth and I had, honestly. We simply got to you first," Seth added in an undertone.

Glory felt a swell of nausea creep up her chest. She took a deep breath, then another. Her heartbeat throbbed against her ears and she tasted something metallic in her mouth. She looked at Eden, who returned her glance with worry and concern. The killer, the murderer sought by the Brothers, had been at Thornhedge — had been in her *room*. Had been near Eden, a woman who had become a sort of family in the intervening months at the Academy.

He had been here. In her *home*.

She couldn't lose her family. Not again.

"Glory!"

Seth's frantic command snapped her eyes to his face. He stood close to her, too close, his hands raised above either of her shoulders, hovering. Seth peered into her face. "Are you alright?"

Glory focused on his face, drawn and pale under his tan with concern and worry. "No. I am not alright."

Seth gave a slow nod. He waited for Glory to continue.

"He was *here*? Or they?" Glory whispered. She glanced at Eden, who looked upset and puzzled. Worried, too. *Everyone looks worried*, Glory thought.

Seth sighed. "Yes. We believe so." A pause. "I'm sorry."

Cold seeped across Glory's shoulders and she gave a quick shudder. "What are we going to do? He knows where we live." Another thought occurred to her. "Wait. The journals in the study — have they been stolen?"

Gareth stepped forward. "The journals are still there, I promise you. As for you and Eden, we can move you to another room in a different hall. Furthermore, we will bespell your room for protection, to hide the location from scrying and to lock the room by magical means. It would only be accessible by you and Miss Eden." He seemed relieved to offer a solution of some sort.

Glory looked Eden. "Do you still want to room with me?" she asked, her tone dull. "After this? I understand if you don't." *Please say yes*, Glory begged inside.

Eden frowned. "Don't be silly. Of course I do." She looked at Gareth. "I assume the vandalism has something to do with the project Glory has worked on with you and the other Mr. Hill?"

Gareth nodded. "Since you are affected by this, as Glory rightly pointed out, I will give you some of the details. Please know that what I'm about to share is strictly confidential and should be kept to yourself and to us." Gareth quickly sketched out the investigation for Eden, though Glory noticed that he abstained from the more macabre details, while Seth guided Glory to a nearby couch.

Glory watched Eden's face during the recital, looking for signs of fear or upset. She waited to Eden to interrupt, to exclaim in fear or dismay. To ask for a separate room after all. Eden did no such thing, to Glory's relief. At the end of Gareth's quick overview, she had only asked one question.

"Would you like some additional assistance with your investigation?"

Glory smiled. The perennial volunteer was back.

Glory and Eden spent the remainder of their day boxing up their belongings in preparation for the move to a new room. As they worked through the debris left behind by the intruder, Glory felt her friend-ship with Eden settle back into its usual patterns of gentle teasing and openness. Despite the mess of the break-in, and the fear she still felt when she thought of the killer in her home, Glory was grateful that at least she had Eden again.

The Hill Brothers came for them later that evening, to escort the young women to their new room. They were accompanied by two additional young men, dressed in patched clothing and with thick boots. The looked like laborers rather than students.

Seth knocked, then stepped through open doorway. "Ready?"

Glory and Eden exchanged a glance. "Yes."

"Then let's go."

The Hill Brothers led Glory and Eden across the twilit campus to another building which stood near the faculty residences. The red brick building stood three stories high, with flower boxes on the first-floor windows and entrances. With quick motions, Gareth and Seth ushered the women inside and up to the second floor. Pulling a key from inside his vest, Seth unlocked a room at the end of a hallway.

Glory and Eden stepped inside. And stopped.

The room was spacious and large, with big windows and a small sit-ting area near the entrance. The furniture consisted of gorgeous woods that shone with recent polish, and the bedding and curtains were done in lush linens. A plush rug covered the wooden floor, muffling the noise of their entrance. Matching beds, dressers, and desks lined either side of the room.

Glory and Eden exchanged an uncertain glance. This was nice. *Too* nice.

Glory turned to Seth. "Are you sure this is the right room?"

Seth met her gaze with his own steady one. "Yes." His voice left no room for argument.

Glory persisted. "This is far too grand for two students."

Seth shrugged. "Then don't tell anyone," he replied. When Glory opened her mouth, he cut in. "Your safety and Miss Eden's is the most important consideration here. We can secure this location. We want you here." A pause. "Please."

She looked at Eden. "Are you comfortable with this?"

Eden had already sat down at her new desk. She looked up at Glory's question. "Oh, yes." She caressed the polished, smooth wood of her study carrel. "I will be quite happy here." She gave an impish grin.

Gareth chuckled. "We'll let you get settled in. With your permission, we'll bespell the room for security and privacy tonight."

Glory nodded, then paused as a thought occurred to her. "When will we return to the investigation?"

The Hill Brothers exchanged a glance. "We thought we'd let you get settled in first."

Glory worried that they were trying to shelter her from the investigation, distance her from the activity in hopes of protecting her. "We will settle in perfectly well," Glory replied. "We should instead focus on finding the others with unique Affinities to warn them. If he can find me, he can find them." A shudder rippled through Glory.

He had been inside her *room*.

Seth stepped forward, concern pleating his brow. "It's possible that he doesn't know about your ability — only your relationship to Juliet." His voice held an edge of doubt, though. Glory understood. The Academy was a sieve: Information and gossip passed through school like a river into a lake. If the killer hadn't known of Glory's ability during the burglary of her room, he would know soon enough.

Gareth spoke from his position near the doorway. "If you're determined to continue alongside us —" he began.

"I am." Glory interrupted, her tone firm.

Gareth smiled. "I didn't expect any other answer, honestly," he admitted. "We have a few leads to pursue, courtesy of Ellison Rote. We had planned to start with Miles Gray, a miner with an Affinity for gemstones who works off a claim about two hours south of Denver." Gareth paused. "Would you like to accompany us?"

Glory nodded. "Just tell us when." She cast a belated glance at Eden. "Are you certain you wish to join us?"

Eden nodded, her face grim. "Yes."

CHAPTER TWENTY

The day dawned with overcast skies that threatened to rain. It reflected her mood: Glory had poorly slept the night prior and awoke with a worse frame of mind.

She and Eden met the Brothers at the Academy stables, as requested by a hasty note last night. It seemed that Rote had finally drafted his list — only to share it with the Brothers, not Glory. That rankled at Glory for some reason but at least the Brothers had informed her. Glory shook her head as they descended the steps of the dormitory. She hoped her sour mood would improve.

When they arrived at the stables, Seth led a mare out to greet them. Glory was startled at his attire: Brown, worn buckskin pants paired with well-worn boots. A cotton shirt and vest, clean but aged by the sun and prior work, were topped by a cowboy hat. A large revolver was strapped to his right thigh. Glory paused. She had only ever seen him in polished, tailored suits that were intended for polite company. The cowboy gear made him look older, harsher. Like a man from back home, in Agate Creek.

"Let's get you mounted." He cast a cursory glance at the young women's outfits, then nodded. They both wore pants in lieu of riding skirts, button down flannel blouses, and wide brimmed hats. The practical clothes were less of a bother, and where they were going, no one would care.

As Eden mounted, Gareth led out a paint mare with an identical saddle. Glory waved away the mounting block, so he held the reins as she pulled herself into the saddle. The Brothers had chosen a pair of dappled greys and mounted with an obvious ease that spoke of long experience. They had already attached the saddlebags with a day's worth of provisions, and they were off. They skirted Denver rather than ride through it, and Glory found her mood improving. South of Denver, they turned slightly west from the main road.

"Where is Ellison Rote sending us?" Glory asked.

Seth nudged his gray alongside her paint mare. "He told us that Miles Black is a gemstone magician about twenty miles southwest of Denver." Seth shook his head. "Rote shared that Black keeps to himself. No one has heard from him in a while." Worry underscored his voice.

"How does his Affinity work?"

Seth squinted at something on the horizon, then turned to her. "I'm not certain but I can hazard a guess: If he has an Affinity for gemstones or minerals, he probably uses that gift to sense and locate the gems. After he finds them, he could determine which ones are of high quality, and so on. It's a good gift to have for the mining regions within the States."

Glory shifted in her saddle. "How much longer, do you think?"

Eden answered before Seth could. "Another hour."

Glory glanced at Eden in surprise, who explained. "I rode on this route when I came to Thornhedge, though I traveled by stagecoach. We might make better time on horseback."

Seth grinned. "Let's hope so. Miss Eden, from where do you hail? Glory mentioned southern Colorado but no further details."

A quick, guarded glance crossed Eden's face, and Glory wondered if Eden would answer. At last, the other woman spoke. "I grew up in a town called Broken Whistle. It's about two days south of Denver, and a bit west."

"Ah." Seth spoke in a neutral tone that matched Eden's guarded expression. "I've heard that area is still a bit... independent."

Eden gave a sudden laugh. "Yes, that's one way to put it." She gave a grim smile. "Lawless and corrupt is another."

Gareth chuckled from ahead of them and called back to Seth. "I thought that was quite tactful of you."

Seth shook his head, a slight smile on his face.

Glory hesitated, then asked in a low voice. "Is it truly terrible?"

Eden winced but nodded. "The town was originally named for the founder, Eugene Chelston. But without nearby law enforcement to serve as back-up, a bad element moved into town. The area served as a gateway of sorts for outlaws and lawless folks — gangs, horse thieves, gambling rings, everything. The turning point occurred when they murdered the sheriff, burned down the jail, and renamed the town Broken Whistle." Eden grimaced. "They wanted it to serve as a warning to outsiders."

"Oh." Glory frowned as worry tugged at her insides. *Eden grew up there?* Agate Creek may have been boring but at least it was safe.

Eden seemed to understand. "Yes, it's awful."

Glory shook her head. "Thank goodness you got out of there."

Eden didn't nod. "I'm grateful for my escape, it's true. But... I worry about my brother. I think he may have an Affinity, too."

Glory thought for a moment. "Can you write to him? Is that safe?"

Eden looked thoughtful. "That might work."

"I will help, whatever is needed," Glory said.

Eden studied Glory for a moment. "Okay," she replied in a small voice.

The sun shone down, bright and unrelenting. The dry air from the high altitude and the early summer meant that dust and wildflowers danced along the trail edges. Glory resettled her hat further on her head, grateful for the shelter of the wide brim. The further from Denver they rode, the more the land changed. Red, yellow, and brown swirled together in layers upon layers of sand, dust, and rock. Sparse bushes and wiry trees huddled together in the poor soil, and grasses sprouted wherever they could find purchase. The trail was quiet. Glory hadn't seen anyone else from their party since just outside Denver.

"Hold up."

At Gareth's call, Glory halted her horse. She saw the others do the same.

Seth consulted a map and muttered under his breath. "I think it's this way." He pointed to the west, and slightly south.

"You think?" Gareth asked, his voice testy. "Or you know?"

Seth glared back. "I think. That's all I *can* know."

"Hmph." Gareth grumbled, surprising Glory. She had never seen him... irritated. Was it nerves? Or something else?

"I know, alright?" Seth seemed to acknowledge an unspoken criticism. "We need to find it and turn back soon. I get it."

Glory cast a sideways glance at Eden, seeking answers.

"We need to hurry." Eden spoke in a low voice, leaning across her saddle. "We're far enough from Denver to attract trouble, and if we do, well, any help we seek will be delayed. Or nonexistent." Eden looked at the Brothers, then back to Glory. "I think they're worried about us. Frankly, I'm surprised they let us travel with them at all."

Fear trickled down her spine, and Glory swallowed hard. She had been so intent on learning more about her mother that she hadn't considered the potential danger to herself — or the danger her presence might bring to others. Guilt gnawed on her insides, and her shoulders hunched down a bit. She was starting to question her decision to come.

"Glory." Eden's voice drew her head up. "Forget I said anything. I'm sure we'll be fine."

Glory shook her head. "No, you spoke the truth."

"But not all of it." Eden gave a half-smile. "They —" she nodded at the Brothers "— understand why you want to know more about your mother's work. Our world is still so new to you. Of course you want to know more."

"But—"

Gareth's call interrupted Glory. "We should move on." He wheeled his horse off the trail, and onto a faint dirt rut. Glory and the others followed in a single file. The rut — for Glory hesitated to call it another trail — was a faint smudge of dirt that showed through the grass. She peered into the distance and saw that they were headed to a series of low hills with rocky bluffs to the east. At the base of the hills, Glory saw the small entrance to a canyon of sorts, which was narrow enough to require them to file into the passage one rider at a time.

Gareth paused. "It must be through here." He peered down the path, which curved out around a bend and out of sight within a few feet. He cast a glance at Seth. "How do you want to do this?"

Seth stared at the path. "One at a time?" he offered, doubt clear in his voice.

"Hmph."

"Yeah."

Glory could read between the lines. "You believe it's a trap?"

Seth and Gareth exchanged another look. "Yes and no. It may not be but if it were, it'd be the perfect place to establish one."

"We can't take the horses through that ravine, right? It's too narrow," Eden said. "Is there another way around?"

"Not without a significant amount of additional time, which we don't have." Seth dismounted. "I'll scout ahead."

"Alone?" Gareth and Glory spoke at once but in different tones. Glory's voice was filled with surprise; Gareth with the familiarity of frequent experience. Glory realized with a start that this *was* a routine activity for the Brothers. She wondered again what they truly got up to when they conducted investigations for the Academies.

"Yes." Seth gave his reins to Gareth before removing the long-barreled revolver from his thigh. He disappeared into the ravine with steps so quiet steps that he hardly disturbed the dust.

Glory and the others waited in silence.

Minutes dragged by.

The only sounds were breaths from Glory and her companions. Without the gentle breeze they felt on the trail, the sun beat down on them. Glory's face flushed from the heat and the worry, and she felt sweat trickle down her back and under her arms. A rock slithered down a canyon wall, and she jumped. She saw Gareth grab his gun, then relax.

It was only a lizard.

At last, Seth appeared at the canyon mouth.

He grinned into their worried faces.

"Clear?" Gareth asked.

Seth nodded. "There's a camp set in a clearing about two hundred feet into this canyon. The fire looks at least a day old, but there are mining tools and supplies hidden in a nearby alcove."

"Should we investigate further?"

Seth shrugged. "I'm not sure. The miner could be further down the ravine. Or in a mine. Or in town. Or —"

A gunshot rang out.

Eden's horse half-reared and lunged into Glory's mount as she came down. Glory's mount staggered sideways, and Glory felt her feet slip the stirrups. Another shot, then another — so close together, how many men were there? Her horse reared.

Glory was flung from the saddle. She slammed into the hard ground beneath her.

"Glory!"

She laid on the ground, stunned. Her breath stuttered in and out in frantic gasps.

"Are you hurt?" Seth had dismounted and now crouched over her, gun in hand. Another shot kicked up the dust five feet left of Glory. Seth returned a shot, then looked down at her.

Glory felt her body in cautious movements. She could feel pain in her elbow and tailbone but didn't seem to be injured anywhere else. "I'm fine. I think."

"Seth!" At Gareth's shout, they both glanced over. Gareth pointed a small overhang with a few trees about thirty feet away. Glory saw a glint of metal through the stone and the shrubbery. "We need to find cover," Gareth yelled.

Seth glanced around, then cursed. "The canyon. It'll have to be the canyon," he yelled.

Gareth looked doubtful.

Another shot rang out.

Gareth dismounted in a smooth, quick motion. He almost pulled Eden off her horse, then he threw the reins at her. "Hold them," he shouted. "Glory, are you hurt?"

Glory shook her head, trying to clear the shock from her system. "I'm fine," she called out. Next to her, or in front of her, Seth returned another shot.

"Get up then and get your horse. We have to move, *now*."

That seems reasonable, Glory thought. She struggled to her feet, wincing as her arm protested. The paint mare stood at the ravine entrance, with trembling legs and her head hung low. Glory crept up to her, scared of the startling the mare into flight. But the horse simply shivered, nervousness apparent in the deep tremors that skittered across her flesh. Glory grabbed the reins, which were thankfully still crossed at the saddle horn.

"Let's go."

Gareth urged Glory into the ravine first, then Eden. The ravine was so narrow that the saddles scraped along the red dust of the sandstone walls, scattering rocks everywhere. Gareth followed, leading both mounts in a single file. Seth remained, and returned fire. He paused to reload his six-gun, then continued to shoot.

Glory pushed forward. She didn't know where she was going but knew she couldn't stop, so she continued. The shooting had stopped. *Seth must be following us now.*

After a few more steps, Glory emerged into a small clearing: A banked campfire laid to Glory's left, next to a small alcove in the rock. Next to the campfire rested a tin dining set that consisted of a plate, a mug, and cutlery, and a bedroll, not rolled up but not laid out, either. Next to the bedroll rested a crate of mining tools. Glory recognized some of the brands from her work with metals. The ravine continued to curve into the rock across the clearing, the narrow tunnel obscured by the turn of the trail.

"Anyone there?" Gareth called out from behind her, worry clear in his voice.

"No." Glory moved her horse across the clearing, to make space for the others to get out of the ravine. Eden came to stand by her, and Gareth and Seth then emerged. They ran quick checks over their horses, running their hands over the hocks and legs of the trembling creatures. Dropping the reins across the saddle horns, they came over to check the other mounts.

Seth came over to Glory's mount and ran his hands over the fatigued paint. Seeing nothing, he turned to Glory — and stilled. "What happened?"

Glory was puzzled. "What do you mean?"

"You're bleeding." Seth stepped closer and examined Glory's arm. Her shirtsleeve had torn, likely when she fell off the horse. Her skin was scraped raw, and fresh blood oozed up to the surface.

"I'll be fine," Glory said. "I didn't even notice."

"We'll clean it when we get a chance." Seth looked up. "Any sign of the shooter?"

Gareth shook his head, his expression grim. "None so far. He also has the advantage. He knows what we look like and where we went but we haven't seen him."

Seth cursed. "Do you think it's the magician? Or someone else?"

Gareth shrugged. "It's hard to know. Miners often shoot on sight and ask questions later. He —"

"Yer goddamn right." A new voice spoke up, slow and deep with a hint of a gravel. "So if you knew you was gonna get shot, why'd you come here?"

Everyone froze.

Glory held her breath. Where was he?

A flicker caught the corner of her eye and she whirled around. A man crouched on a ledge that jutted out from the ravine walls, with his arm braced on his knee. Over his arm laid a long rifle, trained on Gareth. Glory studied his face: Black eyes and hair dominated the face beneath the wide brim of his hat. Red dust coated his skin and stained his mustache. Bristle had bloomed into a scraggly beard, and his clothes had a clay-like coating of the soil she saw everywhere in this region.

The gun glinted in the sunlight, clean and polished, the only thing free from the red dust.

"I'm waitin'." Impatience and anger threaded the man's voice.

Seth spoke. "We mean no harm —"

The man snorted. "I've got a gun on you. So, no, you ain't harmin' me."

Seth tried again. "We're looking for Miles Black."

"Why?"

"He's a magician. One with an Affinity for gems."

"Why are y'all looking for a magic man? 'Specially out here? Yer better off looking in Denver. That's where that magic school is, right?"

"Why would we search for a magician with an Affinity for gems in a city?" Seth shot back. "Looking for a miner in a city is a waste of time."

Glory tensed. She saw Gareth shoot Seth a discreet glare.

Eden looked ill with worry.

"Fair enough." The man shifted the gun on his knee, and turned the muzzle away from Gareth. Glory exhaled a sharp breath of relief.

The man glanced over at her. "I'm not gonna shoot you. Yet. Why are y'all looking for this Black fella?"

Gareth glared again at Seth and spoke before his brother could. "We are looking for Mr. Black because we'd like to ask him some questions about a magician he consulted with around fifteen years ago. We simply want to ask him about his experience, and if he remembers anything unusual about that time."

The crouched man thought over Gareth's words, his eyes disappearing beneath his hat brim for a moment. "Y'all must be from that magic school, yeah?"

Gareth nodded.

"And yer here for research?"

Gareth nodded again.

"You can ask yer questions, then."

Gareth paused, and shot a sideways glance at Seth. "Are you Miles Black?"

"Maybe."

Seth sighed. "Ridiculous. That is *not* helpful."

The man stood. "Don't reach for anything now," he cautioned. "No sudden movement. I don't wanna shoot, 'specially in front of women."

After some shuffling and a few more threats from Maybe Miles, they ended up circled around the banked campfire. The horses had settled from their fright and were eating the proffered hay from their unexpected host. Seth and Gareth had long since holstered their revolvers while Miles cradled his rifles in his arms.

Miles proved recalcitrant to further questions.

"Do you remember the research or any kind of interview with Rue?"

"Which part?" Miles queried.

"Any of it," Seth replied. "The interview, the specific questions — anything that surprised you."

"Hmm."

Seth restrained a sigh. Glory saw Gareth smothered a smile.

"Mind you, it was a while ago," Miles finally said. "I don't remember much. She was excitable, for a learned person. She wanted to know how the gift worked, when I knew I had it, did anyone else in the family have the gift... " Miles shook his head. "Lot of questions."

"Did you share that information with her?"

"Some," Miles admitted. "Not all."

"Why so little information?" Gareth asked.

Miles shot Gareth a scornful look. "You know what people can do to someone with a gift like mine? 'Specially as a kid?" He shook his head. "I'd heard enough tales about folks with gifts working 'gainst their will for a boss they never chose. I ain't signing up for that. So I keep quiet, and I kept my distance from others. That's served me well."

Glory thought of something. "Has anyone else come to ask questions? For research, or maybe for other reasons?"

Miles studied Glory for a moment. "Yeah."

"Recently?" Glory persisted.

"Yeah."

Glory simply waited.

"He was a tall fellow, lanky and pale. 'Cept where he was burned red by the sun." Miles snorted. "No sense at all — didn't even wear a hat. He claimed that he was 'a scholar and a magician' but asked the wrong kind of questions."

Glory frowned. "What do you mean?"

Miles hitched his shoulders up. "The Rue woman asked a lot of questions, true. But they were about the gift, not what I did with it. She took notes, and such. This new man wanted to know how I made money with the gift and what I had accomplished. And he didn't take no notes — no paper or ink in sight." Miles shook his head. "Man was a charlatan. Met him in a bar in Leadville and after the talk, made sure he didn't follow me." He shifted his gun against his arm, his meaning clear.

Glory saw the Brothers exchange a quick glance at this. Could this be a possible lead?

"Do you have any more questions?" Miles squinted up the ravine and at the narrow slice of visible sky. "You'll want to head back to Denver before too long."

Gareth sighed. Glory thought she saw disappointment flicker across his face. "You're quite correct, Mr. Black. Thank you for your time. If you don't mind, we'll gather up the horses and be on our way."

"Don't object to you leavin' at all."

"And you won't shoot us?"

"Nah."

She turned towards the paint mare, then paused. "I have one last question. About the most recent visitor." Glory saw Eden, Seth, and Gareth pause at her words.

Miles gave a short nod.

"Did anything about the man — his clothes or his belongings or what he said — strike you as unusual?"

"Aside from being a lyin' city man in shithole like Leadville?"

"Aside from that, yes."

Maybe Miles thought for a moment. "Come to think of it, yes. He asked if I had known of folks who had gotten the gift later in life." Miles shook his head. "Stupid question. Everyone knows yer born with it or no."

CHAPTER TWENTY ONE

After the disappointing encounter with Maybe Miles, Eden, Seth, and Glory returned to the journals. Gareth had left to investigate a man in San Francisco with an Affinity for culinary arts. They couldn't sift through the rumors to determine the exact nature of the magic, so Gareth had taken the train to investigate.

The journals yielded slow progress. Glory learned that her mother was an astute scholar but a terrible (or at least, inconsistent) cryptographer: Though magic was illegal at the time of the inventory, Juliet had somehow convinced several hundred magicians to speak about their gifts, and in great detail. Her mother had attempted to protect their privacy through mixing the initials of first and surnames (which is how Glory pieced together Miles Gray), or obscuring the name altogether with an alphanumeric combination. In the case of the baker, Eden had discovered that Juliet had amalgamated the first name with the city location and the date of the interview. All in all, Glory wished her mother had chosen a more consistent system.

After an especially painful and fruitless hour, Eden shut the journal she held with a loud thump.

Glory looked up. "Awful?"

"Terrible." Eden agreed.

"Shall we take a break?"

Eden hesitated, then spoke. "We know the journals will take time. I... I may have another lead."

Glory studied Eden. "Oh?" *Why is she so nervous?*

Eden spoke in slow, hesitant words. "I know I haven't spoken much about my family."

Glory waited for Eden to continue.

Eden took a deep breath. "My family is from Broken Whistle. We're... well, we're outlaws." Eden looked Glory, watching her for a reaction.

"All right." Glory gave a neutral nod. She sensed her reaction, or lack thereof, might be important to Eden.

Eden took another deep breath. "My family is... trouble. They specialize in horse thievery, brothels, and bank robbing. They are quite... successful, in their own way." Her lips twisted sideways.

"Are you in contact with them?" Glory ventured.

Eden snorted. "I'm not. They disowned me."

Shock slicked through Glory. "What? Why? Because of your Affinity?" Glory had heard enough tales of families disowning members for a magical ability.

Eden snorted. "No, not at all. To their mind, an Affinity is another opportunity to rob people." She sighed and straightened the stack of journals in front of her. "No, they disowned me because I wouldn't join the family business. It's not right; there's plenty wrong with the world, with poverty and general hardship. I just couldn't do it. I couldn't add to other people's woes."

"I'm so sorry." Glory gave herself a mental kick. Her words were so inadequate in the face of Eden's loss. But she didn't know what else to say.

Eden shook her head. "I'm happy here — much happier than I've ever been. I didn't know I could be this happy." Eden gave a small laugh. "After my escape from Broken Whistle, the magician who paid for my stagecoach fare told me to find Carville's Bookstore. He told me that the owner would help me get into Thornhedge." Eden studied her hands. Her smile grew even bigger and turned sweet. Glory felt as though she were watching a private moment. "I didn't realize that I'd meet Ms. Carville. Her father was my contact at Carville's, the man who helped me get into Thornhedge. They were so kind to me when I arrived."

"You seem close."

Eden looked up. "We are. She... is wonderful." A faint blush stained Eden's cheeks.

Glory grinned. "I can tell," she teased.

Eden was startled. "You... know?"

"It *is* fairly obvious."

"And you accept that?" Eden's uncertainty echoed in her voice and across her face.

"Of course I do," Glory said. "You're together, then?"

"Yes." Eden blushed further but she beamed at Glory. "I'm moving into her home after I graduate from Thornhedge. We will run the bookshop together. Felicity asked me three months ago."

Glory reached over to clasp Eden's hand. "I'm so happy for you both. Truly."

Eden returned her squeeze with both hands. "Thank you." An unspoken question rested in Eden's eyes. "Most people don't approve. We haven't told anyone except a few friends in Denver."

Glory thought for a moment. "I knew a couple in Agate Creek. Two 'bachelors' who lived together above the post office, ran the mail service. They were like every other family in town. When our new pastor came to town, he tried made a few pointed sermons about men and women in the eyes of God. But... I don't know. It's like having an Affinity: We have it or we don't. No one should be punished for something not within their control."

Eden smiled. "Very heretical of you," she teased. After a moment, she seemed to shake herself. "But I told you about my family because I think I may be able to ask my brother for help."

"Your brother?" Glory echoed.

"He's the second in command of Broken Whistle," Eden said, with a wince. "They rob stagecoaches, primarily." Eden shook her head. "But he may know something about the murders."

"What do you mean?"

"Criminals talk." Eden shrugged. "Information is always useful, like a different kind of currency. He may have something for us."

Glory hesitated, then spoke. "Are you sure you want to reconnect with your family? For this? I mean, they abandoned you."

Eden shrugged. "It will be fine. Joseph isn't as... harsh as my mother or my oldest brother. Plus, I'm worried about my youngest brother, Ben. I want to ask after him."

"Why are you worried about him?"

"He's like me," Eden replied.

"A magician?"

Eden chuckled and shook her head. "Yes, but that's not my concern. I'd like to get him to Thornhedge. I mean, he's... like me. And Felicity."

"Oh." Glory felt foolish. She thought of Lily, and how protective she had felt of Lily — when they weren't driving each other crazy with petty arguments. Then she thought of Lily in a town like Broken Whistle, being... different — and worry set in. "Will your family harm him?"

Eden thought for a moment. "None of them know. They aren't... kind to others who are different. As long as he leaves Broken Whistle before too long, he should be safe." Eden shook her head again. "Let me send a note to Joseph tonight. We can ask if he's willing to meet."

"Are you sure you want to do this?" Glory asked.

Eden gave her a pointed look. "Do you want to spend the next several months with these journals as our only lead? And discover more and more bodies?"

Glory thought for a moment, then sighed. "Let me get you a pen."

Eden didn't hear from her brother until four days after she had sent the note. The response was brief and nearly illegible.

"Tomorrow, 9:00, Dusty Rose."

"At night?" Glory echoed.

Eden nodded. "They don't do business during the day."

Glory thought for a moment. "We'll need to find a carriage. Or borrow horses."

Eden looked up from the note. "Will Seth help us?"

"I don't think we'll find a way into Denver without him," Glory said, her tone resigned. "Not that late at night."

Eden winced. "He will not like this."

Glory shook her head. "No."

CHAPTER TWENTY TWO

"Where the hell am I taking you again?" The night air had nothing on the coolness in Seth's voice. *He's still put out,* Glory thought.

Seth had arranged horses for the ride into Denver. Eden had shared the destination but not the purpose with him, and after some reluctant grumbling, he had agreed to accompany them. They had met him at the stables in the garb they wore to find the gemstone miner, the practical clothes still covered in a patina of dust.

"I'll tell you when we're in Denver," Eden replied. She swung up into the saddle and settled in.

"And we're following a lead?" Seth wouldn't let it go.

"Yes." Eden's reply did not encourage further questions. Despite the estranged relationships, Glory knew that Eden was concerned about protecting her family. The young woman was hesitant to answer any questions that would reveal her brother's location or occupation, as it were.

"You can't tell me anything more?" Seth asked. "I'm going into this blind, you know. Will this be dangerous?"

"Seth," Glory said. "We're seeing a man about a lead connected to the journals. Just a few questions, I promise."

"Sure." Seth swung his horse's head towards Denver, his tone curt.

They didn't speak on the ride into Denver. Following the well-worn road that led from the Academy into the city, the dark countryside was lit with bright starlight. A stiff breeze crept beneath Glory's hat and shawl, and caused her skin to pebble into gooseflesh. Slowly, the scenery morphed into gaslight lamps that grew in number the further they rode into the city. Watching the city from beneath the brim, Glory realized that a different part of Denver came alive at night: Loud, tipsy young men and silent, older drunkards stuttered across the street, crisscrossing paths between saloons, brothels, and casinos, weaving a tapestry of revelry and a desperate, almost forced kind of merriment.

At Eden's infrequent direction, they continued through the heart of the city. And then past it. Glory noticed another change: The saloons, brothels, and casinos slowly devolved into their less prosperous cousins. Glory could see the clear poverty in this portion of Denver in the missing shutters and the worn boardwalks that lined bedraggled storefronts, many of which were permanently closed, with dark empty windows that resembled the black eye sockets of a skull.

Soon they arrived at a closed shop, a poor facsimile of the general store she had worked for in Agate Creek. Still, it was slightly less shabby than the buildings that surrounded it. Compared to its environs, the worn shop looked almost palatial. Eden signaled to Seth and Glory to head down the alley. They had barely squeezed through the alley, single file, and had arrived at the back of the building when, suddenly, seven men surrounded the horses. Alarm coursed through Glory. *This doesn't feel good.*

"Carson?" One of the men, with a droopy mustache and a large hat, asked.

Eden nodded.

"Didn't realize you'd bring friends." The quiet menace in his voice chilled Glory further. She cast a quick glance around. It would be hard to escape the alley.

"D'you think I'm an idiot?" Eden retorted. Her voice had taken on a slight nasal twang with different diction than her usual crisp accent. Glory even noticed that Eden slouched a bit more in the saddle. "I ain't travelling on my own into Denver. At night." Scorn dripped off her words.

Droopy mustache glanced at the cowboy with dusty chaps to his right. After a nod from the cowboy, he jerked his head to the back of the shop. "Get down. He's waiting for you."

Glory waited to move until she saw Eden dismount. Then she followed, and as she thumped to the ground, the cowboy with the dusty chaps stepped forward to take the reins. Glory followed Eden into the building, with Seth close behind.

They were stopped in the vestibule just inside. "No weapons," Droopy mustache barked. "Hand 'em over."

Eden knelt down, hiked up her pant leg, and pulled out a knife from her boot. Glory gave her a tight smile. "I'm learning so much about you tonight," she murmured. Eden gave a tight grin.

"You?" Glory looked at Dusty Chaps when he challenged her. "Weapons?"

Glory shook her head. She hadn't brought any visible weapons. She could rely on her Affinity if she needed to. At least, she hoped she could. She had gotten better, more confident since working with Jacinda.

"No weapons?" Disbelief echoed his voice.

"She ain't from our neck of town," Eden said. Glory got the sense that Eden hadn't referred to an actual location but to an understanding of sorts.

Dusty Chaps shook his head. "Helpless fool," he muttered.

Glory turned to see Seth surrounded by three men. Without comment, he handed over his pair of six shooters. *He looks so uneasy*, she thought. *I hope Eden can trust her brother.*

"C'mon." Droopy mustache barked an order.

They followed him further into the building, the narrow hallway forcing them to march single file, and emerged into a resplendent sitting room — far more elegant than the exterior of the building had promised. A refined and sturdy desk stood flanked by two lush armchairs. A small bookcase nestled in one corner but Glory noticed that they looked untouched, the dust thick.

A young man sat in one of the armchairs, snipping the end of a cigar. He didn't stand as Glory and Eden entered, as many men in polite society did; he hadn't even look up when they had entered the room. His clothes were tailored and made from good fabric but were dusty and slightly worn. They matched his surroundings.

"Hello, sweet sister." He stood then, and swept a glance over Eden, his gaze assessing. Eden's brother was of middling height, with a flourishing mustache and bronze, weathered skin that saw a lot of sun and wind. He shared the same black hair, bold cheekbones, and light blue, mischievous eyes as his sister — but the resembled ended there. In Eden, those features had created a pretty young woman. In contrast, her brother was all hard angles and dead eyes. He spared a glance at Seth, dismissing him before his gaze lingered over Glory for a moment. She guessed that he didn't miss much.

"Joseph." Eden's voice was steady. Glory was impressed by the other girl's calm.

"You steal off into the night years ago. Then you never write or send word of your whereabouts," the young man said. He placed a hand upon his chest, the fluttery motion a mocking accent to his words. "We was worried about you." This time, the accent and the tone changed. Rougher, less refined.

"You knew where I was," Eden countered. Her tone and diction had changed to match her brother's. "You coulda found me if you wanted." She stared him down. Glory felt a surge of pride for Eden. She knew this meeting wasn't easy.

Joseph snorted. "No thanks to you. Ungrateful, running from family like that."

Eden snorted back. "You knew I woulda been kicked out at some point." She shrugged. "Ma didn't tolerate backtalk."

"Or freaks." Joseph

Eden stiffened. After a moment, "I don't understand."

Joseph laughed, outright, this time. "You think yer so sly. But since you's already goin' to hell for magic, so your bookstore friend is just a bonus."

Glory watched the color drain from Eden's face, and could see the rapid calculations flash across the other woman's face: How did Joseph know? How long had he known? And what would he do with that information? She stepped forward, and placed a hand to Eden's elbow, offering what comfort she could.

It was a mistake: Joseph swung his gaze on her. "Who's this? Some new *friend*?" He tsk'ed to himself and the other men in the room chuckled. "Eden girl, you do get around."

Eden bristled her brother's tone. "Don't talk to either of us that way. I'm your sister, damnit."

Joseph lit his cigar, then drew a long inhale. He stared at Eden for a moment, then shook his head. "You *was* part of the family. But you ran off, probably cuz you was a freak even then. You know how the Family handles freaks."

Eden stared him down. "I know," her voice toneless. Glory felt the other young woman tremble beneath her hand.

"So's I can't figure out why yer here." Joseph shook his head. "I'm not as mean as the others but I ain't a nice man. You *know* that. Add on that yer a freak?" He shook his head. "I should shoot you myself, spare the family the shame." His hand settled on the butt of one pistol.

Glory felt a wash of ice, then heat, settled over her. *No. No, this cannot happen.*

Eden spoke, her voice angry and incredulous. "*I* bring the family shame? Y'all are nothin' more than thieves, murderers, and con men. Y'all are a *disgrace*. I *remember* what you did to Broken Whistle. This family pillaged that town."

Joseph grinned. "We cleaned house, girl."

Glory watched his next movements as if in slow motion:

Joseph pulled a six gun from his right hostler.

Glory heard Eden gasp.

Swung up to aim at Eden.

Glory saw Seth leap forward.

Cocked the hammer.

Eden stilled, glaring at her brother. Seth struggled against the men who held him.

Placed his finger on the trigger.

A blaze of magic erupted out of Glory. She could feel every sensation in her body: Her rapid heartbeat, the sweat on her brow and under her arms, the chill in her hands and the tickle at her fingertips. She felt... powerful.

Glory twisted her hands. **"Draw."** A whoosh, followed by a series of clicks.

The room stilled, silent.

Glory looked around and almost gasped.

Glory had drawn every gun in the room and trained it upon its owner. The revolvers rested in mid-air, as though held by invisible hands, trained upon the men's faces. Glory's magic had removed Joseph's remaining gun and held it at his temple.

Exclamations and oaths were muttered across the room.

The men trembled in place, unease and fear skittering across their faces.

Glory glanced at the two men who held Seth. "Let him go."

They did. Immediately.

She turned back to Joseph, who had lowered his gun. "Eden has questions for you. You will answer them." Glory nodded at Eden to continue. The other young woman quickly masked her shock. *I hope*

I can keep this up. The drain began to wear on her, a heavy weight that dragged upon her shoulders.

A wide smile broke across Joseph's face, a mirthless and merciless look. "Y'know, if you're looking for work, I have a space for you. You got a unique talent, and I pay well. My men will tell ya."

Glory stared him down, expressionless. "Eden has questions for you," she repeated.

A sneer marred the smile, and Joseph turned to his sister. "So what gives, Eden? What d'ya want? Why pull a prodigal daughter now, after all this time?"

Eden glanced at Glory, then Seth. "We're... looking for information."

"Information has costs," Joseph countered. "Can you afford the costs?" Glory got the sense that Joseph wasn't talking about financials.

Glory focused upon the gun in front of Joseph, and it waggled to and fro. She could feel sweat cascade down her spine, chased by fatigue. She couldn't keep this up for long. "Yes," she answered for Eden.

Eden gave her a small, crooked grin.

Joseph glared at Glory. "Whatcha looking for?"

"There's a string of murders along the West Coast," Eden said. "San Francisco, Portland, Seattle, and now Arizona territories. The victims are usually dissected." Eden saw the furrowed brow on her brother's face and clarified. "Carved open, like a doctor or surgeon would."

Joseph gave a nod. "Yeah, I've heard. Word is it's the work of a religious posse. Doing the Lord's work and all that."

"Religious vigilantes?" Seth asked. "They are much... messier in their executions." He shook his head at Joseph. "These people are precise."

Joseph sneered. "Dead is dead," he said. "One less freak in this world."

Eden glared at him. "So you know nothing?"

"Why in hell should I give a damn about freaks?" Joseph countered. "They don't pay my bills. Screw 'em."

"You don't know anything, then? At all?"

Joseph shook his head. "No."

Eden glanced at Glory, then Seth. She shook her head.

Seth stepped forward. "Thank you for your hospitality but we're leaving. Now. Ladies?"

Eden looked at Joseph and opened her mouth.

He glared back.

Eden gave a sigh and turned to leave the room. Seth sauntered over to Glory, as though without a care in the world but with an urgent question in his eyes: *Could you hold the guns?*

Glory gave a shaky nod. *At least, I hope so,* she thought to herself.

Seth led the way out of the room and back to the horses. Glory walked backwards in slow, steady steps. As she stepped out of the room, Joseph called out to her.

"You eva need a job, you got one. Ya know where to find me."

Glory didn't answer. She turned around and raced down the hall, and out the back door into the courtyard they had arrived into. Eden had already mounted and held the reins of the other two mounts. Glory stumbled as she went down the steps, and Seth caught her.

"Drained?"

She nodded, resting on him.

"Are the guns still trained on them?"

"Yes." Glory looked up at him. Worry and fatigue lanced through her. "I don't know how much longer, though."

"We'll be gone before then," Seth said. He didn't ask permission but instead threw Glory up in the saddle, catching her off guard. Fatigue had turned into a dull ache that crowned her head and shoulders, the weight of the strain crushing down like boulders. Glory rested on the saddle horn while Seth mounted. "Can you stay upright?"

"I think so."

Seth looked dubious. "Let's go."

They navigated the horses out of the alley, and once they hit the main road, Seth spurred the horses to a gallop. Glory hung onto the saddle with her knees and leaned into her horse's neck as they chased the dark road out of and across Denver, and on the way to the Academy. She swayed in the saddle, the magic weighing further and further on her. The edges of her vision faded from gray to black.

Her horse stumbled, and Glory almost pitched out of the saddle. "Stop!"

Panic seized Glory. *Joseph caught up to us. I can't save them.*

The black closed in on her.

Glory came to as hands pulled her off the horse and out of the saddle. She struggled at the touch, and swung her arms and kicked her legs in an attempt to free herself. She was so tired. Scared, too.

"Ow. Ow!" A low curse in a familiar voice. "Glory, Glory, it's us."

Glory stilled, opened her eyes. Light lanced through her squinted eyes and she turned away, pained. After a moment, she tried again. Seth, Gareth, Eden... and Jacinda swam in front of her. She sighed in relief.

"We're carrying you to bed."

Glory gave a single nod. Anything else hurt too much. Instead, she listened to the whispered conversation as someone — Seth? Gareth? — carried her down the hall.

"What happened?" Jacinda's furious voice, low and urgent.

"We were following a lead."

"A lead?!" Jacinda whisper-shouted. "You dragged her into your shenanigans? Absolutely not."

"Like you could stop her." Glory almost smiled at Eden's fierce rejoinder.

"I don't care why she was out tonight. What caused *this*?" Glory could imagine the imperious wave from Jacinda but didn't open her eyes to watch it.

"It was incredible. *She* was incredible." Seth's voice, fervent admiration.

"That doesn't tell me anything." *Jacinda could be very grumpy,* Glory thought.

"We had a confrontation with eight men, and Glory pulled each of their revolvers out of their hostlers — and trained the guns on the men so we could escape. Their own guns. She cocked the hammers, too. I've never seen anything like it." Admiration and awe, edged with worry, from Seth.

Jacinda cursed. "Son of a goddamn rabid squirrel." Seth and Eden fell silent. Glory almost giggled. Jacinda cursed, often and creatively. "No wonder she's exhausted. She had no business using that much magic so early into her training. I'm shocked she's even conscious."

"She saved us," Eden said. "My bro – The leader. He meant business. He would have shot us."

"Well, not Glory. He wanted to give her a job," Seth said.

"What?" Gareth asked. When had he joined them? "What in the world?"

"Had you seen her in action, you would have done the same." Seth retorted. "Hell, I want to hire her myself."

"You are all buffoons." Jacinda's acid words came again.

Glory relaxed into unconsciousness again.

She was home, and safe.

Chapter Twenty Three

G lory awoke in pain the next morning.

Her body felt like it was on fire. Her head issued a low, dull ache. Opening her eyes, the light stabbed at them and she turned her gaze away from the window. She saw that she was in her bed, in the room she shared with Eden. The scents of strong tea and breakfast wrapped around her, and as she breathed deeper of the scents, her unsteady stomach settled. The window had been cracked open. *No birdsong. It must be midday.*

Jacinda came into view. She didn't waste time with greetings. "You'll have a headache, so you'll want this." She gestured to a nearby tray. "Do you need help sitting up?"

Glory managed to struggle into a sitting position. Jacinda adjusted the pillows behind her. "Where are the others?" Glory asked.

"I told Eden to attend morning classes and the Brothers are minding their own business. I knew you'd be out for the night and possibly the day." Jacinda issued a sharp look at Glory as she settled the bed tray over the young woman's lap. "That was dangerous and foolish, what you did last night. So much could have gone wrong."

Glory looked up from a sip of tea. "I know," she said in a quiet voice. "I didn't see another choice. Eden would have been shot by her own *brother.*"

Jacinda brought Glory a napkin. "Family can be a tough business, and I'm sorry for her troubles. Still, don't pull any more stunts like that. Draining your magic is hard on your body — and you're especially vulnerable in dangerous situations."

"But the looks on their faces when I pulled their own guns on them?" Glory grinned. "You should have seen it."

Jacinda raised her eyes skyward and shook her head.

Her grin fading, Glory shook her head. "I can't imagine not loving my own family. Eden deserves more than that lot."

"And she's found it." Jacinda gave Glory a pointed look. "Family can be found, not merely born into. And she now has you and the Hill Brothers."

Warmth suffused through Glory. "That's true," she murmured. After a moment, she continued. "I'm glad Jason has you."

A reluctant smile softened the older woman's face. "Rest up. Your recovery will take longer than you think. Using magic has its costs."

Eden returned from classes in midafternoon. Glory roused from her nap when she heard the door click open.

"How are you feeling?" Eden settled her books onto her small desk before coming over to sit on Glory's bed.

"I hurt." Glory shifted. "Everywhere."

Eden winced. "I bet. Is the headache better?"

"Yes, Jacinda gave me a powder." Glory gave her a curious glance. "How'd you know?"

"Everyone overextends themselves when using magic at one point or another," Eden replied. "The signs are unmistakable: Extreme fatigue, slurred speech, inability to use limbs. Sometimes even fainting. And then a brutal headache. The aftereffects resemble a hangover."

"Swell."

"No, it's not fun," Eden agreed. "How much do you remember of last night?"

"Not much," Glory said. "I don't remember much past pulling the guns on your brother and his men. We got on the horses but..." She shook her head. "Not much more."

Eden grinned, and leaned forward. "That was amazing! The look on that bully's face." Eden sighed in contentment. "Thank you for that, and for rescuing us afterwards."

Glory smirked. "You're welcome. But seriously, what happened afterwards?"

"You made it possible for us to escape by holding the guns on them," Eden said. "After we left the building, Seth threw you into a saddle because you insisted you could stay astride. You almost fell off just outside of Denver, so Seth got up behind you on your mount, to steady you in the saddle. We don't know when your magic stopped but we wanted to be as close to the Academy as possible when that happened. Once we arrived at the Academy, Jacinda and Gareth met us at the stables. Apparently, Seth had left Gareth a note in case he had returned from the Arizona Territory, which he had. Jacinda lectured us something fierce." Eden winced, then shrugged. "Seth and Gareth carried you up here, and you passed out."

Glory thought for a moment. "Goodness."

"You had a busy night."

"I can't believe your brother offered me a job."

"You have a valuable skill. You'd make a great deal of money, though it'd be ill-gotten," Eden said.

Glory shook her head. "Your youngest brother? Benjamin."

"Yes?"

"We have to get him out of there. It's just not safe."

Sudden tears filled Eden's eyes. "I know."

Glory leaned forward and grabbed her hand. "We'll figure it out together. I promise."

The recovery took much longer than Glory expected. The residual headache didn't fade until the following day. Jacinda stated it was because Glory used her magic on eight objects, simultaneously. "That's a great deal of effort for someone as early in their training as you but...

well, I've never met a metal magician before so I'm not sure what to expect," Jacinda had said after the one of the Academy doctors gave Glory an examination.

Gareth visited her on the second day. Visibly uncomfortable as he entered a young woman's room, he brightened when he saw Glory. "Miss Glory, you look much better today."

Glory grinned in welcome, then winced. "I feel better. I can't kick the headache yet but I am better. Truly," she added at Gareth's dubious look. Glory looked beyond Gareth, into the hallway. "Where is Seth?" She looked at Eden, who shrugged, before looking back at Gareth.

Gareth shifted from one foot to another and twisted the hat he held in his hands. "He had an obligation, unfortunately. He sends his regards." He looked up at Glory with an apologetic glance.

"Oh." Disappointment flickered through Glory, catching her by surprise. She pushed it aside, focusing on Gareth. "Well, it is good to see you."

Gareth smiled. "Likewise. What you did that night was remarkable. Dangerous as hell, and I don't approve, but amazing nonetheless."

Eden looked up from her side of the room. "So what's the next step?"

"Pardon?" Gareth looked wary.

"In the investigation," Eden clarified. "After Glory heals up."

"Erm, I'm not quite sure —"

"Gareth," Glory interrupted. "We're—" she gestured between Eden and herself "—already involved. We're not going anywhere. So... what's next?"

Gareth examined Glory as though she were a specimen in a jar. "You aren't... shaken, deterred by this experience?"

"Should I be?" Glory countered, her tone stubborn.

"Yes, frankly." Gareth shook his head. "You both could have been assaulted, killed, sold into slavery." He shot a glance at Eden. "*You* know that. What possessed you to visit your brother, a known outlaw, in a dangerous part of Denver — without telling Seth or myself or anyone what you were getting into?"

"We didn't think the danger was that great," Glory said.

"We are searching for *murderers*," Gareth said in a pointed tone. "Danger is inherent in this exercise. Thus, good judgement and measured risk, not the complete abandon of self-preservation, is necessary." Gareth end on a shout, his words punctuated by deep breaths. The hat brim had been rolled into itself.

Glory stared at Gareth. "You're worried."

Gareth let out an explosive breath. "Of course I'm worried."

"And Seth is, too. That's why he's not here."

Gareth hesitated, then nodded. "He is also angry. At himself, mostly," Gareth added when he saw the effect of his words on Glory and Eden. "He felt as though he didn't do enough to protect you both."

Glory exchanged a glance with Eden, who looked sympathetic. "I will talk with him. We're not his responsibility, and we're quite capable."

Gareth nodded, surprising Glory with his agreement. "You both are quite capable. But these are exceptional circumstances, and you must take every precaution. The danger may seem far away because of where these events are occurring but I assure you it's quite real."

Glory had finally tracked down Seth the following day, the study with her mother's journals. She studied him as he sat on the floor, his shirt sleeves rolled up to his elbows, his vest unbuttoned, and his hair in complete disarray. A scowl puckered his brow, and he rubbed his neck in irritable motions.

"Good morning."

He looked up and did a quick scan over Glory, as though searching for injuries. "You're awake."

"Yes."

"How do you feel?"

"Good, considering. Better than yesterday."

Seth nodded. His next words, measured and even in tone, caught Glory off-guard. "What we did was foolish and dangerous as hell. We could have died."

Glory couldn't disagree. "Yes." After a moment, "I'm sorry for putting you in danger."

Seth shook his head. "Not the apology I'm seeking. I can take care of myself."

"So can I," Glory shot back.

"Yes, you can, and it's as impressive as hell." Seth stood up, scattering journals and a few loose papers in his wake. "But what if they had shot you in the back? What if they had knocked you unconscious? What if you had been killed before you could have pulled the stunt that you did?" His shoulders rose and fell, as heavy breaths stuttered in and out. He was flushed, his eyes dark.

"Gareth mentioned that you were upset. I'm sorry we worried you. We had a lead, and we wanted to contribute to the investigation."

"I don't care about a damn lead," Seth exploded. "It's never worth your safety. Ever."

Glory took a step forward. "I apologize. We should have told you where we were going and what we were getting into."

"Did you not hear what I said?" Seth raised his voice. "Your safety — not mine. Yours."

Glory paused. "Oh."

"Yeah."

Glory thought for a moment. "You know I could get hurt anywhere, right? On the street, falling down some stairs. Even a horse could trample me."

"But you will concede that this last misadventure was especially dangerous, yes?"

Glory smiled, one corner of her mouth picking up. "Yes." Before Seth could respond, she continued. "But I won't sequester myself away in hopes of avoiding danger."

"Will you at least be more careful with your safety?" Seth muttered, his head bent as he studied the floor.

"I can do that."

Seth cast her a skeptical glance.

"I will try," she amended. He grinned, the first since she arrived in the room.

"Are we...?" Glory didn't know how to phrase it.

"We're fine," Seth said. "I just worry. I don't want anything to happen to you."

A warmth stole through Glory. "Do you feel that way because you brought me here? To Thornhedge?"

Seth studied her before shaking his head.

"Because we're friends?"

"We are friends, yes." Seth paused. He studied her face, his eyes roaming as though he sought answers. Glory felt breathless, and her hands shook under his steady gaze. She clenched them, to keep them still.

Finally, he spoke. "Yes. You are a... cherished friend."

"Seth, Glory, there you are." Gareth's voice interrupted the fragile space between them, and Glory jumped at the sound. Seth stepped back and bent to pick up the papers that had scattered on the floor. Glory looked at Gareth, and saw Eden stood behind him. Eden glanced between Glory and Seth, and cast a quick look at Glory, a question in her eyes. Glory gave a minute shake of her head.

"What is it, Gary?" Did Glory imagine that edge to Seth's voice?

Gareth looked up from the journal in his hands. "We found a new lead: Leadville."

Seth thought the statement over, then shook his head. "I don't know anything about Leadville."

"It's a mining town, south of here." Gareth waved the journal in his hands. "There is a woman with a precognitive Affinity, the first that Rue ever recorded. Apparently, she is the genuine article."

"A precognitive Affinity?" Glory echoed. "She can predict the future?"

"Yes, and no." Gareth waved the journal. "Your mother wrote that she could foretell large scale disasters only, and that she has never made a prediction for herself."

"I wonder how that works," Seth muttered. "That gift must be hell."

"What does she do for a living?" Glory asked.

Gareth winced. "Cardsharp, and other assorted hobbies."

Seth laughed. "She can foretell the future, and she cheats at cards? Rather brilliant, really."

"Leadville is a rough town," Eden murmured. "If she is still there, she must be a smart and formidable woman to make her own way for this long."

"*Is* she still in Leadville?" Glory asked.

"I've contacted my source, and they confirmed that, yes, she's still there. She owns a saloon now, which is called The Fortune Teller." Gareth shook his head. "A bit on the nose, I fear."

"When do we leave?" Glory asked.

Gareth frowned. "Are you recovered sufficiently for this? You may not realize this but you could have injured yourself. You will need more time to heal."

Glory shrugged. "I don't plan on using my Affinity this time."

"No one plans on using their Affinity during an emergency," Gareth retorted. His irritation made him seem younger, heightened his resemblance to his brother. "It just happens. That's why you need to rest up."

Irritation flashed through Glory. "I'll be fine, I promise." She looked at Eden, then Seth. "Right?"

Both of them shook their heads.

"Traitors," Glory muttered.

"Glory, you need to rest," Seth said, his tone so gentle that it stirred butterflies in her stomach.

Eden shot a quick, considering glance at him. Then she pointed a gleeful grin at Glory, who blushed.

"Well, when may we go?" Glory asked, her voice a little shaky. The butterflies hadn't settled.

"In a few days, right?" Eden interjected. "The healer said Glory should recover in two more days."

Glory seized on the interruption and cast Eden a grateful glance. "Perfect. We can go then."

Seth and Gareth sighed, at the same time.

They decided to go to Leadville three days later. Not due to Glory's recovery but rather the weather: Always unpredictable, the Denver region had experienced rainfall, thunderstorms, some enormous hail, and then blue skies with bright sunlight. All of them elected to postpone the trip rather than be besieged by the weather. The designated day dawned, and Glory watched Eden rise to dress in skirts and a pretty blouse. Worn breeches that still hadn't seen the last of the dust from the Maybe Miles adventure in hands, Glory paused. "We're not riding horseback?" she queried.

Eden looked taken aback but then shook her head. "Oh, no. Leadville is far enough from Denver to warrant a train ride. But it's also close enough to be quick trip, too."

Delight filtered through Glory. "Then we're not riding horseback?" She wished she were one of those young ladies who adored horses but could not see the appeal. Glory knew the basics but the saddle hurt her hips and thighs, and she sat so high off the ground...

Eden gave a crack of laughter. "No, you're safe."

"Thank god," Glory muttered. She shoved the breeches back into the dresser cabinet and got dressed in a simple skirt and blouse. Glory snagged a quick breakfast for the four of them in the dining room, wrapping biscuits and bacon in clean napkins and tucking them into a rucksack, before meeting the others at the coach station near the edge of the Academy. She passed out the still-warm parcels of food and inquired about the status of their carriage.

"Soon," Gareth answered, the only one of them whose mouth wasn't currently full. "Then Leadville is approximately an hour by train."

The train station bustled with midmorning activity when they arrived. Metallic screeches rent the air, and whistles groaned through the hubbub of the station in intermittent bursts. They boarded the train and settled into the seats without further ado. The Brothers Hill insisted that Glory and Eden take the window seats, to shelter them from passersby on the full train. They chatted about nearly everything: coursework, post-graduation plans, the wonderful and exciting places the Brothers had seen around the States and the Territories. Glory particularly wanted to know about the West Coast. She had never seen an ocean apart from drawings in books and couldn't quite imagine it.

Eden was quiet about her post-graduation plans, simply saying that she wanted to open a shop. Glory understood her caution. It was wise to be cautious in a city and a country rife with a religion that forbade any love beyond that of a man and a woman.

As for herself, Glory couldn't imagine what she would do after Thornhedge. She hadn't known its existence until a few months ago, hadn't known that magic was available to her — that it was indeed a part of her heritage. And once Glory had arrived at Thornhedge, she hadn't thought past mastering the basics in a hurry; she had been so worried that she wasn't a real magician. But she was strangely at peace with not knowing her future, post-Thornhedge plans.

If she had become a magician only a few short months ago, what else might her future hold for her?

INTERLUDE

I t wasn't working.

None of it had worked.

He sat down on the rotted chair, his trembling hands resting between his knees. Yet another body lay upon another table only two feet away — another failure.

There were eleven of them. Eleven people he had tracked, killed, and examined. Number twelve lay on the table in the dark room, the smell of a corpse who had soiled herself ripe in the musty, damp air.

And all for nothing.

He couldn't determine the source of the Affinity.

He stood, lunged forward, and flipped the table with a roar. The body and the viscera tumbled and slipped off the surface and onto the floor in a broken heap of limbs. The sight of the useless carcass incensed him, and he snarled. With a sudden yank, he ripped a leg off the table and surged forward, swinging the firm wooden pole against the body again and again, the sounds of thuds upon flesh a second, ersatz heartbeat to the one that played in his ears and thrummed in his head.

After several minutes, he rose and straightened. *No one will be able to identify her now.* He took several deep breaths. The wooden pole tumbled from his now lax grip.

This was simply a setback. He simply needed new leads, fresh ideas.

He could do this.

He had to.

CHAPTER TWENTY FOUR

L eadville was a dump.

There was no other word for it.

After they had emerged from the rundown train depot, covered in dust and tracked with mud, and onto the streets, the four paused at street's edge to observe. The streets were just wide enough to admit two wagons' worth of space. The hitching posts and the exteriors of even the most prosperous of stores were made sun-bleached wood covered in mud and speckled in old sawdust. Miners, identified by the mud- and clay-encrusted clothes and boots, wandered into saloons and barbershops but hurried into the three banks that lined the main street. Each bank had a pair of private guards stationed at the doors, rifles held in hand and at the ready. Peering past, Glory saw more guards within the banks.

The banks clearly knew who their customers were — and took precautions.

"What a hellhole," Seth muttered. Gareth shot an irate glance at his younger brother and Glory smiled to herself. *Such a stickler for not swearing in front of women.*

"Where do we go from here?" Glory asked, stepping out of the path of a swaying and possibly drunk miner.

"She should be inside the Fortune Teller, a saloon."

Eden glanced around. "That won't limit our options, unfortunately."

"Do we know what she looks like?" Glory asked.

Gareth shrugged. "The report was vague, unfortunately."

Glory sighed. *This may take a while.*

They stepped around debris and potholes while walking on the street, and onto the worn boardwalk with splintered timbers and tracks of mud. Men spilled out of the shops and saloons in an untidy sprawl. Glory saw very few women on the streets; instead, the working women festooned on the balconies above.

Seth stopped in front of a saloon, which bore a large wooden sign that read, *The Lucky Broad.* "I'll inquire about her in here."

Glory started to follow but Eden and Gareth pulled her back. Eden pointed at a small sign posted below the name of the saloon: No Genteel Women Allowed Inside.

Glory frowned at the sign. "Are we genteel?"

Eden snorted. "Usually, no. But here? Yes. Only saloon girls are welcome inside." They stood to the side of the double doors, under an awning. More miners stumbled and strutted into the saloon, casting side glances at the motley group composed of Eden, Glory, and Gareth. Seth returned in a few moments, looking disheveled. He shook his head before tugging his jacket back into place. Dismay spread through her chest, and she tried to ignore it. *We're here to work,* she reminded herself.

"She's not here," Seth said in a harried tone. "They said the Fortune Teller is two streets over and four down."

"Did you have any trouble in there?" Gareth smirked at his brother.

Seth shot him a quick glare. "Let's move on."

The Fortune Teller failed to impress. The gold had long flaked off the large sign above the door, leaving behind a mottled effect that looked somewhat diseased. The windows were thick with dust and one of the double doors hung crooked, making it impossible to open one door without holding the other steady.

"She's in there?" Eden asked, doubt clear in her voice.

"That's what they said." Despite his words, Seth didn't sound convinced.

As they walked up to the doors, Glory searched for a sign that forbade "genteel women" from entering and found none. She nudged Eden. "We should be able to go in here, yes?"

Gareth overheard. "No. Please, no." Discomfort prompted a sudden flush to his face, and the man shook his head with vigorous motions. "You don't know what you will find in there."

Glory simply looked back at Gareth. Seth chuckled. "Come on, Gareth, let's go in."

The saloon was clean inside, or at least cleaner than the exterior. Chairs clustered around the round tables in the room and men of all ages and social status sat in them, attention focused on the alcohol and the games in front of them. Worn green felt covered a few tables, which were largely ignored in favor of the card games. Glory had a limited knowledge of the games; it wasn't considered proper for young women to play them. A counter ran the length of the back of the bar, and bottles and jars of all sizes and content lined the shelves behind. Glory glanced around and felt...disappointment. This *is a saloon?* She wrinkled her nose. She wasn't impressed. Glancing at Eden and the Brothers, she saw that none of them looked surprised or dismayed. *Must be normal.*

A loud shout, followed by a round of cheers and groans, emerged from one corner of the saloon. Glory followed the sounds with her eyes. There sat a woman in chaps, trousers, and a blouse, and a cowboy hat hung from the back of her chair. Glory could see a revolver strapped to one leg and a Bowie knife laced against the other. A cloud of reddish blond curls cascaded around the woman's face.

"That must be her," Glory murmured. "Or, at least, there aren't any other women around."

"Yes," Gareth agreed. Glory saw him glance at Seth. "Do you want to make the approach? Or shall I?"

"Why don't you go this time?"

Gareth started forward, and Glory watched the older brother change before her eyes: He removed his hat and adjusted the guns at his side. His usual businesslike stride switched to saunter, and he wandered from table to table, as though interested in the various games. Finally, he walked by the woman's card game and paused to observe. The men who noticed Gareth shifted, and held their cards a little closer. The woman didn't bother to glance up from her cards.

Her next words startled Glory. "You lookin' for the Fortune Teller?"

Gareth paused. "Yes."

"This ain't a place for ladies." She jerked her head at Glory and Eden. "Get 'em out of here. Better yet, leave town."

"We need to speak with you." Gareth's voice was firm.

"Yeah, all y'all do. I can't predict yer future so yer wasting time — mine and yers."

"This is a different matter," Gareth said. "It's about... well, a series of murders."

The woman shrugged. "Happens all the time. Unfortunate and all."

"The murders of magicians," Gareth pressed.

The table went still as men paused in their shuffling. Others in the room had finally noticed the interaction between the woman and Gareth, and had paused activity to listen into the conversation. Noticing their scrutiny, Gareth shifted so his back was to the wall rather a room of strangers. Seth pulled Glory and Eden closer to the door, then unstrapped his sixgun as quiet as possible.

The woman looked up at Gareth, and Glory stifled a gasp: The Fortune Teller had one black eye and one blue eye. Both stared into Gareth, as though searching for answers. Finally, she spoke.

"The game is near done." She jerked her head back. "There's a sitting room behind the bar. Wait there."

"Thank you." Gareth inclined his head.

The woman glanced around the room, mismatched eyes missing nothing. "What?" she shouted. "Y'all don't have yer own affairs to mind?"

Noise erupted throughout the room. Gareth waved them forward, and they made their way around the saloon edges and into a small, surprisingly clean room with comfortable furniture located behind a door next to the long wooden bar. Glory and Eden sat on the settee while Gareth stood near the door. Seth paced the room, back and forth. The minutes crawled while they waited for the woman.

"Is this a trap?" Gareth muttered to Seth.

"Doesn't feel like one but..." He shrugged.

The door flew open, and Gareth took a hasty step back to avoid getting hit in the face.

The Fortune Teller paused in the doorway. She glanced at Gareth her face expressionless. "Oops." She did not sound concerned, or worried.

Seth stepped forward. "Thank you for your willingness to —"

"I'll stop ya right there," the Fortune Teller said. She stepped further into the room, and then shut the door. A lock clicked into place. "Yer here for the magician killer."

"Yes," Glory said.

The Fortune Teller switched her focus from Seth to Glory. "A girl searchin' for a killer? You crazy, bored, or stupid?"

Glory gave a grim smile despite the harsh words. "Scared, mostly."

"Hmm." The Fortune Teller studied Eden, then back to Seth and Gareth. "Like I said out there, I can't predict a person's future — just general disasters and widespread misfortune. I don't know much about this killer yer lookin' for."

"But you know something?" Glory pressed.

The woman nodded. "Rumors started circulatin' across the rail lines about six or seven months ago. Someone's been cuttin' up magicians, and not just any of the strange folk. Special ones. Those with unique gifts. Same rumors say that the bodies have missing pieces."

"'Missing pieces'?" Eden echoed, puzzlement on her face. "Like limbs? Or appendages? And why on earth?"

The Fortune Teller shrugged. "Ears, innards, limbs. Once even a heart. As fer why, who knows? He could be doin' experiments." The older woman winced. "Could be eatin' them, though that ain't a pleasant thought."

Horror washed across Glory, and she could feel the bile rising in her throat. From the corner of her eye, she saw the Brothers exchange a glance. They weren't surprised or upset, just...calculating. *They knew,* Glory thought. *They have always known that this is a possibility.*

"That's what the rumors say." The Fortune Teller looked contemplative for a moment. Then she tapped her temple. "The gift, it says something different about this one. Nothin' good, that's fer sure."

They all waited.

"Yer lookin' for him to put a stop to his work, yeah?" The Fortune Teller studied her hands.

"Of course." Gareth sputtered.

"Him?" Seth echoed. "Not them?"

The Fortune Teller dropped her hands and looked up. "Yeah, him. Women don't go for that kind of crazy. But if you want to stop him, yer gonna have to kill him. He ain't fit for jail or an asylum of some kind. Kill him and be done with it."

No one spoke.

"Yer all so taken aback." The Fortune Teller shook her head. "How did you think this was gonna end? You'd call the sheriff, lock him up, and saunter into the sunset, pleased with yer efforts? Yer gonna have to kill him. He won't stop, and he's comin' east. Following the rail lines like he's chasing the rumors."

"Is this what your Affinity tells you?" Glory asked.

"Yes." The older woman nodded. "Typical omens, I get as dreams and nightmares. This killer? Visions, square in the middle of the day. Awful ones." She shuddered, her gaze going distant. "He's comin', and he needs killing."

"He's coming east? Or to a specific destination?" Seth asked.

Irritation crossed the Fortune Teller's face. "I don't know. He's just comin'. And if yer with the magician school, you better lock it down. Add safeguards and what. That's a ripe killing ground for him."

"Do you know why he does it?" Glory asked, surprising herself. "Why he kills, I mean?"

The Fortune Teller shrugged, her face turning sad. "He's sick. Broken. He wants what he can't have and doesn't *feel* the difference between right and wrong." She stood up straight, as though to shake off the morose conversation. "I got a card game I gotta get back to. One of my last before I jump town."

"You're leaving?"

"Yep. East," the Fortune Teller replied. "Don't ask me where. I ain't tellin'."

Glory reflected on that information for a moment. *She's so scared that she's leaving town.*

"That means you all need to get out. Yer wastin' my time." The Fortune Teller was clearly done with them.

"One last question," Glory interjected. "Do you think it's the God's Word movement?"

The Fortune Teller scoffed. "Not likely. Their kills aren't precise. They're... messy. Needy. This one, he's precise."

A chill rippled over Glory.

"Thank you for the information," Seth offered.

"Don't care. Get out. Please." The Fortune Teller tacked on the late courtesy.

Glory trailed behind Seth as they filed out of the eponymous saloon, Eden and Gareth bringing up the rear. Outside, the mid-afternoon sun beat down, merciless without a soothing wind. They walked to the train station and purchased tickets for the return trip to Denver, subdued and worried.

EXCERPT

Research Notes, J. Rue

August 13, 1878

Boston, Massachusetts

I picked the worst time to come to Boston. Late summer, when the heat and the humidity conspire to show Boston at its worst: Smelly, hazy, and miserable. This setting may account for the uncharitable account that follows.

I came to Boston at the express invitation of a prominent family with a long lineage of Affinities. They had heard of my research (word gets around in the magical community, faster than the telegram it seems) and had urged me to interview their youngest daughter, a woman with an Affinity for manipulating weather. Intrigued but somewhat reserved with my optimism, I added Boston to my route.

When I met the family, I regretted my choice.

They live in a wealthy neighborhood, one of the best in Boston, in a lavish home festooned with all the obvious trappings of wealth: polished silver, lush rugs, exquisite tea service, and extravagant furniture. They were a family of five, the husband and the wife having had three children, all of whom had fairly powerful abilities. The youngest, however, had a remarkably unique one — and it was abundantly clear how much pride both the parents and the young woman took in this fact.

Over a long, long afternoon filled with often replenished tea and nibbles, they regaled me with the family's long history of strong and unique Affinities:

"We've never had a non-magical child in this family." (I highly doubted that. Families like this simply sequestered "problem children" away).

"The B. family has always thrown powerful affinities, and unique ones, too. My grandmother had the same ability for weather; my grandfather had the gift for gemstones." (This was shared with such patently false modesty that I had almost choked on my tea).

"We are quite proud to continue the tradition of fine breeding and to perpetuate the best magical bloodlines." (I smiled through my teeth at this nonsense).

When I was finally able to question the young woman, named F., she proved a somewhat disappointing subject. As many families are wont to do, the parents had neglected F.'s education in favor of finishing schools and the fine art of household management in preparation for marriage. This lack of education hindered F.'s ability to share how her gift worked, though to her credit she managed to convey some details. According to F., after feeling what elements were present, she would then be able to manifest certain weather patterns. It did have a downside: Manipulating the weather in Boston apparently could have an adverse effect on local microclimates. Drought had been reported in neighboring counties. When asked under which circumstances F. used this gift, she smiled and admitted that the family had never had a garden party or outdoor event rained on. They were the envy of the society matrons and had often been prevailed upon to share the gift.

I think my facade of polite interest cracked then.

At that moment, I felt some disgust. That incredible and powerful gift, being used on garden parties and society gatherings for the already rich and powerful of Boston. What a profoundly limited application of that ability. I had almost shaken my head but managed to still busy myself with taking notes.

I wrapped up the interview as quickly as I could. The sense of pride and the overpowering self-satisfaction that the B. family marinated themselves in became oppressive and suffocating. All that posturing and nonsense for something over which they had no control. One does breed for Affinities: Either the child has one or doesn't. Inheritance is still a mystery to our community and for a brief moment, I despised the B. family for telling themselves self-serving lies about their own magnificence.

I shouldn't judge so harshly, I know. It's only human to seek meaning and to understand one's place in the world. But I despair at the old wives tales and nonsense I hear about magical inheritance because it hinders true understanding of the facts — of which we have very little. It's possible the magical inheritance is simply too magical to understand through the lens of the scientific method, and I'm prepared to accept that conclusion should I arrive at it. However, clouding the issue with false attribution and social climbing is frustrating at best and dangerous at worst.

I think I'm ready to go home.

—J. Rue

CHAPTER TWENTY FIVE

The failed trip to the Fortune Teller seemed to cast a pall upon their subsequent investigatory efforts. Each visit with a potential lead seemed to be worse than the last and Bertha Weintraub was no exception to this pattern.

A robust German grandmother located just outside of Denver, Bertha had an Affinity for fibers. This allowed her to manipulate wools, most yarn, and many fabrics. Glory wasn't surprised to learn that the older woman ran a seamstress shop while still in her mid-seventies. The shopfront had gleaming windows, lined with attractive dresses and bolts of fabric. The interior smelled of floor polish and starch.

When Seth and Glory stepped into her shop, Bertha cast a sweeping glance over them. "I don't need anything from that school," she barked at them before she hustled to the other side of the shop. She began sorting a pile of linens.

Seth and Glory had exchanged puzzled glances, taken aback by the unusual greeting.

Seth stepped forward. "Uh, ma'am, we simply wish —" he started.

"Wishin' doesn't pay my bills."

"I understand, ma'am, but if we could —"

"Not buying anything? Then good day."

"Ma'am."

"Get out."

Glory had had enough. "Mrs. Weintraub! Have you had any disturbing visitors lately?" she called out. Glory caught Seth by the arm when he would have stepped forward again. She gave a short shake at his questioning look.

Mrs. Weintraub stared at Glory, her gaze pointed and eyebrows raised. "Aside from you?"

Glory almost grinned despite her own irritation. "Aside from us. Ones that are... dangerous."

The eyebrows came down into a sudden furrow. "No. We keep a quiet shop here. No demonstrations of magic. The gift? It invites trouble from the mundanes."

Glory nodded. "So you haven't seen or heard anything unusual? No rumors of any kind?"

"I said so, didn't I?" Mrs. Weintraub shook her head. "Now buy something. Or get out."

Seth found his voice. "Thank you, ma'am. We'll take our leave now."

Outside the shop, Glory paused and glanced at Seth. "That didn't go well."

Seth shrugged. A crooked smile crept on his face. "Well, I think we can count her as safe from the killer. No one would cross that woman."

Glory jotted down a few notes down on the papers she had pulled from her satchel. "On to the next one?"

Seth nodded, a defeated look on his face.

Glory repressed a sigh.

The news reached Thornhedge on Thursday morning.

The good Pastor Brown's flock had encircled the encampment of the World-Renowned E. W. Forster & Sons Circus. Incensed by the obvious, flamboyant, and celebratory presence of a group of magicians camped in the center of Denver, most of the protestors alternated between singing hymns and chanting poorly rhymed cries that denounced the magicians. Other members of the flock held pitchforks, torches, and sandwich board signs, the latter of which consigned magic users to hell in one form or another.

Only the presence of the Sheriff, and a hastily recruited posse, forestalled any violence that evening. However, the members of the World-Renowned E. W. Forster & Sons Circus awoke to find a gallows erected in front of the circus entrance on Thursday morning. Three rope nooses swung in the slight morning wind. *The Denver Tribune* captured the eerie image with an artist's sketch. The newspaper had delivered the eerie tidings to Thornhedge early the next morning and had cast a pall on the breakfast meal.

Hushed conversations whispered through the common room. Glory could see worried and frightened faces throughout the room; even Eliza Hicks seemed subdued.

Glory looked at Eden. "What does this mean for us? For Thornhedge?"

"I don't know." Eden gripped her tea, knuckles white.

Glory swallowed hard, then sipped her cold tea.

The Brothers returned the next day.

"Did you find anything in Tucson?"

Gareth shook his head. *He looks exhausted*, Glory thought. She glanced at Seth. *He looks angry.*

They sat in a private dining room adjacent to the common mess halls. Tea and a lunch lay untouched before the Brothers and Glory. Eden was in Denver, visiting with Ms. Carville.

"Unfortunately, no. We learned nothing new in Tucson." Gareth gave a weary sigh.

"We merely arrived in time for another killing," Seth muttered. A pained grimace covered his face, and he pushed his chair back further from the table, jostling the furniture with his sudden movement.

Glory's shoulders tightened. "The same as the others?"

"Of course." Seth shook his head. "No mistaking that signature."

"That's awful."

"Yes. It damn well is."

"Seth." Gareth's tone bore a warning.

"Oh, give over, Gary." Seth nodded at Glory. "I've heard worse from her."

"He has." Glory assured Gareth.

Gareth gave a weak chuckle. "I didn't think I'd find anything amusing after Tucson. But you two..." He chuckled again, shaking his head.

Seth sighed again.

Glory studied Seth, then Gareth. "What else happened? You aren't only upset about Tucson." It was a guess but a good one: Gareth and Seth exchanged a quick look that spoke volumes.

"She is sharp," Gareth murmured.

"Told you, didn't I?" Seth replied.

"Well?" Glory prompted.

Gareth sighed. "We've —" he gestured between Seth and himself "— been upbraided for our lack of progress on this matter. The mundanes are starting to notice the murders and that never bodes well for the Affinity community. As well..." He trailed off, studying the floor.

"Yes?"

"We were chastised for involving you."

Seth grunted. "Foolish bastards," he muttered.

"Seth." Weary resignation from Gareth this time.

"Let it go, Gar."

Glory studied the ivy pattern that wrapped around her teacup. She felt an odd sense of shame, which was chased by frustration. The Brothers had revealed her true nature to her, then gave her a future. In short, they had changed her life. She couldn't imagine being at Thornhedge without the Brothers in her life. That they had been chastised for involving her in their life, their investigation, *hurt*.

"Involving you in the pursuit of the murders, really," Gareth clarified. "Not for bringing you to Thornhedge."

Seth shook his head. "They are fools," he repeated. "Glory provided us with fresh leads and a sound mind for the investigation."

Gareth shook his head, frustration marring his brow. "Seth, you needn't defend Glory to me. She's as dear as a sister. And yes, we wouldn't be nearly as far along as we are without her."

"And Eden," Glory reminded them.

"And Eden." Gareth smiled at Glory before turning back to Seth. "Remember, they don't *know* her. Thus, they cannot know how capable or formidable she is."

Glory felt a blush stain her cheeks. The hurt that she felt a few moments ago dissipated in the evidence of Gareth's obvious confidence and affection. But she had remaining concerns.

"What does this mean for me?"

Gareth and Seth exchanged another look. Then Gareth spoke. "They told us to keep you away from the remainder of the investigation."

Glory looked from Gareth's neutral expression to Seth's mutinous one. "And do you plan to comply?"

"No," Gareth said.

Glory took a deep breath. Relief cascaded through her.

Seth grinned. "I knew you had it in you, Gar," he chortled.

"I'm not celebrating this disobedience," Gareth said, his tone grumpy. "We are keeping this quiet, you hear? They are not to find out about her continued presence."

Glory and Seth nodded, barely stifling grins.

"So what's next?" Glory asked.

"Back to the journals, I'm afraid," Seth sighed. "We need fresh leads."

That plan was short-lived.

Glory stopped at the entrance of the Brothers' private study. Shock froze her; worry washed over her.

Seth bumped into her from behind. "Oops, my pardon, Glory. What —" His voice trailed off as he saw the scene before him.

As if from a long distance, Glory heard Gareth's exclamation. "What on earth?"

The private study had been ransacked, violated. The furniture had been overturned, books pulled off the shelves and tossed upon the floors. Scattered pages from her mother's journals littered the floor. An inkpot stained the corner of the Aubusson rug.

The trunks were missing. Glory swallowed past the painful lump in her throat. Her mother's journals were gone.

Seth swore.

Gareth didn't chastise him, stunned into disbelief.

The Brothers pushed past Glory, gently setting her to the side. Glory watched as they paced the edges of the room in brisk methodical motions, searching for any intact journals and picking up relevant pages left behind. The search didn't take them long: The thief had left little behind.

Seth swore again. Gareth ran his hands through his hair.

"He's here," Glory said. *Who else would want the journals?*

Seth looked up. "What?"

"The killer. He's here. Or was. In Thornhedge." A shiver echoed down her spine. Glory hugged herself, trying to chase away the cold fear that settled into her bones. She watched the realization dawn across the Brothers' faces.

Gareth started forward. "I need to alert the Provost. We need to lock down the Academy."

"What about the magicians in Denver?" Glory looked up. Her shaky voice firmed. "Eden is in Denver. We need to warn her."

Seth strode over to Glory, grasped her arm. "Gareth, can you handle Thornhedge? Glory and I can ride into Denver, alert everyone through Carville's network."

"Yes, I've got this. Go," Gareth urged. "Be safe."

Seth and Glory parted outside the building.

"I'll meet you at the stables in a moment," Glory said.

"I'll have the horses ready."

Glory raced across the courtyards, disturbing a small group of picnickers. Once she reached her dorm, she vaulted the stairs up to the room she shared with Eden and tumbled through the doorway, tripping over her skirts. She hardly shut the door before tearing off her dress to scramble into trousers and a shirt. Boots were next, with an iron ingot inserted into each boot along the exterior of her leg. *Better than knives — I can make anything with these.* She settled her blacksmith's belt across her body like a bandolier. Hammers, metal ingots, and other tools rested on her back, the weight a calming comfort to her unsteady state. *Just in case.*

Back at the stables, Seth stood with the reins in his hands. He scanned her appearance in a thorough sweep from head to toe, not even missing the hidden metal ingots in her boots. "Good — you're prepared." Glory saw that he had added a pair of revolvers on either hip. A rifle rested in a saddle case upon his mount.

He held her mount steady. "Need a lift up?"

Glory swung into the saddle. "No."

"Then let's go."

The ride into Denver was short and brutal; Glory felt terrible for the horses. But mostly she felt fear. She hoped that Eden and Felicity were safe. That this killer would be caught.

Once in Denver, they were obliged to slow due to traffic. Of a sudden, Seth stopped. Glory pulled up her mount and looked at him. "What's wrong?"

Seth nodded into the distance. "That."

Glory followed his gaze. A large group of people in their Sunday best blocked the roads ahead. Religious hymns saturated the air, and after searching for a moment, Glory could see Reverend Brown leading his flock. The crowd, thick with protestors and signs, was too dense to pass.

A frisson of fear skittered across her scalp.

Seth wheeled his mount aside. "We won't get through to Carville's down this road. This way." Glory followed him down a short side road. They wove in and out of alleys, dusty lanes, and even through the courtyard of a hotel, much to the shouted dismay of the hostlers. They arrived at the back entrance of Carville's Books shortly after. Glory fell rather than dismounted from her horse, and after hitching the horse to the post, she ran after Seth into the bookshop.

Eden and Felicity were moving the furniture in front of the windows. *Anticipating another riot,* Glory thought as she ran up to Eden, grasped her arm. "Are you safe?" She watched Seth run up to Felicity, murmur something to her, then they both ran off in separate directions — Seth out the front door, Felicity towards the back of the shop.

Eden paused. "Safe? Glory, what's wrong?"

"The killer was at Thornhedge."

Eden's complexion blanched white. "What?" She said, her voice strangled.

"He ransacked the study," Glory said. Her breath sawed in and out, and her hands trembled. "Stole the journals."

"Oh, Glory." Eden gave her a quick embrace. "I'm sorry."

"Never mind that," Glory said, her tone urgent. She could hear the crowd of protestors outside the circus, eclipsed by angry shouts between the pastor and another man, with a deeper voice. Reverend Brown, Glory recognized. "We don't know where he is. We came to warn you, to send an alert through Carville's network. Gareth has notified the Academy."

Eden shook her head, as though to clear her thoughts. "I don't understand. He's here? How will we find him? Let alone stop him?"

"Eden." Felicity's strangled voice drew their attention — and held it.

A tall, thin man stood next to Felicity, a revolver with a long barrel pointed at her temple. "You won't need to look for me," he said. "I'm right here."

Glory felt her heart jump into her throat. Shock chilled her body, and she studied the man before her with dazed eyes. Her voice trembled as she spoke a single word.

"Jason?"

Glory hardly dared to breathe.

Gone was the anxious, eager to please man from Jacinda Eldredge's study. Instead, a stranger stood before her: Gaunt and pale, with unwashed hair, and tattered and unkempt clothes. She could smell him from where she stood. Dark circles carved themselves underneath his eyes, which were a feverish bright blue. *He looks ill.*

"Jason, what are you doing?" Glory asked.

"You know him?" Eden hissed.

"Yes," Glory replied without looking away from the gun at Felicity's head. "He is Jacinda's nephew, and her secretary." Glory shook her head. "I don't understand. Jason, what is going on?"

Finally, Jason spoke. "I understand you've been searching for me." The gun wavered in his unsteady hand. His eyes were dark, dead, empty.

Recognition wrapped around Glory like an unwanted embrace. "No," she whispered. "Please, no." *It's him. He's the killer.*

"To stop me from my research, yes?"

"Jason, no." Glory gave a shake of her head, denial a metallic taste on her tongue. *What will I tell Jacinda?* "You don't do this. Right? This isn't you. You didn't murder anyone."

Jason gazed at her, unperturbed. Empty. "Science comes with casualties."

Her shoulders sank. *Oh, Jacinda. I'm so sorry.* "Jason, you're not a scientist," Glory replied. "You're a murderer."

Eden grabbed her hand, then squeezed. *Don't antagonize him*, her eyes warned.

"You wouldn't understand." Jason sneered.

"You're right," Glory said. "I don't."

"You have a rare Affinity. You are *special*." His face contorted and he looked less than human for a moment, envy making his sneering features monstrous. "Do you know what it's like to lack an Affinity in a magical family? Of course you don't. The daughter of the grand Juliet Rue, of the famed Rue Inventory. You don't have the first clue what it means to be the freak of the family." The tall man scoffed.

"I don't understand." Glory looked Jason, her heart in her eyes. *If Felicity dies, Eden will be heartbroken.* "Will you put down the gun, explain it to me?"

The gun barrel lifted a bit higher. "No. I'm here to get what's mine."

Glory looked at Eden, then Felicity. Puzzlement and fear mirrored in their faces. "What do you mean?"

"Are you truly that daft?" Jason shouted. "I want my birthright. I want an Affinity."

Silence reigned over the shop after that pronouncement. Glory could hear the protestors directly outside the shop, loud and angry.

"But..." Eden stuttered. "How-how will you get an Affinity if you weren't born with one?"

Horror swamped over Glory as she finally understood. "The dissections. He is looking for the location of the Affinity. And he's seeking the rare ones for the prestige, in case he manages to transfer the gift."

A stunned expression crossed the other women's faces.

Nausea roiled within.

Glory swallowed hard, choking back the nausea that filled her mouth.

Jason studied Glory, surprised yet pleased. "Yes," he admitted. "That's exactly it."

"But you must know..." Glory started, her tone gentle and with an eye on Felicity. *Don't upset him.* "It won't work. There is no guarantee that Affinities are in the brain or the heart or anywhere in the body, really. We don't know the source of magic. We may never know."

The gun swung in her direction. "I'll take the chance."

Glory stared down the barrel. Ice congealed in her chest but she pushed Eden away from her. Eden made a sound of protest, but Glory held up her hand. *Stay.* At the periphery of her vision, she saw Felicity inch away from Jason.

"Even if you find the source of the Affinity, how will you transfer it?"

"Magic."

Glory stared at him in astonishment. *He is insane.* "That's not how Affinities work."

Jason cocked the hammer. "I will make it work."

Glory closed her eyes. *Calm,* she thought. *Be calm. For Seth. For Eden.*

He squeezed the trigger (Glory heard Eden shout).

The hammer struck the firing pin. (Seth burst into the shop, his gun raised).

"Stop."

A flash blinded Glory. (Was that a second shot she heard?).

A body slumped to the floor. Glory opened her eyes.

A bullet quivered in mid-air, inches in front of her face.

Jason lay on the floor, limbs splayed. Blood seeped from his chest.

CHAPTER TWENTY SIX

Denver recovered swiftly from the near riot that had almost occurred outside of the E. W. Forster & Sons Circus. The sheriff had arrived to disperse the crowd shortly before Seth had run into the shop to shoot Jason August. The gunshots inside the shop had frightened away the participants, and far faster than the presence of the sheriff. The protest itself only merited a small, two-inch column in the back of *The Denver Tribune* in the next day's newspaper.

No gunshots were mentioned.

When informed of the string of murders, and her nephew's involvement, Jacinda — the sensible and stern taskmaster who Glory once suspected could take on the world — had almost collapsed. She staggered at the news, her face rending itself in grief. She seemed to age a decade overnight, as though heartbreak and worry and shame had siphoned the color and life from the woman. Glory wished she could shoulder some of the burden for her teacher.

Jacinda decided against a funeral for her nephew.

"He caused enough damage and heartbreak during his life," Jacinda had asserted to Glory, sorting through paperwork at her desk within her study. "His death deserves no attention from anyone." She had him buried outside of the cemetery perimeter, north of Thornhedge Academy, in the dusty patch of earth reserved for criminals.

Gareth escorted Glory and Eden to the Provost's Office at the Academy a few days after Jason had died. The Brothers had shared that they were expected to make a report to the Academy leadership and were asked to bring along the other magicians present at the shooting. Glory followed the others into a large building to which she had never entered before, and up the stairs until they reached the top floors.

Eden glanced around, her expression puzzled. "Why isn't Seth here?"

Glory hid a smile. She hoped Seth would be able to explain later.

Gareth cleared his throat and avoided Eden's gaze. "Uh, he may join us later." He knocked on the ornate doors.

"Enter," a deep voice called.

Gareth pushed the doors and held them open for everyone to file into the room; once inside, Glory spotted Jacinda sitting near the end of a large table. Four older men lined the table. Glory recognized Provost Burst from her first meeting with him; when their eyes met, he gave a solemn nod of recognition. Glory took a quick glance around the room. The lush carpet, polished wooden bookshelves, long oak table, and stained-glass windows bespoke wealth and privilege. The very air seemed laden with power, both magical and social.

"Thank you for joining us today." The Provost spoke, focusing upon Seth and Gareth. "We will read the report you've tendered in due time. But first, can you walk us through the bones of what happened?"

Gareth launched into an overview of his investigation in partnership with Seth: How the Brothers had become involved after their cousin Jeremy's murder, had learned of the first murders in the Washington Territory, and had followed them down the West Coast. After realizing that Jason had targeted rare Affinities but unable to discern his motivations, they had consulted the published Rue Inventory in hopes of seeking more knowledge about the types of abilities Jason seemed to seek. The Brothers soon learned that Jules had carefully obscured the identities of all the magicians to protect their privacy. Thus, they couldn't issue a warning to the individuals themselves. And for obvious reasons, the Brothers hadn't wanted to publicize the serial murders throughout the Affinity or the mundane communities. Too much panic for the former group, and the wrong kind of attention from the latter.

Once the Brothers had exhausted the published Inventories, Seth had suggested they seek out Jules' family. Surely her research notes would be able to offer insight into the killer's motivations? Alas, they were too late, and only found the remaining Rue daughter in a grave-yard.

"Though we missed conferring with Abraham, it was soon clear to us that Miss Rue belonged at Thornhedge," Gareth said. "Her rare Affinity and her keen mind made her a natural fit for us." Gareth beamed at Glory.

"Yes, yes. We know you enrolled Miss Rue at Thornhedge." The man who sat to the right of the Provost shook his head. "But what possessed you to involve a girl in a murder investigation? Especially one with such potential for tragedy?"

Gareth rocked back on his heels, cleared his throat.

Glory beat him to it. "They are not at fault. They wished to read the journals my mother used during his research. When they refused to explain why they needed my family's journals, I refused them access." Glory stared down the man who had spoken.

The man *harumphed*.

Gareth stepped forward. "Miss Rue proved an invaluable asset to this investigation, as did Miss Eden Carson. My brother and I couldn't have made the progress we did without them."

The Provost waved a hand, weary resignation etched across his face. "Carry on with the report."

Gareth continued with the narrative, providing extra details to the events that led up to the confrontation with Jason Eldredge. The man to the right of the Provost scoffed when Gareth reported Glory's trick with the bullet.

"Balderdash." He looked to the Provost. "Are you willing to entertain this nonsense?"

"It's true," Eden said, anger clear on her face.

"Vickers, let it go." The Provost nodded at Gareth. "Continue."

"Well, there isn't much more to report, Provost Burst. After Jason Eldredge passed, we brought the body back to Thornhedge and used the confusion caused by the incident in Denver to hide our activities."

Provost Burst nodded. "Well done." He looked down the table at which he sat. "Any further questions for any of our investigators?"

All heads shook back and forth, except for Glory's mentor and the now visibly angry man who sat to the right of Provost Burst. Glory watched Jacinda, sadness and hurt warring inside. The woman hadn't looked away from a wall sconce during the entire recital.

Gareth stepped forward once more. "One last thing, if I may: We did locate and search through Jason Eldredge's rooms at a boarding house in the southwest area of Denver." He named a neighborhood with which Glory was unfamiliar. "We are still going through his notes, papers, and belongings." Gareth shook his head, sorrow on his face. "Seth and I are confident that we can notify most of the affected families that we found the killer and bring closure to a few more who may not have known how their loved ones had died."

Outside, the late afternoon sunlight had cleared the morning storm clouds. Gareth held the door open for Eden and Glory, then followed them down the steps. At the base of the stairs, he pulled out a pocket watch. He looked at Glory. "His telegram said he would be here by now."

"He'll come." Glory was sure of it.

Eden looked between Gareth and Glory, her brows pleated in confusion. "Are you talking about Seth? Where is he?"

Gareth stared into the distance for a moment, then gave a sudden grin. "Over there," he replied. He nodded to the south.

Glory looked over — and her heart leaped into her throat. Seth walked towards them with a small suitcase in one hand. At his side, a boy of about twelve or thirteen years of age, with black hair, tan skin, and blue eyes, chattered up at him. The boy's clothes were new, if somewhat dusty, as were his shoes.

He did it. He brought Ben home.

Besides her, Eden made a broken sound. Then she ran towards her little brother and gathered him into her arms. She buried her face into his hair and cried. Her brother wrapped his arms tight around Eden and hid his face against her shoulder.

Tears slipped down Glory's face. The moment felt private, intense, and she turned to look away, up at Seth. He sported a black eye the left side of his face and a scratch along his cheekbone on the other side. Glory frowned and wiped away her tears. "What happened?"

"They didn't want to let him go at first," Seth replied. He shook his head with a half-smile. "Don't worry about it. I've only got a shiner. We managed to get away quickly."

Glory looked at Eden, who now rained kisses on her brother's face against his laughing protests. She had never seen her friend so unguarded, so relaxed. Joyful. She swallowed against the emotion that choked her and looked back at Seth. "Thank you. So m-much." Her voice broke on the last word.

Seth stared down at her, his eyes warm and his face serious. "You're welcome."

After Eden left to enroll Ben in the Academy, Glory sat next to Seth on a stone bench in the courtyard directly behind her dorm. The sunlight and the warmth of the summer day promised better weather than the dark clouds on the western horizon would deliver. But she closed her eyes and enjoyed the sunlight on her face while she could.

"What will you do with the journals?" she heard Seth ask. "Now that Gareth and I have stopped pestering you for the use of them?"

She smiled, not opening her eyes. "I talked it over with Jacinda. I'm going to donate them to the archives here at Thornhedge. They are best suited to care for them, protect and preserve them — and then my mother's notes can benefit scholars and researchers." A cool wind ruffled her hair. Had the storm already arrived? She opened her eyes to look, and found Seth's gaze on her face, his eyes intent as he traveled from her eyes to her hair and lips, and then back to her eyes. Glory flushed, then cleared her throat.

She looked at small garden that filled the courtyard. "How long until you and Gareth are off on another investigation?"

"We're taking some time away from the investigations." Seth's voice had an odd tone.

Glory tore her gaze away from the rows of roses, gave him a sharp look. "You weren't punished, were you? Because of me?"

Seth looked puzzled, then his brow cleared. "What? No, no. Not at all." Seth cleared his throat. "I asked that we turn down assignments for a while. I want to stay at Thornhedge, see how... I want to... Damn," he muttered.

Glory leaned forward. "What is it?" She had never seen Seth so flustered.

Seth looked up — and Glory realized just how close he was. He smiled, and the tender expression on his face caused her breath to stutter in her chest. Slowly, giving her a chance to object should she want to, he raised his hand to cup her face.

After a moment, Glory pressed her face into the palm of his hand.

Seth grinned, delight and wonder clear on his face.

Glory grinned back. "This is why you wanted to stay at Thornhedge?"

"Absolutely."

She leaned forward, her lips hovering above his. "Good."

She felt his smile as he kissed her, cradling her head with gentle hands. He deepened the kiss, and Glory felt her own grin melt into his. He tasted of ginger and honey, smelled of sandalwood and something that was unique to him. After a moment, Seth pulled back, slightly panting and with disheveled hair. Had she done that?

He studied her face for a moment. "Damn, you're lovely."

Glory grinned. "Tell me more about that."

"How about I show you instead?" Seth leaned forward for another kiss.

ACKNOWLEDGEMENTS

My deepest gratitude goes to the fantastic cover artist, MIBLArt; my mentor with the Write Team Mentorship Program, Courtney Gould; and my beta readers. You all helped transform this project into something special and I'm thrilled I was able to work with you. Thank you for sharing the gift of your skill and talent with me.

My friends and family have long championed me. Their unwavering belief, support, humor, and kindness has helped me in innumerable ways, especially when I went through the hardest years of my life. I wish everyone in this world were as lucky in their community as I am in mine.

A heartfelt thank you goes out to Rachel. You've read everything I've sent your way, even the earliest, shittiest drafts, and your incredible insight, superb GIF reactions to our meme exchanges, and stalwart support have been a blessing. Thank you for everything.

Any man who makes you cupcakes, with festive pennants that match the colors of your book cover, during an ice storm and then traverses said ice storm to deliver these treats in order to celebrate the release of your debut novel is a treasure indeed. I'm very lucky to have you in my life, Grant, for this reason and many more. Thank you for being wonderful.

Katie, your tireless enthusiasm and positivity is a joy to behold. I'm thrilled for your future and I cannot wait for the world to see what you will share. Thank you for being my friend.

Lastly, I deeply appreciate you, the reader. I became a writer to share the joy that comes from an excellent story and I'm grateful that I get to this work. I hope you've loved your time with this novel. Thank you so very much for your support through your purchases and reviews. It means the world to me.

About the Author

Rebecca Rook designs tabletop games, manages a little free library dedicated to sequential art and comics, writes young adult fiction, and lives in the Pacific Northwest with two wonderful dogs. A 2021-2022 Hugo House Fellow in Seattle, WA, she also attended the 2021 Tin House YA Fiction Workshop in Portland, OR. Prior to this, she completed the wonderful Yearlong Workshop for Young Adult and Middle Grade Fiction at Hugo House. The author of the award-winning novel, *The Penance of Valentine Cash*, she writes young adult fiction in the fantasy, thriller, and horror genres.

Learn more here: https://byrebeccarook.com/
Instagram: https://www.instagram.com/byrebeccarook/

Sign up for her email newsletter, The Rookery, to stay up to date with new releases, giveaways, and more!

WHAT REVIEWERS ARE SAYING…

The Penance of Valentine Cash — <u>Order Here</u>

"Author Rebecca Rook has crafted an atmospheric and immersive fantasy novel that was a truly captivating experience from beginning to end. I adored the slick and intelligent blend of mythology and contemporary themes, creating a narrative that captures contemporary YA readers but also feels suitably grand in its proportions as it resonates with the struggles and triumphs of the human condition.

A STRANGE AFFINITY

Valentine's journey is both fantastical and deeply relatable, exploring themes of redemption, identity, and the interconnectedness of lives through emotively penned narrative moments and some really excellent speech and thought presentation. Thanks to the confidence and delicacy of the author's narrative structure, this novel goes beyond the simplicity of a modern retelling to produce a poignant reflection on the consequences of one's choices and the transformative nature of redemption, all in a format that is easily digestible and still action-packed for its target YA crowd. Overall, I would not hesitate to recommend The Penance of Valentine Cash for fantasy fans everywhere, and I cannot wait to see what more this talented author has to offer." — Five Star Review from *Reader's Favorite*

"Good God was this book utterly amazing! I honestly picked it up on a whim, and I cannot express just how delighted I am that I did so, because I loved it so so much! The story of an up-and-coming musician forced to complete a series of harrowing tasks to earn a return to life, The Penance of Valentine Cash is the Americana urban fantasy I didn't know I needed until I read it. Despite the clear inspiration from The Twelve Labors of Hercules, this book draws from an eclectic mix of American folklore for its fantasy elements, which is an angle that I surprisingly don't see too much of these days! Not to mention it's backed up with fantastic characters, with the titular Valentine Cash being an absolute standout. Her grappling with not only the supernatural challenges she has to undertake, but also with the weight of her actions and whether or not she really deserves a second chance is the core of the story, and it makes the magic feel so much more real! And shout out to Six, who is the best personification of an American highway I've ever seen in fiction. All in all, an utterly enchanting novel, and one that I heartily recommend!" — *NetGalley Reviewer*

"This debut author knows how to write books! Incredible story-telling, the characters were so well developed. I even shed some tears. I read this in less than a day. It flowed so beautifully. Very very good." — *Goodreads Reviewer*

"Such a great story and loved the characters, especially Six. I was rooting for her more and more as the story went on... definitely worth the read." — *Goodreads Reviewer*

"This book was WOW!... The adventure, the fear, the courage and self doubts that Valentine experienced...the unlikely relationships she made while on penance...made her a legend in my eyes... and also very human. I had cheered for her, feared for, wept with her and my heart breaks for her and with her." — *Goodreads Reviewer*

False Haven — <u>Order Here</u>

"Excellent read! Scary, suspenseful, and entertaining!" — *Goodreads Reviewer*

"As I read this book, I truly felt like I had become Vivienne and was her throughout the entire ordeal. I felt cold, wet and muggy...like I'd been the one doing all the heavy work. I felt the pain of losing a parent. I felt the disappointment of being unseen by the remaining parent. I felt the desperation of needing a break. Most of all I feel her fears, her despairs and her hopes for a potential future. Any book that made you feel this way is so worth the read. Highly recommended!" — *Goodreads Reviewer*

"This was everything that I was looking for from this type of book, it had everything that I was looking for in a horror element. The characters were what I was hoping for and were written perfectly and worked with the universe. I was on the edge of my seat from beginning to end and glad it worked with the story. Rebecca Rook has a great writing style and [I] enjoyed how strong the story was." — *Goodreads Reviewer*

COMING SOON: CITY OF GRAVES

Finch Marlowe is gifted and privileged.

She knows she's lucky. Except her wealthy parents have high expectations for her future. Every extracurricular activity and every volunteer endeavor contributes to the never ending quest for a perfect college application – and Finch feels every bit of that pressure. Failure is not an option.

But Finch has a secret: She belongs to the city's urban exploration community – a dangerous and thrilling pastime that involves exploring abandoned buildings. Moving through these forgotten places gives

Finch with a sense of freedom she's never experienced at home, and she begins to unearth her real self in this new community.

However, everything changes when Finch finds a body in one of the buildings. Then Finch discovers a chilling connection between the victim and the urban exploration community that has become so important to her, and her newfound world begins to crumble. As Finch becomes the target of a killer, she finds herself questioning everything she knows in a desperate attempt to save herself.

City of Graves is a young adult thriller that will appeal to fans of *I Hunt Killers* by Barry Lyga, *None Shall Sleep* by Ellie Marney, and *Paper Valentine* by Brenna Yovanoff.

Available June 18, 2024, in paperback and e-book.

Pre-order today!